**Bracknell
Forest
Council**

'An historical novel dripping with menace'
                    Shari Lapena, author of *The End of Her*

'Utterly brilliant . . . full of secrets and deliciously creepy, I raced
through it'   **Lisa Hall, author of** *The Perfect Couple*

'A spooky treat, which had me turning the pages faster and faster'
                    Cass Green, author of *In a Cottage in a Wood*

'A powerful, spine-tingling, beautifully written gothic mystery
full of real, complex characters, smart, dark twists and utterly
immersive historical detail'   **Hayley Webster**

'It's twisty and atmospheric, seriously creepy, and has an inspiring
central character I was rooting for'   **Cressida McLaughlin**

'A creepy, evocative mystery'   *Heat*

'If you like gothic mystery, buckle up! This atmospheric read has
it all'   *Woman Magazine*

Rhiannon Ward is the pseudonym for Sarah Ward, the bestselling and critically acclaimed crime author. Sarah has a masters degree in religious history and has long been fascinated by the long tradition of spiritualism in England and is a member of the Institute of Psychical Research. Sarah is also a crime reviewer and book blogger at Crimepieces.

THE QUICKENING

Rhiannon Ward

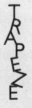

First published in Great Britain in 2020 by Trapeze
This paperback edition published in 2021 by Trapeze
an imprint of The Orion Publishing Group Ltd
Carmelite House, 50 Victoria Embankment
London EC4Y ODZ

An Hachette UK Company

1 3 5 7 9 10 8 6 4 2

A CIP catalogue record for this book is
available from the British Library.

ISBN (Mass Market Paperback) 978 1 4091 9218 3

Typeset by Input Data Services Ltd, Somerset

Printed and bound in Great Britain by Clays Ltd, Elcograf S.p.A.

MIX
Paper from
responsible sources
FSC
www.fsc.org   FSC® C104740

www.orionbooks.co.uk

For Anita, Anwen, and in memory of Lynn.

Quickening is one of the most important signs of pregnancy . . . a lady at this time frequently feels faint or actually faints away; she is often giddy, or sick, or nervous, and in some instances even hysterically.

Searchlights on Health: The Science of Eugenics, 1920

The deaths occurring in almost every family in the land brought a sudden and concentrated interest in the life after death. People not only asked the question, 'If a man dies shall he live again?' but they eagerly sought to know if communication was possible with the dear ones they had lost. They sought for 'the touch of a vanished hand, and the sound of a voice that is still'.

The History of Spiritualism by Arthur Conan Doyle, 1926

Chapter One

January mornings are the worst times to greet the living when you'd rather be amongst the departed. My fractured night hadn't helped. I dreamt I was still pregnant with Hugh and Philip. One of them was kicking my ribs, a reminder that he'd soon be bursting out into the world. I was swollen to massive proportions and Bertie, his hand on my stomach, was teasing me that I was delivering an elephant. How had we not noticed there were two? Afterwards, in the maternity hospital, Bertie, stiff and shy in his unfamiliar uniform, had promised to return unscathed to me and the children. Standing at the ward window I watched him go, though I'd been warned not to leave my bed. My breath frosted the square panes of glass as he crossed the courtyard and disappeared into the world beyond the hush of the hospital.

I dreamt on, alert to the monstrous deception and the knowledge that, when I awoke, I'd find myself alone in the desolate bed. A second kick brought me to my senses and into the room with its thin, floral curtains barely hiding the winter morning light. The sheets smelt of human warmth, fusty and sour, and I swallowed down the familiar rush of nausea. This new, strange child inhabiting my body kicked once more and settled.

Edwin was moving around downstairs, preparing his tea. If he was in a good mood, which was rare, he'd bring me up a cup, allowing me a few more minutes in bed before I had to face the cold house. Otherwise, he'd leave without saying goodbye, with the tea cooling and the fire in the living room unlit. I pulled back the covers when I heard the front door shut with a click and, thirsty from my dreams, went downstairs. My feet slapped on the bare stair boards, the air so icy that my soles stuck to the wood, leaving faint, tacky imprints.

In the kitchen, I threw the damp tea leaves into the sink and put the kettle on the range, listening to the hiss of the water. The day spread out, dull and empty. Edwin's mother had promised to call and would bring provisions with her. It would save me the trouble of deciding what to cook for the weekend, worrying if the remaining housekeeping money would stretch to the cost of food. Glancing in the mirror hanging on the window above the sink, I barely recognised my grey features and defeated expression in the glass.

As the kettle began to whistle, there was a tentative rap on the front door. Not expecting anyone so early, I ignored it until a more insistent knock shook the frame.

'Telegram for Louisa Drew!'

At the sight of the uniformed messenger boy, his brass buttons glinting in the winter sun, I took a step back. No one who has lived through the war is able to receive a telegram without fearing what tragedy it might contain. My hands trembled as I ripped open the envelope, although, in fact, I had no one left to lose.

REQUIRED AT MARSHAM AND CLIVE OFFICES
9AM TODAY LEO

'Any reply?' The boy was impatient to leave, his hands already grasping the handlebars of his bike.

I shook my head and shut the door, reading again the

unexpected message. In the distance, I could hear the clock ticking in the living room, telling me to hurry if I was to make the appointment. Instead of brewing tea, I used the hot water to wash and even the act of passing the steaming flannel up and down my arms lifted my mood. Afterwards, I put on the only decent dress which still fitted. It was the one I'd bought for my wedding to Edwin, its modern lines forgiving to my swollen stomach. I took two pennies from the housekeeping tin which would pay for the bus into town and paused, weighing up whether to leave a note. Edwin occasionally came home for his lunch and might wonder where I'd gone. In the end, I left the telegram in the middle of the table for him to see. I checked my camera case and tripod were still at the back of the broom cupboard. During an argument, Edwin had threatened to pawn the tools of my trade and I'd hidden them, first in the loft and then, noticing my husband relax as my work dried up, behind the brushes and dustpans.

The morning was dry enough for me to sit on the open deck of the bus and I had the level to myself. Office workers, keen to keep their clothes pristine, were enjoying the comfort of the lower floor, which was hot and steamy in the cold day. The fresh air kept at bay the nausea still plaguing my mornings. It hadn't lasted nearly as long with the twins, but the doctor assured me that every confinement was different. I looked at my watch and, realising I was early, got off at Shaftesbury Avenue to walk the rest of the way. London was waking up, although, in the distance, I could hear the sounds of the barrow boys at Covent Garden calling to each other, their own day nearly done. At Seven Dials, I passed a coffee seller and hurried past the aroma, sickly to me, watching the ground for patches of ice at my feet.

Patty, Leo Marsham's secretary, was climbing the stairs in front of me as I arrived at the studio. Leo's office was high above the bustle of the photography work below, but nothing went on in the business that he didn't get to hear of. Patty turned and raised a pencilled eyebrow at my presence, her make-up imitating the faces of the celluloid heroines she worshipped every evening at the picture house. I followed her rayon-stockinged legs up the steps into the reception where my former employer, perched on a desk, was waiting for me.

'Ah, Louisa, you're here. Come through into my room.'

He pulled out a chair, his gallantry immediately putting me on my guard. Leo had made a point of warning me that work would be scarce, probably non-existent for a woman in my condition – and yet, here I was, being made comfortable in a space usually reserved for select clients. He coughed and pulled out a handkerchief from his trouser pocket to blow his nose.

'We have a rather unusual commission,' he said at last, picking up a photograph from his untidy desk and placing it in front of me. 'I've been asked if you'd be willing to go down to a house in Sussex. The family are selling up and moving abroad, to India, I think. The house and its contents will be going to auction and they want someone to photograph the rooms and the items for sale.'

I glanced down at the image, recognising it as a Victorian print. Not bad, but with a gritty quality which I could easily improve on.

'The client is . . .?'

'The auction house, naturally.'

'And they asked for *me*?' I couldn't keep the incredulity from my voice.

'No, not them.' He took off his jacket, sweating slightly despite the meagre fire in the grate which was failing to heat the room. 'It was the family who requested you. They were quite insistent, I believe. Do you know a Colonel Felix Clewer? Or perhaps his wife, Helene?'

I shook my head. 'I've never heard of them. They know of my work?'

'They must, as they specifically asked for you. I'm sure you'll be able to find out more from the family yourself if you accept the commission.'

I was hardly well known outside the photographic world. My images had made it into newspapers and journals, but I'd had no exhibition to make my mark on society. A mystery, then, why they wanted me, but as I'd been requested, perhaps the fee would be decent. I wondered if it was a little early to bring up the subject of money . . .

'How long do you think it will take me?'

'About a week. You should be home by next weekend.'

I looked out of the window at the gloom of the morning. Even getting up early, I would only have five hours of good daylight to take my photographs. Less, if the days remained overcast. I turned back to Leo, his expression an unfamiliar blend of appeal and embarrassment.

'Can you do it?' He had his eyes on my stomach. Leo was a Victorian in age and attitude and I remembered the fight I'd had to secure my original position in his business.

'When would you want me to leave?'

'Later today would be ideal. Tomorrow at the latest.'

'Where's the house exactly?'

'Around ten miles from Brighton. Clewer Hall – perhaps you recognise the name?' He searched my face, looking for a response. His manner struck me as false, his usual expansive cheerfulness sounding forced.

Puzzled, I picked up the photo and looked at it more closely. The house was an austere red-brick building, dominated by a row of tall chimneys. A five-sided wooden turret, topped by a weathervane, was just visible at the back. I could feel my mood dropping as I gazed at the angular, forbidding home. Although the picture had been taken in summer – I could tell by the froths

5

of wisteria hanging from creeping tendrils – part of the house was shrouded in darkness. Perhaps it was the photographer's ineptitude, but I wasn't so sure. An underexposed image shouldn't be dark at a single point. I pulled up the collar of my coat to mask the chill which was creeping over me.

'So, what do you think? The auction house is prepared to pay well. There must be items of value in the collection, given the size of the commission.'

'The fee is?'

Leo placed in front of me a sheet of paper, headed with the name of J.C. Stephens, an auctioneer who'd once commissioned me to photograph a butterfly taxidermy collection. He pointed to a figure quoted in the second paragraph and I peered closer to check I wasn't mistaken. It was a sizeable amount. Three years ago, I'd have taken the commission in a heartbeat. Now, I had a new husband to consider, a man made short-tempered and needy by his experiences in Kitchener's Army. Edwin would be furious when he discovered I'd be gone for over a week. I had so little to do at home but my presence in the silent house was taken for granted.

Then there was the baby. I had taken photographs while expecting the twins, but these had been small jobs, easily completed in an afternoon. I was twelve years older now and this was likely to be a significant commission, judging by the sum of money on offer. Perhaps I should just accept and be damned. The thought of retrieving my camera equipment from the cupboard and inhaling again the sharp tang of my developing chemicals was intoxicating. I took a deep breath.

'I'll be glad of the assignment.'

As I looked up, I caught an expression of worry cross Leo's face. He hid it at once and made another effort at joviality. 'A bit of a change from Kentish Town, as you can see.'

'Have you been there?'

'Alas, no. I've heard of Clewer Hall, of course. The family were well known at one time but it's a different era now, as my children keep telling me.'

'Well known for what in particular?'

Leo frowned. 'Helene Clewer was a renowned hostess at the turn of the century. Her soirées were often featured in the society pages. Before your time, obviously. Her husband, Felix, was a collector of curios and antiques. If I recall correctly, he had a collection of marble hands which caused quite a stir at the time.'

'Marble hands? Sounds very Victorian.'

'Doesn't it just?' Leo was making an effort to relax as he leant back in his chair. 'They're presumably part of the sale. I have some papers to give you so you can see what the auction house is keen to have recorded.'

Leo's unnatural demeanour had put me on edge and I rubbed the grooved arms of my chair, trying to make sense of his manner.

'There's nothing untoward with the commission, is there? Something else I should know about the family?'

He laughed, avoiding my eye, and pulled open a drawer, taking out a sheaf of paper. 'Nothing to worry about. I shall send a telegram to tell the family to expect your arrival. The house is much changed, I believe.'

'Changed?'

'And the family, come to that. They lost all three sons in the war. I can rely on you for your tact and understanding in relation to this.'

I nodded, unable to speak.

'There's a train at two. Is that too early?'

'I'll be on it.'

'Wonderful. I can give you some glass plates to take with you for your camera but you'll need to stop at a pharmacy to purchase the necessary chemicals.' He stopped, his gaze sliding away from mine. 'There are plenty of stories attached to the family. Don't . . .'

'Don't what?' I couldn't fathom what the matter with Leo was. He wasn't a man to hold back, usually.

He shook his head. 'It doesn't matter.'

As I left the building and stepped out into the crowded street, Leo's altered manner and cryptic farewell left me uneasy. I pushed my concerns to one side. Leo had his failings but I was sure he wouldn't send me on an assignment where I might be compromised in any way. On the bus home, I plotted my escape and the best way to avoid Edwin's fury. In the end, I took the coward's way out and was waiting in the hall in my travelling coat when his mother came to call, carrying a basket full of pies which Edwin adored.

'I called in at the—' She stopped dead when she saw me. 'What's happened?'

'I'm sorry, Dorothy, but I have to go away for a week or so. I've been given an assignment and I can't turn it down.'

'You're *working*?'

Her incredulity only made me more determined to leave immediately. I picked up my case.

'We need the money, Dorothy. How else am I to pay for the baby things? I've bought nothing yet.'

She opened her mouth and closed it. For a moment, I thought she was going to berate me for not keeping the items from when my boys were babies, but she stayed silent. She tried another tack.

'You can't leave Edwin here on his own for a week. He needs you.'

He does not, I thought. My husband was the most self-sufficient man I had ever met.

'He'll have you, Dorothy – and, as I said, we need the money. I'll write when I get to Clewer Hall. I can't wait for Edwin to come home, I need to catch the two o'clock tra—.' I faltered at the sight of her face. 'What's the matter?'

'You're going to that den of heathens?' Her voice oozed scorn.

'You mean the Hall? I heard there were once a lot of parties.'

I followed her retreating back into the kitchen where she began to unpack her basket. 'It's not parties I'm referring to. I go to *parties* with the church and suchlike. I've nothing against people enjoying themselves. It's the other stuff.'

'What other stuff?'

But she wouldn't say. Her round face was red with indignation as she pulled out a chair and opened her copy of the *Daily Mirror.*

'You'll tell Edwin for me, then? And let him know the fee will keep us going until the baby is weaned.'

'I'll wait here until he gets home.' Her mouth settled in a line as she made a show of putting on her glasses to read the inside page.

A prickle of disquiet began to creep over me as I remembered Leo's manner. 'Is there something I need to know before I go to the Hall, Dorothy?'

She looked up at me, her birdlike brown eyes holding mine. We'd never been close, in spite of our common experience of grief and loss, or perhaps because of it. Tragedy, I found, didn't necessarily bring people together.

'You're a good girl, Louisa, but the artistic type, so you're probably easily led. This is a Christian household. There are some things which went on in the Hall that were the devil's work. Take your photos and come home again.'

Chapter Two

As the train sped through the Sussex countryside, my nausea was replaced by a knot of apprehension as I tried to make sense of both Leo's and my mother-in-law's reaction to Clewer Hall. I closed my eyes, surrendering myself to the rocking of the train, and the image of the house I'd seen in the photo appeared for a moment, its stern facade brooding over the lush garden.

I sat up as the train groaned on its approach to Brighton station, its wheels squealing against the iron rails, and I used my gloved hand to wipe away the dripping condensation from the window. Peering onto the brightly lit platform, I gaped at the flurry of activity visible through the glass. I'd naively assumed I'd be deposited in a parochial backwater with plenty of people on hand to assist me, but the bustle of the station rivalled that of Paddington. Engines hissed and doors slammed, and I felt some of the tightness in my chest loosen at the familiar sounds as I pulled at the window.

'Porter. Porter!'

My shouts were swallowed up into the clatter which echoed around the arched roof and a pair of uniformed employees rushed past, hurrying towards the first-class carriage. I dragged my cases, camera and tripod from the compartment and caught the eye of another porter, who made to move on, then, I thought, took pity on my plight. We fought our way to the entrance where, together, we looked for a car which might be for me. It was the chauffeur who spotted us first, tapping me on the shoulder.

'This way, miss.' I followed his limping figure to an ageing Wolseley, where I drew envious glances as I was deposited in the back with a blanket over my legs.

It was a miserable day near the coast, warmer than London but with a sky full of slate-coloured clouds stretching out as far as the eye could see. The car bumped along through the country-side which became a blur of high hedgerows and tiny lanes. We passed through a village consisting of a cluster of houses, a small garage with a shop attached and a post office, outside which a huddle of women stood talking. I envied their camaraderie, even though they turned to stare at me as we went by, continuing to follow our progress as we slowed and passed through a gap in a row of tall conifers.

Away from the open road, the day darkened in the overgrown foliage and I was glad of the blanket which I pulled tighter around me. Tentacles of wild dogwood crept underneath the car's hood, jabbing at my arms and straining for my face, and I suppressed the urge to cry out. The driver appeared not to notice my dis-tress, concentrating on the engine which had begun to sputter as we climbed the lane. The house had not yet come into view, but as we navigated the driveway, pockmarked with puddles and fis-sures, I felt the same chill I'd first experienced in Leo's office. The sensation of a cold finger on my heart, and heavy hands pressing on my head as my ears roared at the drop in pressure. The baby responded to my unease, squirming in protest until I shifted my weight so I was leaning on one hip as the car lurched from side to side.

Finally, Clewer Hall appeared and I drew back into the hood, hiding my face in case anyone was watching for my arrival. I was glad of the privacy as I took in the house. Leo had warned me I would find it changed from the photograph, but the once austerely imposing Hall had become a wreck of itself. The bare bones were still there – the angular design, the tall chimneys and the long, imposing windows reflecting back my gaze. Through the drizzle, though, I could see where mortar had fallen away from around the bricks, encouraging seeping damp which stained the orange-red walls. The roof was missing some of its slates, which had been left to lie shattered where they'd fallen onto the gravelled path. Even the wisteria had failed to survive the march of time. All that remained was a web of veins where the suckers had once clung to the walls.

I counted three storeys. The ground floor, with four large bay windows bulging out onto the path; an upper level, where one of the rooms in the east wing was clearly the former nursery, complete with rusted iron bars to protect the family's young; and a row of mean, small glass panes sunk into the roof indicating the servants' sleeping quarters. The kitchen and other working rooms must be at the back of the house, hidden from visitors. The gardens had once had money spent on them. I could make out the traces of extensive landscaping and a network of formal planting made indistinct by neglect and the passage of time. I was distracted from my inspection by a rustle in the scrubby, overgrown lawn. A fox, making its way through the long grass, stopped for a moment to watch our progress before disappearing out of sight.

Although we'd left the overhanging shrubbery behind us, the day was still dark, and I saw, as in the photo, that part of the house was in shadow. I looked up to see what was throwing its shade onto the Hall but saw only the watery sun hanging low in the sky, straining to lighten the day. I could see nothing which would explain the outline darkening the eastern wing which cast such a gloomy pall. Frowning, I leant forward and the image dissipated, leaving me with just the ruin to contemplate. I rubbed a hand over my face, wondering if a migraine was imminent.

The driver pulled up outside the front door which opened immediately and a tall, elderly man in a black dress coat gestured for the car to continue along the drive. His eyes, coal-black pebbles in a lined face dominated by an oversized nose, met mine.

'I don't think he wants me to enter through the front door.'

I felt a wave of hysteria rise up in my chest. Once, Bertie and I would have laughed at such old-fashioned sentiments in the life we were making for ourselves. We were proud to be neither gentry nor servant class but working people, beholden to no one. Now, with my nerves stretched, I was afraid to laugh, unsure that if I started, I'd be able to stop.

I caught the driver looking at me in the side mirror. Mistaking my mood, he winked. 'Not to worry. You'll get a better welcome round the back.'

The wheels of the car slipped along the gravel as we continued round the side of the house. The driver stopped at a door which, judging by the lingering smell of cooking vegetables, led through into the kitchen. I hoped the interior of the house wouldn't be as unwelcoming as the facade. My feet were frozen and the sleeves of my coat damp. What I needed was a warm fire and to change my clothes.

The driver didn't get out but continued to look at me in the mirror. I saw concern in his expression and guessed this was my only opportunity to arm myself against what might await me inside. I leant forward.

'Is this house well known? My mother-in-law knew of it but couldn't remember why.' A white lie, and I felt a flush creeping up my face as I spoke.

'She probably meant the séance, miss. Years ago now, but it was attended by Mr Conan Doyle. You know, the detective writer?

Caused quite a stir at the time – it even made it into the London papers.'

'Why was it so famous?'

I saw him hesitate. 'A gentleman wrote down every word so the details were there, plain to see, in the newspaper. Tales of long-dead friends and relatives come back to communicate with the living. None of us liked it below stairs but some people don't have any sense.'

He switched off the engine and turned to me. I saw, for the first time, the scar which ran from the top of his temple, down past his ear and under his collar. It was puckered in places, inexpertly sewn in the trenches, I assumed, like the wounds of so many others.

'If you don't mind me saying, miss. You'd be best off staying away from all that. There's some things not to be tampered with.'

Chapter Three

I sat thinking as the driver padded around the car to open my door. A famous séance. So that was what had so upset Dorothy. Well, I can't say I was surprised. She and her church friends were hardly likely to approve of communicating with the dead. The devil's work, she'd called it. It didn't explain Leo's reaction, though, nor the warning the driver had been at pains to convey. The Victorian liking for séances was well known and hardly newsworthy. My mother had attended a couple, I remembered, when I was a child. I'd awaited her return with bated breath, watching through the bannisters from my spot on the landing, but she'd come back from the evenings laughing at the absurdity of it all. Séances were not to be feared. There must be something more.

I took a deep breath and, accepting the driver's offer of an arm, avoided looking up at the house looming over me as I stepped out of the car. We'd parked next to a rose garden. The bushes tilting in the beds were lifeless and the heads of the summer flowers had been left to decay and freeze on the stems. There couldn't be a gardener on the staff any longer as no self-respecting plants-man would have left roses in such a state. Above the garden was a terrace which must once have been impressive. Now, the stucco was peeling and unswept leaves gathered in the corners. Two sparrows rested on the balustrade, their heads to one side as they watched me straighten my coat, and I became aware of the sensation of pressure dropping once more, a consciousness of all the energy being sucked out of the day, leaving only silence. I began to fear I might be falling ill, which would be disastrous for my commission. Whatever happened, I would need to hide any signs of weakness from the family. I shook my head and the noises of the garden returned, the sparrows quarrelling as they flapped away.

'Go on through to the kitchen and I'll let Colonel Clewer know you've arrived. You can leave your bags with me.' The driver began unstrapping my case from the back of the car.

'I'd rather take the camera myself. The rest I'll leave to you, although you will need to be careful with my boxes of glass plates.'

'Camera?'

I pointed at the square leather box on the back seat. 'I'll carry this myself.'

There were footsteps behind me and a female voice, clear and refined, spoke. 'Miss Drew?'

I spun round to see a woman in her late forties walking towards the car, her face etched with fine lines. Her faded hair and pale eyes reminded me of the roses in the garden, distressed but with a hint of former beauty. I found my anxieties dissipating at her smile, such a contrast to the dark Hall and unwelcoming elderly servant.

'Why didn't you drop her at the front of the house?' she asked the driver. 'Oh, don't tell me, Horwick sent you round here. Never mind.' She came towards me and held out a hand. 'I'm Lily Clewer. Let me take you into the sitting room for some tea.'

I lifted my camera from the car and my coat slipped open, revealing my ungainly shape. 'It's *Mrs* Drew.'

Lily's eyes went from my stomach to my face and she took a step backwards. 'This way. My father's looking forward to meeting you.'

She turned, but not before I'd heard the tremor in her voice and seen the flash of concern on her face. The driver was also looking at me in alarm but wouldn't catch my eye as he disappeared with my case.

'When is your baby due?' Lily's words were infused with suppressed emotion as I heaved my camera behind her, struggling to keep up with her brisk pace.

'Not for another six weeks.'

Her shoulders relaxed a little. 'Your first?'

'No, but I have none living.'

She faltered and looked round, glancing down at my bag.

'I prefer to carry my camera.'

'I'll be careful.' She prised the handle from my fingers and my aching back loosened as I was relieved of the weight.

'You'll be gone by next weekend at the latest,' she said, her eyes once more on my stomach. I wondered who in the family had insisted on me taking up the commission if my pregnancy was so unnerving for this woman.

I followed Lily into a hall, the vibrant colours of the interior a surprise after the dreariness of the outside. The walls were painted a deep bottle green and, at the far end, two ornate pillars rose to the ceiling, framing a drawing room full of glass cabinets beyond. My photographs would bring out the rooms in all their splendour, with no hint of the smell of damp which infused the air. We had entered through the porch at the centre of the house, which meant the wing which had appeared in shadow outside was to my right. I could see very little, just a long corridor which was brightly lit. The first door off the passage was ajar, revealing part of a wall covered in a crewelwork design of brown swirls.

I stepped towards it, pulled by an indefinable sense of sadness I could detect coming from the wing. I could recognise a grieving house – God knows, I knew how that felt – but this was something more.

'Not that way.' Lily stopped and peered down at me. 'Is everything all right? Perhaps you need to rest first?'

I shook my head. 'No, really. Everything's fine.'

She hurried me away to the left and we passed, without introductions, a widow in her mourning weeds ensconced in the drawing room. Fat and squat in her chair, she sat at a mahogany table opposite a wan woman in a loose-fitting dress who pondered over a row of picture cards. The pair were wrapped in a cloak of complicity for, apart from a brief glance in my direction, neither acknowledged my presence as I hurried through the room. Lily, too, appeared keen to avoid introductions, and I felt rather as I had done on the day Edwin took me to church to meet his mother and she had snubbed me to continue a conversation with one of her acquaintances.

We entered a more homely sitting room, furnished in a style fashionable two decades earlier. A man was sitting in one of the far chairs and, as I followed Lily to meet her father, I marvelled at how, in this frozen house, something inside me was coming to life.

Curiosity killed the cat, my mother used to say when I'd got into another scrape at home, usually ending with a grazed knee or a cuff from my older brother. But inquisitiveness can help you overcome a lot of things in life, I've found. It was curiosity, after all, that first made me accept the offer of a camera to see if I could take a decent portrait of a brother who has long been lost to me. I'd learnt, in my new life, to quash all my inquisitiveness, but in Clewer Hall I felt the stirrings of that suppressed side of my nature.

I was curious to discover the identities of the two women Lily had not introduced me to, hastening me past as if I were something shameful. The squat widow's glance might have been brief as I hurried by but, as our eyes had met, a silent communication passed between us. I had only just arrived in this decaying house, and here was another dismayed at my presence.

Chapter Four

CLEWER HALL
25 June 1896
9.07 p.m.

As the air cleared, Ada Watkins stifled the urge to cough. She slipped a peppermint into her mouth, its sticky sweetness soothing her throat, raw from speaking in several voices. The smoking candle had been a blessing, its choking fumes thickening the air and compensating for the bright gas lamp the journalist had insisted on placing in the middle of the table. Watching the young newspaperman opposite her, she traced with her fingertips the carved pattern of berries and leaves on the Whitby jet mourning brooch pinned to her chest. It was a design chosen so as not to offend any of her clients, although she'd noticed the spoilt madam two places to her left staring at it during the séance.

The journalist was struggling to finish his transcription. His shorthand was too slow for the speed of her messages, something that he, if not Ada, had failed to anticipate. If there were problems later, she would claim he hadn't accurately transcribed her words and had been forced to rely on his memory at the end of the session. Through the table light, she could see a sheen of sweat on his face from the hot room. Henry Storey would go far in his profession, she was sure. He had the ability, unusual in Ada's experience of men, of being able to do more than one task at any given time. He'd carefully written down her communications from the previous hour while watching for any movement he might be able to report to his London readers as trickery.

The mood in the room was subdued. The great detective writer was the first to stand, patting his evening jacket for his cigar case before slipping off into the night. During the séance his expression had been both bored and watchful. She'd heard he was a believer, but he too had kept an eye on Ada's hands. She watched him extinguish the smoking candle with his fingertips and disappear through the door which gave onto the terrace.

From experience, Ada knew it was best to stay at the table while the guests departed. It prolonged the air of intimacy and ensured there were no embarrassing scenes on the way out. She kept her eyes on the wall opposite where the pattern on the embossed leather covering danced in the haze, smelling faintly of the stables. Her eyes focused on an image of a small chimpanzee squatting amongst the branches, its expression mocking.

At the sound of a choked sob, she turned her head. Helene Clewer was being helped from the table by her daughter, Lily, who shot Ada a venomous glance as she passed through the door. Their neighbour, Sir Thomas Jensen, hurried after them, his mood dark, leaving her alone with the journalist. Henry had finished his transcription and was gazing at her as he drew a sketch on the back of his notes.

She frowned. 'That's not going in the newspaper, is it?'

'It's just for me. We can use the photograph we printed last year.'

She watched him for a moment as he filled the paper with thick, violent strokes. 'Why are you angry?'

'That was contemptible, wasn't it? Mentioning the children.'

'I simply pass on what my spirit guide tells me.'

'Of course, Mrs Watkins.' Henry slammed the pencil on the

table. 'If you'll excuse me.'

Ada rose, smoothing out the creases in her skirt and extracting the pin she'd hidden in her sleeve earlier that day. She bent it back into its usual shape and slipped it into her hair. Picking up her father's pocket watch, she saw she had twenty minutes until the trap arrived – time for some night air before the journey back to London. She passed through into the orangery and opened the doors, letting in the warm evening air filled with the scent of tobacco and lush roses in full bloom. Her eyes were alert, darting around to find the source of her earlier unease, but all she could hear was the sound of hushed voices talking on the terrace. She crept along the side of the house, unseen by the speakers and spotted, through the light from the storm lantern, Conan Doyle inhaling deeply on his cigar.

'You didn't feel inspired to join us, Felix?'

Felix Clewer leant back against the wall, also smoking, keeping one hand in his pocket and his eyes on the darkening garden. He picked a shard of tobacco from his moustache. 'I'm happy to indulge my wife, but I draw the line at taking part in an obvious charade.' He took a final puff of his cigar and placed the stub on the ash stand. 'Why was Helene crying?'

Conan Doyle leant forward and his words were lost to Ada. She waited, unconcerned at the consternation she'd caused. Spirits were an unreliable lot. You never knew what they'd communicate to you and sometimes you had to embellish a little.

Felix jerked back at Conan Doyle's words. 'I knew this evening would end in folly.'

'You have to keep a clear head about these things, Felix. For every honest medium there's a fake. Ada Watkins . . . well, let's just say I didn't see any obvious forms of trickery, but some are better at hiding it than others.'

'Do you think she's even a widow?'

'It's possible, although anyone can wear a black gown.'

Ada made to leave, infuriated at their tone.

'Odd, though.'

Ada stopped and held her breath in the shadows.

'What was?' asked Felix.

'I don't suppose it's anything. There was a strange atmosphere this evening. You made the right decision to stay out of there.'

So he'd felt it too. Brooding, Ada made her way to the front of the house in time to see Sir Thomas snatch his hat from Horwick's outstretched hand. She could feel the force of the man's displeasure, as could Horwick, whose nervousness was making him stammer.

'L-leaving so soon? I should mention your departure to C-colonel Clewer.'

'Don't bother.' Sir Thomas moved off down the drive. 'I'll call round in the morning to make my apologies. I've had quite enough for this evening.'

Ada hesitated, watching the man's departing back. Sir Thomas was taking the shortcut through the gardens to his neighbouring property. He moved briskly across the lawn and, in the moonlight, she could see the man's cane lashing up and down.

Horwick spotted her and moved back in distaste. 'You'll want your payment.' He left her briefly in the hall and returned with a pile of coins which he slid into her hand. She checked to ensure they were all sovereigns.

'I can hear the trap coming up the drive.' Another who was anxious to be rid of her.

'I need to get my things.'

She hurried through to the darkening room, opened her reticule and placed the coins, along with the small handbell and her father's watch, into her black beaded bag. The table was bare, with the exception of a piece of paper left behind by the young reporter. Perhaps he had gifted her the portrait he had drawn of her? It was unlikely to be flattering, but no matter. The public would only see the photograph she'd had taken in the Soho studio.

Curious, Ada reached out, noticing that, unlike the dark cream notepaper used by Henry, this leaf was pale blue and lightly scented. Not her portrait, then. Ada unfolded the paper and looked at the message.

'CHARLATAN.'

Chapter Five

Felix Clewer took my hand, the strength of his grip pulling me slightly towards him. With any other, the gesture would have been alarming but, as I steadied myself, I saw he was smiling, his eyes taking in my appearance with none of his daughter's discomposure. He was slightly built, standing only a little taller than me, sporting a Hussar moustache which I always associated with the military. This was the man who'd amassed the collection I was to photograph in advance of its disposal to buyers from around the world.

'You'll have some tea? There's cake, too.' He pointed towards a delicate porcelain tea set laid out on the table, the cups shimmering with a pale blue glaze.

'Thank you. I haven't eaten all day.'

Lily frowned and picked up a small handbell, its high-pitched chime echoing around the room. 'You'll need more than seed cake if this is your first meal.' She saw my eyes on the bell. 'We've been unable to use the servants' system since the main copper wire snapped. In any case, there's just Horwick, and Janet who comes in from the village every day to help out. They're never far away during the daytime. You'll find a bell in each room if you need to get their attention.'

'I shouldn't need to trouble them too much.'

Felix returned to his armchair with its view over the darkening garden. Lily took one of the sofas, her usual spot, judging by the pile of books and a pair of reading glasses on the side table. I hesitated and eased myself onto the other sofa, the springs creaking at my weight.

'We kept meaning to change the bell system to electric when we had a generator put in but it doesn't matter now. Perhaps the Hall's new owners will install it – if they can find the staff, of course.'

'Those currently here aren't staying?'

Lily set the cups on their saucers. The china was without a single blemish, a set incongruous amongst the faded furnishings.

'Horwick's retiring to his sister's boarding house in Bournemouth. Janet may stay but I'm sure she's had better offers elsewhere. She remains with us because her mother was a maid in the house, thirty or so years ago. I'm not sure her loyalty will stretch to new owners.'

'And the driver who brought me here?'

'Quinlivan? He might be persuaded to remain. He's very useful to have around – he helps out in the house, getting involved in everything Horwick is now too old to manage. And there's cook, of course, but Mrs Wherry is also looking to retire soon.'

The door opened and the elderly man who'd shooed me to the back of the house appeared. I could see, from his openly curious expression as he stared at my swollen form that they'd been talking about me in the servants' quarters.

'Horwick, could you ask cook to arrange some sandwiches for our visitor? Bring them in here. I'm sure I could manage one or two as well.'

He bowed slightly, his eyes still on me, and retreated from the room. Lily, I noticed, was relaxing in the presence of her father. As she busied herself pouring the tea, I took the chance to study her more closely. Her unremarkable but well-cut outfit, a powder-blue bouclé skirt and cardigan set, should have suited her fair hair but instead made her look insipid and, in the garden, she hadn't struck me as that. My mother would have observed that she needed to make more of herself.

'I was told you'd specifically requested me to photograph your home. Are you familiar with my work?'

Lily paused in her task as she considered my question.

'We knew of you as a lady photographer operating in London. I asked Mr Stephens to see if you were available.'

'But who—?'

'Please help yourself to cake.' Lily handed me a cup. 'We asked for you at the auction house as Louisa Drew. I hadn't realised you were married.'

She was evading my question but I didn't press the matter as mention of my past, which I so rarely discussed, produced a flash of anguish. *Stay in London*, I told the grief. *Let me forget for a moment in this house.* I took a deep breath.

'Drew was the name of my first husband. It's how I've always been known professionally, although I was widowed in the war. J.C. Stephens will simply have contacted my employer to find me.'

'You've remarried, then? What name do you go by now?'

I paused. 'My last name now is Tandy but I see no reason to change my name for my work.'

I saw Lily glance at her father and I wasn't surprised. The vote might have been extended to some of us women but keeping the name of your dead husband, even for professional purposes, was hardly conventional.

'I'd prefer it if you called me Louisa.'

'Louisa it is, then – that's settled.' Felix reached into his jacket pocket and pulled out a thin cigar. 'Do you mind if I smoke while you have tea? It's too chilly to open a window but I can go outside if you prefer.'

I looked towards the door which led onto a terrace faintly lit by an ancient storm lamp. From here I could see, despite the cracked casings, that the windows were clean, the opaqueness of the glass due only to the gathering dusk. I caught the smell of beeswax and vinegar and wondered if the family had cleaned the room for my arrival.

'Please feel free to enjoy your cigar.'

I braced myself for a return of the nausea but the curls of smoke which drifted over to me produced a comforting fug. The room had a gentle peace to it, the only noise the clink of coals rolling in the fireplace hidden behind an embroidered screen and Felix's occasional draw on his cigar. It made a nonsense of my apprehension – but I couldn't shake the creep of dread on my skin. The fear had retreated for a moment, although I was sure it was only for a moment. In a room far beyond us, I could hear a woman, or child possibly, singing to a tune on the piano, their off-key pitch oddly beautiful.

Lily watched me take a sip of the tea which was infused with a taste of peaches and damp bark.

'Do you like it? It's from a plantation in Darjeeling close to where we're moving to. Father has taken a five-year lease on a house in the region.'

'It tastes wonderful.' This wasn't strictly true. The infusion had a bitter aftertaste, but this might have been caused by pregnancy, which distorted some flavours.

Lily leant back, her expression relieved. 'I've never visited India but, in my most anxious moments, I think about the smell of the tea and am reassured everything will be fine with the move.'

'Why that part of India?'

Felix studied the glowing tip of his cigar. 'I spent time in the region when Lily was very young and we were at war with the Afghans. Our garrison was stationed in Jalapahar, a town of green hills and wide skies. In the afternoon, the cloud would come down and it was like heaven on earth. It was made all the more memorable in contrast to the horror which came after it.'

'Horror?'

'Sorry, I'm being fanciful. It must be the time of day. I meant war. I was sent to Afghanistan.'

I remembered the driver's mention of Conan Doyle. 'Like Dr Watson.'

I caught Lily glance across at her father but he didn't look up from his cigar. 'Yes, exactly. Although unlike the fictional Watson, I returned uninjured.' He winced, the gesture of a survivor. 'Later, on my return trip to England, I passed through the region again and stayed with some friends who'll be our new neighbours. They wrote to me about the house coming available.'

'You're looking forward to it?' I asked Lily, half my attention still on the singing. It was a child, I was sure. I tried to make out the tune but it remained just out of reach, an old-fashioned melody I recalled from my nursery days.

'Once we've persuaded Mother it's not such a bad thing, I'll find leaving everything easier. This house is too big for us. We all need a fresh start.'

The room fell silent again, the easy comfort between father and daughter gone. Lily passed me a piece of cake, I'd been too polite to help myself, and I took a mouthful of the dry, seedy slice.

'After tea, I'll take you to your room. I think we can wait until tomorrow for you to start work. Janet has agreed to give you a tour of the house, but it's best Father shows you the items from his collection. You have a list from the auctioneers, I think.'

'I have.'

'And you think your photographs will take around a week?'

'At most. It depends on the light and how much I can get done each day. I'll develop the images as I go along. I just need somewhere dark to process the plates, a cellar, for example.'

Lily made a face. 'The cellars are very damp. Perhaps one of the outbuildings will be better. Quinlivan can help you cover up any windows.'

'Then I'll speak to him in the morning.'

'I'm pleased your husband could spare you at short notice.' She hesitated. 'He was happy for you to come?'

Edwin. Well, I'd hardly given him the chance to object, leaving so suddenly. My sneaky departure wasn't anything to be proud of but I could never explain myself properly to Edwin. Words froze in my throat once I received one of his withering glances. I looked at the ormolu clock on the mantelpiece. He would be home from work soon and Dorothy would have the job of explaining to him the reasons for my sudden flight.

'I'll try to telephone him at his place of work tomorrow. He'll be relieved to hear I've arrived safely.'

'I'm sorry we left it so late – everything is rather rushed at the moment. We'll have a houseful of guests next week. It'll be like old times.'

'I can keep out of your way, if it's inconvenient.'

'Not inconvenient, no. I just hope we don't get in *your* way.'

Horwick came in carrying a plate of sandwiches which he placed in front of me on the table. I took two triangles and bit into one of them, my teeth sinking into the soft bread until they reached the crunch of the cucumber. I put the other aside, trying not to look greedy.

'Is it a celebration? The gathering, I mean.'

Lily frowned but, before she could answer, the singing abruptly stopped and I heard a shout of distress from the adjoining room. After a moment the door opened and the elderly widow I'd passed earlier stood on the threshold, her bulk filling the frame.

'Mrs Clewer's had an upset.'

Lily hurried out of the room while Felix, nodding apologies in my direction, opened the door onto the garden and stepped out into the blackened afternoon. I was left alone with the widow in her bombazine mourning dress which showed signs of extensive mending. We stared at each other without speaking, the dismay I'd caught as I hurried past her in the central drawing room still showing in her expression. She was about the age my mother would have been, had cancer not robbed me of her comforting presence. Like my mother, she wore her hair in a pompadour style, hopelessly out of date, of course, but with a reassuring Edwardian elegance.

I found myself unable to stop staring at her as the silence stretched thin, with just the sound of our breathing and the crackling of the fire. Finally, determined to take the initiative, I stood, making more of a fuss of getting to my feet than I'd have liked.

'I'm Louisa.'

Instead of taking my outstretched hand, she leant forward and put a powdered cheek to mine. I could smell the camphor of mothballs mixed with the woman's cheap perfume, a sickly combination which caused acid to rise in my throat.

She kept her face close to mine. 'You've been here before, I think.' She clutched my arm. 'Haven't you?'

I shook my head, modulating my voice to show that she had nothing to fear from me. 'This is my first visit to the Hall. Why do you ask?'

'Are you sure?' I felt her fingers tighten. Her face was still next to mine, her peppermint breath brushing my cheek.

'The house is very distinctive. I'd know if I'd visited in the past.'

She relaxed and released me from her grip, her brow still furrowed. I saw that the fringe of her shawl was frayed, a single thread trailing to the floor. Without asking, she reached down for my stomach and let her hand slide over the swelling.

'How far gone?'

'Seven, nearly eight months.'

I could hear the alarm in her voice as she stepped away. 'I thought it all made sense but now I'm not so sure. It never occurred to me you might be expecting. I wish I'd known about the baby first.'

Chapter Six

I was saved from further scrutiny by a servant in a cocoa-brown housedress opening the door. She entered without knocking, frowning when she saw my companion. This must be Janet, whose mother had once been a servant at the Hall. I'd expected a capped maid, all deference and curiosity but Janet, although aged around twenty, had the dress and assurance of an experienced housekeeper. Her face was flushed, two spots of carmine staining her cheeks.

'Miss Lily has asked me to show you upstairs.'

I picked up my camera, still unsettled by the widow's reaction to my presence. I touched her briefly on the shoulder before I left the room and she reacted to my gesture of comfort by reaching up to grasp my hand. The baby sensed her unease, kicking at my abdomen, and I put my free hand over the swelling, trying to soothe the child. Janet led me up wide oak stairs covered by a strip of narrow Persian carpet, worn in places, but the colours undimmed against the wood.

'Who was the woman with me in the sitting room?'

'Mrs Ada Watkins, ma'am.' She paused. 'A friend of the family.'

As I looked down over the balustrade, I could see Ada taking her seat again at the mahogany table and reaching for the picture cards. I paused, taking in the scene. The glass cabinets were out of sight, tucked under where the great stairs met the upper gallery. I had a better view of the wide drawing room and the wing I had seen in shadow outside. The passageway to the east still pulsated with repressed energy and I'd have lingered if Ada hadn't looked up with a flash of concern. I couldn't understand her fears. Her words suggested that she had played a role in my appointment but was now regretting it. My head pounded as I tried to make sense of it all.

I hurried to catch up with Janet, who had stopped outside a room at the end of a passageway directly over the wing of the house which so repelled me. There was nothing up here to account for my fears. It was a little chilly, perhaps, but then I'd been thawed by the sitting room fire.

'I'm putting you next to the old nursery. It means we won't have to move you when the guests come. The Colonel always put a good store in his children's education, so the governess had decent living quarters.'

She pushed at a door which opened onto a large room, the walls papered with rose-pink stripes. A heavy iron bed dominated the space, a bolster stretching its span on top of a plump floral eiderdown. The only other furniture was a set of drawers, a bedside table with a lamp on it, the bulb occasionally flickering, and a washstand.

Janet snapped the curtains across the window, fussing to ensure they were hanging straight. 'If I'd known you were expecting I'd have suggested a room on the other side of the house with the bathroom. Here, there's only a privy across the landing.'

'That will be fine.'

'Do you like the room?'

I forced a smile. 'It's lovely.' But it wasn't. Unlike the shabby warmth of the sitting room, this space had an icy sharpness to it. Underneath the handsome fire surround there were sticks of kindling and shrivelled pine cones in the hob grate, wait-ing for a match to light the tinder. Perhaps the room needed warmth. Janet made no move towards the hearth, confirming my status as neither guest nor servant. I'd be expected to look after myself during my stay here. I lifted my camera onto the chest of drawers while Janet gazed at the bed where my suitcase had been placed, causing the counterpane to pucker around its edges.

'Dinner will be at seven. You'll hear the gong up here. Sound carries in this house. The first, at ten minutes to, as a reminder, and the second time, on the hour.'

After she left, I sank into the bed and rested my arm on my case, taking in the atmosphere. A room occupied by a succession of governesses, most likely teaching Lily into adulthood and the boys until they went to school. The place must have once been a riot of sounds, which made the silence now all the more unbearable. I needed to shake away my gloomy thoughts by some physical activity. If this was to be my room for the next week, I might as well try to make myself comfortable. I unpacked my case – what little I had in it – and checked that the photographic plates, the chemicals and the zinc processing bath had survived the trip to the Hall. Nothing had spilt, but as I opened the clasp, the foul tang of the potassium bromide made me swoon with heady memories.

I needed another table to place my camera on each evening but I didn't want to disturb the family so soon into my stay. Surely one of the other rooms would have a spare piece of furniture? I opened the door of my room and surveyed the empty corridor. Janet had told me my bedroom was next to the old nursery and I tried the door on my right. It stuck for a moment, then yielded, a fusty smell rushing at my face as I fumbled for the light switch. Although bare of toys, it was still recognisably a place for children. At one end, near the barred window overlooking the front garden, was a round table, its top scarred with age, surrounded by worm-ridden chairs. Towards the back of the room were the remains of dismantled beds: a heap of white metal and stained mattresses. None of the furniture would be suitable for my purpose.

I crossed to the window, straining to look out onto the night, but could only see my reflection in the glass. My dark hair, bobbed to Edwin's dismay last summer, had grown to my shoulders but I still preferred it to the heavy bun I'd worn during my last pregnancy. I smiled at my reflection, split by the rusting metal bars outside the window, enjoying the sense of freedom in this wreck of a house.

My smile fell away as I became aware of that same drop of pressure I'd experienced earlier. The faint creak of the house and the tread of feet on wooden steps replaced by a feeling of weight against my scalp, as if a pair of hands was pushing me under water. As I stared at the glass, my reflection faded to be replaced by nothing, just the blackness of the night. I might not be there – my face had disappeared. For a moment, and it went to show how tired my eyes were, I thought I saw the outline of a child in the room behind me. A silhouette, that was all, but when I spun round, it was the same desolate, empty space. Confused, I rubbed my eyes as the outside sounds returned. First, the patter of rain on the glass and then the sound of the front door closing with a heavy thud. When I looked again, my reflection had reappeared in the window.

Embarrassed at the effect of the long journey on me, I crossed the room towards my own. I needed to rest so I didn't appear a half-wit at dinner that evening. I slipped off my shoes and rolled down my stockings, draping them over the washstand. My body heavy, I took out from the drawer my travelling clock, a present from Bertie long ago; I could hear the mechanism ticking which was odd as I was sure I hadn't wound it up before my journey.

I must have been mistaken, because when I turned the spring, I found it fully coiled. I set the alarm for six, which would give me ample time to change for dinner. Slipping off my dress, I got underneath the covers and submitted to the pull of sleep.

Chapter Seven

When I awoke, I thought I'd gone blind. I'd forgotten about the deep, still black of the countryside. For the first time in months, I'd dreamt of nothing, but instead of feeling rested, my eyelids were as if weighted with coins. Worse, I was so desperate for water I could barely swallow. It must have been the Darjeeling. I hadn't enjoyed the bitter aftertaste of the brew and it had left me with a raging thirst. I fumbled for the lamp and found the switch on the twisted twine, confused because I was sure I'd gone to bed with the light on. Picking up my clock, I saw it was nearly eleven. I'd slept through my alarm and through dinner, and no one had thought to come for me.

Annoyed with myself, I crossed to the washstand and shook the pitcher. There was water in the jug for me to wash but I couldn't guarantee it was fresh enough to drink. One friend who lived in the country told me they drew the water for the bedroom ewers from a stream and I couldn't take the chance with the baby.

With unsteady legs, I put my dress back on and found the water closet, a small windowless cupboard between two rooms. I took a few handfuls of water from the tap and, revived, groped my way down the stairs lit only by a faint strip of moonlight coming in through the front window. In the drawing room, I half expected Ada to still be there, pondering over her cards but the space was empty, with only the smell of camphor in the air. Across the room I could see the passageway, still emitting its fetid invitation.

I turned my back on the passage, allowing my eyes to grow accustomed to the shadows thrown by the faint light.

I reached out to the wall, hoping to find a light switch but flinched as my hands came into contact with the fur of the flock wallpaper. Next to an oil lamp on the table I found a glass jar of matches and struck one, lighting the wick and replacing the glass shade with shaking hands. A faint breeze – from a gap in the window, possibly – made the flame flicker as I lifted the lamp to survey the room. Illuminated was a maze of doors, all shut, with no clue as to which one would lead me down into the kitchen. Remembering the cooking smell from the afternoon, I calculated I'd need to enter the wing on my right.

I crept towards the passageway, conscious of my heart thudding in my chest, my throat parched once more, trying to ignore the pressure of nausea which increased with each step. I found my footsteps slowing and the crawl of dread creeping up my skin. Cutting across the oppressive silence came the sudden roar of something being dislodged from the walls deep within the passage and shattering to the ground. I panicked, tripping over my feet as I fled, pulling at the front door to escape into the frosty night.

In the garden, the icy night air brought me to my senses. Used to the din of the city, I was reassured a little by the sound of an owl hooting in the distance and the stab of sharp wind on my cheek. I nearly laughed at my folly, although I hadn't recovered enough to re-enter the house. I took a deep breath, considering my options. I knew that if I retraced my path from earlier in the day, I would find the tradesmen's entrance and the way into the kitchen. Servants are often the last to go to bed and, as the front door was unlocked, at least one must be awake. My feet crunched on glittering gravel stones as I went along the front of the house, passing a row of tall cypresses whose tips bent in the strong breeze. As I brushed against them, their needles dropped spears of ice onto my dress, hurrying me forward towards the anticipated warmth.

I was alert to every sound, my heart stopping at a rustling in the nearby bushes and the crack of twigs snapping.

'Hello?'

I heard a footstep behind me and turned to see a shadow run across the path. It bumped into me, I was sure, forcing me to grasp one of the fragrant pines to stop myself tumbling to the floor. Nearby, an animal shrieked. Bertie, a country boy, would have recognised it but I only knew that, fox or badger, it was the desperate cry of an animal in pain.

'Who's there?' There was no response, only the whoosh of the wind amongst the leaves. 'Hello?'

I cursed my stupidity at coming out in the freezing night.

'Are you all right, miss?'

I swung round, still holding the swinging branch. It was Quinlivan, whose breath, misting across me in the dark, held a trace of whisky I remembered well from my father.

'I saw something in the undergrowth, a shape which came out of the trees. There was a cry, too.' I could hardly get the words out, my breathing laboured and my child somersaulting inside me.

'The cat, perhaps? We have a mouser who lives in the kitchen.'

'Larger than a cat. The size of a child or monkey.'

'A monkey?'

His tone released the tension and I started to laugh. 'I didn't mean an actual monkey.'

'That's a relief at least. Let me get you inside before you catch your death. What are you doing out here?'

'I overslept and then couldn't find my way around the house to the kitchen. I thought it might be easier from the outside.'

Fearing his ridicule, I made no mention of the passage.

'We lock up every evening about this time. You could have been outside all night if I hadn't seen you. Are you hungry?'

'Famished.'

'Cook is still up. We were going to leave a tray for you.'

He steered me back into the drawing room and through a door in the far corner. I looked towards the passageway.

'I heard something dropping from along that wing.'

'That's the worst part of the Hall. It was probably plaster falling from a wall. The rooms at the end have nearly rotted away. You'll soon get used to strange sounds around this house.'

So it had been a chunk of wall hitting the floor which had so startled me. I could have kicked myself for my idiocy. At least I'd only made a fool of myself in front of Quinlivan, who was taking it all in his stride. He steered me through a door which opened onto a corridor with a vaulted ceiling, impressive except for the patches of mildew staining the whitewashed walls.

'Be careful, the floor's uneven.'

He kept his hand on my back as we descended stone steps until I felt the heat of the kitchen summoning me with its warmth. I blinked as we emerged into the light of the range and saw, next to it, an elderly woman sitting in a spindle-back chair nursing a cup of tea.

'This is Mrs Drew.' Quinlivan pulled out a seat for me. 'I think she could do with some food.'

Unlike cooks in overwrought novels, Mrs Wherry was thin, the lines around her eyes showing the years of hard work and poor light.

'I've made up a cold collation. You'll have something hot in the morning.' She nodded towards a tray. 'You can eat it here or in your room, if you prefer.'

I lifted the cloth and saw a dish of ham and potatoes with a sliced tomato, not dissimilar to the type of meal I made at home.

'I'll join you, if you don't mind.'

Quinlivan drew a cup from a big brown teapot, set it in front of me and poured one for himself.

'She was outside trying to find her way around the house.'

Mrs Wherry held her cup out for another. 'I'd have got Horwick to call you for dinner. I was the same with my two. Half asleep during the day, then I'd be up in the night, ravenous. What were you going to do in a strange house? But Miss Lily told us to let you sleep and there's no arguing with her.'

'I'd have preferred to be woken.'

'Of course you would,' said Mrs Wherry, happy to have been proved right. I picked up my knife and fork and began to eat.

'You'll have to call me Alice – none of this Mrs Wherry nonsense. There's precious few of us servants left to stand on ceremony. Come down here any time you feel peckish. It's a shame the family want you to eat with them. You'd find it more comfortable in the warmth.'

'I'm sure, but they've made me feel very welcome so far. I've been put in the old governess's room.'

She made a face. 'It's a nice room, even if it's a sad reminder of better times.'

'The family lost sons in the war, didn't they?' I was talking with my mouth full but was too hungry to care.

'All three.' Alice pulled off her cap, ruffling her wispy grey hair. 'Although the Clewers aren't the only gentry around here to have lost their heirs.'

'Were they in the same regiment? I heard towards the end of the war they were trying to split brothers up to spare one for their parents.'

Quinlivan put his cup down with a thud on the table. Alice glanced at him but turned to me, happy to talk about the lost children. 'The eldest two were. Archie was a regular. He'd set his heart on a military career like his father and joined the Royal Sussex from school. He was the first to die at Ypres. Richard volunteered after Archie's death, although the mistress pleaded with him to stay. He was lost at Boar's Head.'

I looked at Quinlivan. 'Boar's Head?'

He rubbed his face. 'It was a push against the German line. A smaller battle, but the Sussex lost a lot of men in the counter-attack.'

'And the youngest?'

Alice made a face. 'Cecil had bad asthma and was rejected by the army. One day he was handed a white feather by a woman who saw he wasn't in uniform. He liked the sea and asked at the recruitment office to join the Navy, who enlisted him despite his bad chest. Towards the end of the war, they were taking anyone. He drowned in the Aegean on the *Louvain*.'

'Terrible to lose all three,' I said, picking up my cup. I assumed Helene Clewer, their mother, was the pale-looking woman I had seen opposite Ada. We were linked by the loss of our sons, although she had paid little notice of me as I'd passed.

The tea was unexpectedly strong and reviving, a contrast to the Darjeeling earlier which hadn't agreed with me. Alice looked at my empty plate with approval.

'I have a son of my own but he came back, thank God. What about you? Did you lose anyone?'

I made a face, the tea turning sour in my throat.

'Perhaps she doesn't want to talk about it,' suggested Quinlivan.

I looked again at the wound, the wide band of scar tissue suggesting a hurried repair to his face. 'You were injured in the trenches?'

'A piece of shrap. The chap next to me lost most of the top of his head but was still breathing when I was lying next to him.

They gave me brandy while they stitched me up and shipped me back to Blighty to recuperate. Five months later I was back at the front.'

I set down my cup, twisting my wedding ring around my finger. For my second marriage I'd reused the one Bertie had given me, a betrayal I'd never forgive myself for. But times were lean and it was a bittersweet reminder that I had once known happiness.

'I wonder what the next generation will think of our tragedy? I'd hate to think that it's only us going to remember.'

'No one's going to forget – we just don't want to live in the past.' Quinlivan had clearly had enough of the subject.

Alice, her cup halfway to her mouth, said, 'I hear you met Ada Watkins earlier.'

'We had a brief chat in the sitting room.' The woman's odd reaction to my presence came rushing back. I paused, wondering how much I should reveal to this pair so early on in our acquaintance. I decided, for the moment, to be discreet. 'Janet told me she was a friend of the family.'

'Friend? That's one way of putting it,' said Alice. 'She's sponged off them for years. The master wouldn't have her anywhere near the place if he could put his foot down. Sometimes I think the only reason he's taking them to India is to get away from that woman.'

'She's financially dependent on the family?' I asked, remembering the unkempt gardens and ageing automobile. The Clewers hadn't struck me as people with money to spare.

'Ada Watkins is a medium,' said Alice, watching my reaction.

Of course. Quinlivan had mentioned a séance. I thought of Dorothy's face again and tried not to smile. 'Mrs Clewer talks to her dead sons?'

Quinlivan stood, his scar suddenly inflamed. 'I told you in the car about the séance. It was that woman's doing. When her predictions made it into the papers, she got rich off it all. The famous Ada Watkins. She'd tour the country, visiting houses, playing to packed theatres. All from that one night.'

I remembered the patched dress. 'She appears in reduced circumstances now.'

'But still she won't leave them alone. It happened before I was here, of course, but she's been a visitor for as long as I can remember.'

Alice pulled at Quinlivan's arm, a motherly gesture, but he shook her off. 'It'll be her last time here but she's certainly going out with a fanfare.'

'What do you mean?' I asked.

Quinlivan retreated into the scullery. I heard the clank of his mug against the sink and he reappeared wiping his hands with a towel.

'They didn't tell you? They're going to recreate the séance next week. Same people as in 1896, the ones still alive that is, although those which aren't might make their presence felt in their own way. Because one thing's for sure: either Ada's got a direct line to the dead or her predictions on that evening when the old queen was on the throne were a bloody good guess.'

Chapter Eight

25 June 1896
9.33 p.m.

'This is your fault.' Lily placed a compress soaked in lavender-infused water on her mother's forehead. Daisy, Helene's maid, was hovering by the door, her eyes alight with curiosity. The speed with which she'd appeared to help Lily take Helene up the stairs suggested she had been hovering near the Adelaide Room, waiting for catastrophe to strike.

'We'll be all right now, thank you, Daisy. Can you ask cook to prepare mother's infusion? Gladys can bring up the tray. I'll ring for you when Mrs Clewer needs undressing.'

Helene was leaning against the bolster, her faint not helped by the bodice of her dress drawn tight against her chest. Loosening her mother's stays would help, but for that she needed Daisy, and there were a few things they needed to discuss first. The details of the séance would be common knowledge below stairs soon enough. Everyone talked and, where facts were missing, they soon created myths which were impossible to refute.

'I told you not to invite that woman into our house. She's so showy. Did you see she wore her mourning brooch on the right side of her blouse? She doesn't even know the basic dress conventions.'

Lily watched her mother turn away and shade her eyes from

the candle flickering on the nightstand. Helene still liked old-fashioned light in her bedroom, although she lived in fear of her bed sheets catching fire. 'She came recommended and I so wanted to please Mr Conan Doyle.'

'If he hadn't been here, then that rude journalist would never have come. He didn't stop staring at me the whole evening.'

'Are you sure? He seemed preoccupied with making his notes.' Even in her swoon, her mother's voice had a malicious trace.

Lily, irked, moved to the dressing table and lifted the lid of Helene's jewellery box, listening to the plaintive rendition of 'Für Elise'. 'Why are you so upset? You surely don't believe her predictions?'

'She threatened my family. How am I supposed to feel?'

Lily picked up the horsehair brush and pulled out the pins in her mother's hair. Helene's fair ringlets fell down her back and Lily began to brush, as she'd done countless times when, as a girl and unable to sleep, Helene had encouraged her to creep past the closed door of her governess, Miss Lewis, taking Lily into her chamber and letting her play with her bedroom trinkets. Lily felt her mother relax, her coiled tautness unwinding as she untangled the tresses.

'The fact that Mr Conan Doyle is a believer doesn't mean Ada is genuine. I'm sure—'

'What? What are you sure about?'

Lily, remembering the forthcoming newspaper article, shook her head. 'It doesn't matter.'

'But the spirit's warning was directed at *me*.'

'Mrs Watkins is a fraud who plays on our fears. She must have read up on the family before she came.'

Helene grasped Lily by the wrist. 'Then how did she know about *you*?'

Lily tried to pull out of her mother's grip but Helene held on tight. 'The servants talk. You said it yourself. We've discussed this before.'

'But the first voice she spoke in – that was my grandmother, I'm sure. She talked about my baby voice and how I used to sit on her knee in her garden.'

Helene had loosened her grasp and Lily pulled away. In the séance, Ada's voice had assumed that of an early Victorian gentlewoman, old-fashioned sentiments and endearments pouring out of her mouth, a message everyone present could have made something of. She looked at her mother's distraught face and tried again.

'Some things were applicable to everyone and some were random guesses that missed the mark. She talked about "my little egg". No one knew what she meant. She just struck lucky a few times, that's all.'

'And her reference to a child? How would you explain that?'

Helene rose from the bed, making her way towards the window. The afternoon was warm and Lily watched small rivulets of sweat trickle down her mother's back. She should call for Daisy. Her mother would feel better after her Vin Mariani, a tincture of cocaine popular amongst Sussex society women.

'I ought to go down to see the guests. I heard Sir Thomas leave, but there's still Henry Storey to entertain,' Lily said.

'Felix can look after the men.' Helene's voice was sharp.

At the sound of horses' hooves on the gravel, Lily joined her mother at the window. The Crow Man, Lily had once called old Fletcher who drove the trap from Brighton. He was always dressed in a black cloak and a tall topper, regardless of the wind blowing off the channel. They watched as Ada approached the carriage, her widow's weeds making them look like a pair of harpies. In the heat of the evening, Ada's eyes were roaming the gardens as the trap turned in front of the porch and disappeared down the drive.

'She's gone now, Mother. We don't need to see her again.'

Helene continued to look out of the window, her eyes fixed on a spot in the distance. 'We might make alternative plans for Christmas.'

'You don't believe her, Mother! Tell me you don't believe her?'

Helene, in a trance, began to twist her handkerchief. 'We might make alternative plans,' she repeated.

Chapter Nine

I woke to the sound of the clock shrilling at a pitch impossible to ignore. In my stupor, I must have forgotten to set the alarm yesterday afternoon. There was no way I could have slept through that clatter, no matter how tired I was after the journey to Sussex. I lay in the bed listening for the sound of movement in the house. I wasn't sure how to get hold of hot water to wash myself. Lily had mentioned a handbell to summon help but there was no evidence of it in my room. I should have asked Alice about arrangements during our chat in the kitchen, but Quinlivan had clammed up after his cryptic comments about Ada's predictions and we'd gone our separate ways soon after.

I washed in cold water from the ewer and dressed quickly, pulling on my faithful Holland jacket over my clothes. Once belonging to Bertie, it had long lost his smell. Bertie . . . I paused. My first husband had been a stonemason, a true craftsman tempted away from the countryside by an employer keen to utilise his skills in churches around London. His practical nature had appealed to me when we'd met and, after his death, I'd taken comfort from the fact that I was carrying on the artisan tradition with my photography. I had hoped to pass on our practical talents to our sons. It was not to be. For a moment, I closed my eyes and allowed myself the fantasy that it was Bertie's child I was carrying. How glorious that would be. Another chance of new life sprung from our happiness. As if to assert its independence, the child inside me jumped and I laughed. *Fair enough, little thing,* I thought. You shall be your own person.

After I left the bedroom I hesitated for a moment outside the nursery and, on a whim, pushed open the door. The room was as I'd left it the previous evening, fusty and still. Closing the door softly behind me, I made my way to the dining room for the promised hot breakfast.

Felix must have already eaten. I passed him in the sitting room, his ironed copy of the *Daily Telegraph* held up in front of his face. Horwick, his manner friendlier than the previous day, took me into the dining room and sat me down at the huge table.

'The mistress and Miss Clewer will be taking breakfast in their rooms.' I noticed he made no reference to Ada.

There was hot food, not much of it – a few devilled kidneys, the blood seeping into the silver tray and grilled tomatoes. I took two slices of charred toast and ate them dry with a cup of tea weakened with water from a small jug.

'Is Janet around?' I asked Horwick, remembering Lily's instructions that she was to show me the house.

'She starts at midday on a Saturday.'

I couldn't waste the morning's light waiting for her to arrive. I took another slug of tea, thankfully not Darjeeling, and went to Felix.

'I'm ready to start if you're available.'

He put down the paper. 'Excellent.'

He made no mention of my absence from dinner, guiding me instead into the drawing room and to the cluster of cabinets towards the back of the room. The first of them, filled with a collection of scarab amulets and seals from Ancient Egypt, took my breath away. They were dazzling in their intensity, ranging from obsidian black to copper-gold. Even a set of dull, pebble-like brooches had their own rustic charm, like the buttons on a child's coat.

'These are recent acquisitions?' I was thinking of the popularity of all things Egyptian after Howard Carter's opening of the tomb of King Tut.

Felix unfastened the cabinet and pulled out a ring, placing it into my palm. 'Egyptian amulets have been popular for centuries. I started my collection before I married. I would have acquired more but I was continually outbid in the Sussex auction house by Mr Phipps at Rye. He may be one of the buyers of some items in this collection.'

'They're being sold individually?'

'That's the plan.'

I studied the ring. The shank was fastened into the shape of a horseshoe with a navy scarab on a hinge at its head. I couldn't help myself and slipped it on my little finger, ignoring the thrill of apprehension. A small pulse began to sound in my ear, like a child's drum beating far in a distant room, drawing my eyes away from the item of jewellery towards the passageway to the east of the house. I wanted to take the ring off immediately but Felix had taken my hand and was studying it.

'It doesn't suit you. Egypt is all dust and heat. Let me show you something I would think more to your taste.'

I put the ring back in the cabinet, glad to take it off my finger. I wouldn't be able to photograph each item individually. Although I had three dozen glass plates with me, an unusually plentiful amount, I would need to arrange the objects to fit the catalogue the auctioneers put so much effort into producing. Felix, I saw, was waiting for me next to a huge four-door cabinet. I studied the grotesque creatures he thought would be more to my taste.

'These are kylins, mythical Chinese beasts. They have the head of a dragon and the body of a deer.'

Unlike the scarabs, there was little to differentiate each animal. They reminded me of the pampered dogs Hugh and Pip had loved petting when they saw them in Regent's Park. An army of tiny Pekinese puppies with their little pug faces and bulging eyes.

'They're . . . well, strange . . .'

Felix smiled. 'Not to your taste, then?' He gestured around the room. 'I could show you more but I know you're keen to get started. Each cabinet is given over to a separate group of collectibles. If you've any questions, come and find me. I'll leave it to you as to how they're best presented. First, I must show you the Adelaide Room which houses more of the collection.'

He led me out of the large drawing room towards the wing I so dreaded entering. I stopped as the tiny throb I'd felt in my ears began to get louder until I could barely hear Felix next to me.

'Is anything the matter?'

Feeling idiotic, I shook my head. 'Nothing, really.' I caught the smell of damp and a fetid, earthy odour which was harder to identify. 'Are these rooms used regularly?'

'Hardly at all. We've already shut off a few of the rooms in advance of the sale. I wouldn't go near the ones at the end of the passage. Are you sure everything is all right?'

'Yes, of course. Please lead the way.' I took a deep breath and followed him into the corridor.

The passageway was an extension of the main drawing room, a long oblong shape with an arched window at the end. In the winter sunlight, dust particles hung suspended in the corridor, creating a grimy haze. They were illuminated by a row of lamps hanging from the ceiling which also revealed six doors in the passageway, all closed. Feeling a little like Alice in Wonderland, I looked around, but could find nothing to account for my fears and followed Felix into the room on the left.

At first, I was disconcerted by the walls. It was as if a hundred banners of dripping fur had been pegged out to dry around the room. When I looked closer, however, I saw it was merely wallpaper decorated with a clashing assortment of fruits and animals.

'Do you like it?' asked Felix. 'The embossed pattern is leather. Quite a feature, don't you think?'

'Leather wallpaper?' I stood back and let the riot of images assail me. 'It's very powerful.' The intricacy of the pattern was impressive and my children would have loved the little chimpanzees and preening birds. There was even a tiny snail amongst the foliage.

'Why is it called the Adelaide Room?'

'Like the Australian city, our room was named after the young wife of William the Fourth. She was a rather tragic figure, much younger than her husband and life wasn't easy for her.' He began to say something and stopped. 'I'm pretty sure she never made it to Australia, but she did stay here not long after her marriage and she particularly liked this room.'

Even this fantastical wallpaper? I wondered. There were two cabinets on the far wall, filled mainly with porcelain from the Orient. Next to them was a glass case of Italian cameos depicting classical scenes and a set of jade figures, perhaps picked up by Felix in India. It was a dazzling collection and I would need steady hands to photograph it. I looked around for a place to put my camera while I assembled the objects.

The door on the other side of the room opened onto an orangery, bare except for a few desiccated plants in ornamental tubs. I stood at the spot where I thought I would set my camera and my eyes fell on a waist-height cabinet with a hinged lid. Through it, I could see the severed arms of seven children lying on burgundy velvet cushions, resembling the waste from amputation surgery.

'These are unusual.' I tried to mask my distaste from the man who'd thought the monstrosities worth collecting.

Felix was looking out of the window but knew at once what items I was talking about. 'Four of them are my own children's forearms. They're marble sculptures copied from casts we took from the children. Queen Victoria began the trend with her own offspring and I had similar ones done for all mine. The trick was keeping them quiet while the plaster of Paris was applied for the casts. It was best done when they were asleep.'

'And the others?'

'Children of various servants.'

'And you're not keeping them?' I couldn't keep the disapproval from my voice.

Felix stiffened but continued to look out of the window. 'It has to be a new start. Lily isn't interested and Helene can't bear to look at them. What else am I to do?'

I could hardly condemn him. As I had done the once unimaginable thing of wearing my Bertie's ring for another man's wedding, so Felix was disposing of these small relics to start afresh.

'I think I'll start in here. I need to find a way to bring in more light, but I'll take an image of the wallpaper and then look at the individual cabinets.'

He nodded and went from the room, leaving me alone with his collection. I caught the eye of a small creature in the leather wallpaper.

'Time to begin,' I told the chimpanzee who continued to scrutinise me, its brow furrowed.

Chapter Ten

As I opened up my leather case, I thought my heart would burst with joy. My camera felt weightless as I placed it on the tripod, excited by the promise of new beginnings. The pounding in my ears had subsided once more but I couldn't shake the feeling that the pulse of energy was in some way connected to my presence in the Adelaide Room. The space had the stillness of catastrophe delayed, the restless sleep of the night before battle. I was surprised by my fancies. My pregnancy had been marked by nausea and inertia, but I wasn't usually whimsical.

My first photo was an image of the whole space, showing the unusual wallpaper off to full advantage. I took a single shot, carefully staged as my plates were precious. Next, I decided to get the marble arms out of the way and cross them off my list. I lifted the lid and stood my tripod over the cabinet, angling the lens down at the velvet cushion. I was worried about the dark background and would need to be careful when I developed the plates to ensure the outline of the arms was clear. Perhaps placing them on the table would have been better, but I couldn't bring myself to move each little fat limb.

With this task completed, I relaxed. Outside, there was a flurry of activity around the Hall although the first visitor wasn't expected until Monday. The servants, Horwick in particular, had perked up at the thought of famous guests, although his role appeared to be that of supervising the work of first Quinlivan and then Janet, giving orders with his precise, faded voice.

He came in to see me once, checking up on me, I thought. He didn't knock – my status didn't require it – but he did cough to indicate his presence. I spun to greet him, but he had his back to me, retrieving an item of silver from the mahogany cupboard.

'Lunch is at one,' he announced, still intent on his task. 'The family have said you'll be dining with them.'

'I'd rather carry on with my work. Will you send my apologies?'

He straightened, turning to face me and I realised, despite his leanness, that he was around my height.

'Very well, Miss Drew.' His eyes dropped to my stomach and I felt myself turning pink.

'I'd prefer to be called Louisa but my formal name is *Mrs* Drew. Address me by whichever you wish, but I'm not a Miss.'

I watched him in turn redden and incline his head in assent. I decided to make use of my advantage.

'Do you call Ada by her first name or Mrs Watkins?'

Horwick looked down at the little creamer he had in his hand, shaped in the form of a cow. 'Mrs Watkins, above and below stairs.'

'You've known her long?'

'Long enough.' He turned to go.

I couldn't understand his antipathy towards a woman who had struck me as pitiable rather than inspiring dislike. I called over to him before he could leave the room. 'She's come back to recreate the séance, I believe. Quinlivan mentioned it last night.'

He hesitated, his hand on the doorknob. 'It'll be the last time Mrs Watkins can upset the family. We should be grateful for small mercies.'

'Was the original séance so awful?'

'I wasn't present. Perhaps one of the guests will give you their recollections, if you're minded to know.' He paused. 'Best not to ask Mrs Clewer, though.'

Helene Clewer, a woman I was yet to be introduced to. I was hardly in a position to be pestering her with my questions. I returned to my camera, my head full of the bliss of images seen through the lens. Photo fever, we call it. I saw the world in black and white, my eyes inside the camera as I judged each frame.

Eventually, around three o'clock, the light began to fail and my reddened eyes persuaded me to finish for the day. The room was still; I hadn't realised how still while I'd been at my work, but now I was aware of the frigid quality of the air. I stopped and looked at my fingers which were beginning to turn blue. While the rest of the house was cold, here the temperature was glacial. I had been so absorbed in my work, I hadn't thought to ask for a fire to be lit and no one had considered I might need some warmth in the room. It was a house where family and servants were used to living with the cold, I suspected. Now, I had a choice. Either I could begin to develop the shots in a makeshift darkroom or I could rest, as I was exhausted.

It was the restless movement of the baby which made up my mind. I tidied up and left the passageway to put my camera back in my room. Did that part of the house breathe a sigh of relief as I left it? I felt a breeze on my cheek; a split in the plasterwork perhaps letting in the cold air? In any case, I was glad to leave the east wing and I think it wanted rid of me, too.

In the drawing room at the bottom of the stairs I spotted Mrs Clewer, who was hovering underneath a huge painting, a landscape of a river with a reed bed where a child huddled on a branch in the foreground. A pastoral scene, but there was nothing idyllic about it; the expression of the child suggesting disappointment and exclusion.

'Is everything all right?'

She started as I spoke, her eyes widening in surprise. She looked me up and down, as if seeing me for the first time. 'It's Louisa, isn't it?'

'It is, Mrs Clewer.'

'Oh, call me Helene.' I saw her hands were trembling, a sure sign of shot nerves. 'Have you seen Ada?'

'I've only seen Horwick this morning.'

'I don't want *him*.' Her voice rose. 'I've told Lily and Ada I'm not to be left alone. Where are they?'

I looked around me, the weight of my equipment making me clumsy.

'I can look for them once I've put my things away.'

She shook her head as she took a step away from me, moving towards the wall so her thin body pressed against the painting. I saw that the little boy depicted in oils had the legs, not of a child, but of a goat. He was a Pan in miniature, without the malice of adult representations but with the weary eyes of one who'd seen too much. I pressed past her, feeling like a pack horse in full load as I struggled up the stairs.

I had nearly made it to the upper floor when I heard the music again, a piano playing below me in the wing of the house where I'd spent the morning. A high voice picked up the tune; a lament again, familiar to me, although the title of the song was hard to recall. The plaintive song unsettled me and, laden with my equipment, I wobbled, almost losing my balance.

'Who's playing the piano?'

I turned in time to see Helene freeze. 'The piano?' she asked. 'I hear no piano.'

I was saved from further explanation by the arrival of Lily in the drawing room. She saw her mother still poised at the bottom of the stairs and hurried to meet her. It was only when Helene turned that I saw the effect my words had on her. She stood at the bottom of the stairs, ignoring Lily's attempts to steer me into the sitting room, regarding me with disbelief.

Chapter Eleven

'What are you doing?'

Janet was standing in the passageway as I reached the top of the stairs. 'You surely shouldn't be carrying all that stuff with you in your condition!'

She reached down and took my tripod and plates from me.

'I was wondering who I heard singing downstairs.'

'Singing?'

'I can hear someone playing the piano and singing along to it. Can't you?'

We both listened to the silence broken only by the muffled sound of wind rattling the front door.

'I don't hear anything. In any case, the only piano in the house is too rotten to be played,' said Janet as I followed her along the corridor into my room. I saw she'd tidied the space, folding up my nightgown and taking away the dirty washing water from the bowl. On my bedside table was a small brass handbell.

'We didn't realise you'd be up so early this morning. I'll bring you hot water at eight tomorrow. If you want it any earlier, ring the bell and Quinlivan can carry it up.'

'I'd appreciate that.'

'And I can arrange a bath before the visitors arrive. Let me know which day you want it and I'll have it brought up and put in front of the fire.'

'Are you able to give me a tour of the house tomorrow? I'm

making good progress on the collection but I need to take photos of some of the bedrooms.'

Janet frowned. 'I don't think the family are upstairs at the moment, so I could show you them now.'

I followed her out into the passageway. She paused at a door opposite and pushed it open. It led, not into a room, but to stairs made of inferior pine and scuffed from years of heavy tread. A means for generations of servants to travel up and down the house, out of sight of the family.

'I know you're not a servant, but you might find these easier if you need to get to the Adelaide Room. They'll also take you down into the kitchen if you need something in the night.'

We both turned at the sound of a door opening. Ada emerged from a room near the central stairs, curious, possibly, at the sound of our voices. She was wearing the same dress as the previous day and was again surrounded by the scent of mothballs. Instead of her cheap perfume, however, I could detect a sweeter smell, spiced apple, perhaps, drifting towards us. She closed the door behind her, holding onto the handle.

'Janet, is that you? I need a hand with Mother.' Lily's voice carried up the stairs.

'I might have more time tomorrow,' she whispered and hurried towards her mistress.

I thought Ada might follow her but she stayed, regarding me with the same concern as she had in the sitting room. I was torn between heading into my room for the nap which I desperately craved and finding out more about what was preoccupying the medium. I still couldn't understand the servants' antipathy towards her. Hovering uncertainly in the fading afternoon light, she looked like a great-aunt of mine, all double chins and whiskery kisses.

I saw she was holding a pack of cards, the same set she'd laid on the table in the drawing room. 'You do readings?'

Ada regarded the pack. 'You recognise the tarot?'

A memory from before the war, long buried, came rushing back. One of the board members of the *Lady's Realm*, a magazine which had first featured my work, was married to a mountaineer. It was she who'd suggested I photograph a pockmarked man who'd made an unsuccessful attempt on a Himalayan peak ten years earlier. Aleister Crowley had told me about the tarot then but I'd declined his offer of a reading. He'd later fallen out of favour and I couldn't imagine him gracing a women's magazine these days. I was glad, though, I'd refused a reading, for God knows what would have shown in those cards on the eve of my catastrophe.

Ada was watching me. 'You know of them?'

'I once turned down the offer of a reading.'

'And now?'

I hesitated, emboldened by my successful afternoon. 'I'd be interested in seeing what they say. I'd prefer not to do it down-stairs, though.'

Ada inclined her head in assent, probably used to women wishing to hide their activities from the men in the household, and I followed her into her room. I saw it was no larger than my bedroom, although a little better furnished. Here the sweet smell was stronger and I saw a dark brown bottle, inadequately stop-pered, on her bedside table, the label facing away from me.

Ada put the bottle on the windowsill with a brief glance at me and pulled the nightstand to the end of the bed.

'Sit.'

I sank onto the mattress as she took a tub chair from the other side of the room and sat opposite me, shuffling her cards. Her fingers were as fat as the marble arms I'd photographed earlier, one of them bearing the imprint of where a ring had once pressed itself into the flesh. She laid about twenty cards, like their owner a little worn around the edges, face down on the table.

'Choose one. Don't think too much about it.'

I paused, trying to detect any energy in the cards until, defeated, I pointed to one at the bottom right corner which Ada flipped over. The image was of an elderly, cloaked man carrying a staff in one hand and holding up a lamp in the other. The picture reminded me a little of Holman Hunt's painting *The Light of the World* which I once saw at St Paul's Cathedral. As I studied it more closely, however, I noticed that inside the lamp was a six-pointed star. Ada was fumbling in her pocket and finally pulled out a pair of metal spectacles with pebble lenses. She hooked them over her ears and regarded my choice.

'The Hermit.' Ada's voice was complacent. 'He carries the lamp as a seeker of truth. Now is the time for inner reflection and the hermit will guide you as you pursue the knowledge you seek.'

'Knowledge of what?'

I must have sounded flippant as Ada's face fell. 'Take the reading. Sometimes it takes a while for the meaning to become clear. Pick another.'

I hesitated too long and the cards began to blur as I tried to choose. In desperation, I selected one in the middle and turned it rather than wait for Ada.

The act unsettled her. She lightly tapped the card with her finger, as if to claim it back from my touch. The image was of a man in medieval costume hanging by one foot, the other tucked behind his leg.

'The Hanged Man,' said Ada although I could have worked that out for myself. 'He represents an upheaval and a change beyond your control.'

I thought of the baby. 'Will it be a good change?'

'I can't tell you that, dear. It's not clear to me at the moment. We'll have a final card, I think.'

I pointed, without thinking, to one at the top and Ada revealed another medieval image, this time a burning turret topped by a crown from which three bodies descended into darkness.

'The Tower.' Ada was reflective. 'It represents revelation, usually accompanied by destruction. I've not been wrong, then. Your presence here will unlock secrets.'

'I hardly think I'll be here long enough for that.'

'We'll see.'

Exasperated, I shook my head. 'Ada. What is all this about? Everyone's reaction to me feels odd. First Lily's when I arrived, then yours in the sitting room and, just now, Helene looked at me as if I was possessed. Why am I here?'

'You've been employed to take photographs.'

I sighed. Ada was clearly a woman used to dodging questions she didn't care to answer. I liked her bravado although I suspected there was much Ada hid from the world. Now I studied her face, I saw her pupils were tiny in her hazel eyes. From where I was sitting I could now read the label of the bottle – laudanum, a tincture my mother had occasionally used when she was laid low but had certainly not kept in her bedroom. While my mother was alive, I'd never been allowed near the bottle, even as an adult. The perfume conjured up memories of female illness and illicit remedies.

'When's the séance, Ada?' I asked.

'You've heard of our plans?'

'It was mentioned in the kitchen yesterday. I heard you were intending to recreate the evening from the last century.'

'It's a fancy of Helene's and I don't see any harm in it.' Ada gathered the cards, placing the pack in a neat pile on the table.

'But surely, after the notoriety last time, you don't wish for that type of scrutiny again? The world has moved on.'

'Has it? Not as much as you might think. You don't approve of séances, I see.'

'It makes no difference to me.'

'You never considered trying to contact your sons?'

I pushed myself up off the bed, knocking over a glass which dropped to the floor and rolled towards the door. I again caught the scent of spiced apples.

'My sons are in peace,' I said, trying to hide my anger. 'Why would I need to contact them?'

Ada remained seated. This couldn't have been the first time she'd been rebuked for her beliefs but I saw, to my shame, her eyes dampen. She reached into the depths of her skirt and pulled out an off-white handkerchief to dab her eyes.

'No need to raise your voice. Children are the hardest to contact. It saps all the energy from you. *You* have nothing to fear from your little ones, I'm sure.'

Except they might be in that half-world and not resting in their graves . . . Their spot in the churchyard was a solace to me, a place to leave flowers once a month even if I had to hide the expense from Edwin.

'But people do fear your messages, don't they? What about that first time? Quinlivan hinted at a tragedy. Were the messages so awful?'

Ada replaced her handkerchief and I saw her hands tremble. In that moment, I pitied her. 'Terrible and accurate. Did Quinlivan tell you what was predicted?'

I shook my head.

'Well, you'll find out soon enough. I don't like to talk afterwards about what the spirits communicate.' She studied my face and reached for my hand. 'Not to worry. I hope you'll still be here when the séance takes place. I think the house has something to say to you yet. In fact, I'm sure of it.'

Chapter Twelve

I dressed for dinner in an outfit which would have to do for evenings as I'd brought precious few clothes with me. I felt faded and dowdy, and yet I remembered feeling like a ship set in full sail when I'd been carrying my twins. It was times like this, conscious of my burgeoning stomach, that I missed my mother the most. She'd been full of practical advice during my first pregnancy and I desperately would have liked to talk to her about the strange sensation of carrying a new, growing child while still grieving for my lost sons. At times, I was overwhelmed with optimism for the future of my baby until I remembered the cage I'd built myself in my home with Edwin in Kentish Town.

I heard the faint, low sound of the gong at ten minutes to seven and arrived at the top of the stairs at the same time as Felix, who was straightening his cuffs and looking on the scene below with distaste. Ada and Helene were huddled together on a sofa, their heads almost touching, and Lily was talking to a large, barrel-chested man, still attractive, in his late sixties.

Lily called up to me. 'Louisa, come and meet Sir Thomas. He's our nearest neighbour.'

As I descended the stairs, Sir Thomas smiled across at me but his eyes looked past mine to Felix, who he hurried to greet. They moved to a large cabinet filled with Sèvres vases which perhaps Sir Thomas was hoping to purchase before the auction. Lily and I drifted over to Helene and Ada. Helene was dwarfed by her dress, an apple-green crêpe de Chine. I couldn't imagine this woman as a society beauty, but then I came from a long line of capable women and found it difficult to identify with lacklustre pallor. Ada had changed into an ostrich feather affair, more flamboyant than her black dress but still of a period a decade or so earlier.

Lily spotted Janet hovering by the door and hurried to speak to her. I was left with Ada and Helene, neither of whom were inclined to question me as I was used to when people realised I was pregnant. *When's the baby due? Are you hoping for a girl or a boy? Is it your first?* We sat in silence, the two women getting up at the sound of the second gong with evident relief.

I was placed next to Sir Thomas for dinner. For the first time, I thought the house magnificent in its decline. Candles were placed not only on the table but also the buffet stand and mantelpiece, light leaping between the polished silver sticks. Sir Thomas drank steadily and heavily with Horwick, an unlikely ally, I thought, making sure his glass was continually topped up. I found the Clewers' neighbour to be forthright and opinionated but clearly fond of the family.

'You've started your photographs then?' he asked me, tucking into his mutton cutlet with gusto.

'I spent the day in the Adelaide Room. It's the room most dependent on good light and today has been bright.'

'We've had a dull, wet winter this year. I'll be glad of the snow that's forecast.'

I thought of my photographs. 'Snow's not good news for me. The clouds will be low in the sky.'

Sir Thomas grunted. 'I have the grandchildren coming on Tuesday. They'll love it, of course. I shall have to get their sledges oiled ready.'

'You have many children?'

He glanced up at me, frowning. 'Just the one, Samuel. My wife was gravely ill after him and we had no more. Pity she's not around to see the grandchildren because Samuel has sired four sons. She'd have enjoyed having young ones around her.'

I caught Lily's eye and she flushed and looked to her plate, her food hardly touched. Helene had also been listening to our exchange, a sheen of sweat on her face. Perhaps it was the mention of grandchildren which had unsettled her, for she was now unlikely to have any of her own. For the first time since my arrival, I had her full attention.

'Do you like the Adelaide Room?' she asked.

'It has an unusual atmosphere,' I ventured. 'It's very silent.'

Helene nodded. 'Yes, I feel it too. It always calms me when I'm in there.'

It wasn't what I meant. As the chimpanzees had watched me furtively from the wallpaper, I couldn't shake the feeling the walls were inspecting me too.

'It's where we'll be having the séance later this week. Lily has told you about it, I suppose?'

Sir Thomas gave Ada a malevolent look which she ignored, cutting a potato in half.

'I don't think we've mentioned it to Louisa yet,' said Lily.

I saw Horwick listen for my reply, remembering our conversation earlier. 'Are these the guests you mentioned?' I asked Lily. 'They're arriving for the séance?'

'There will be three additions in total. Mr Conan Doyle will be coming down from Windlesham with his wife Jean. We've had a bit of trouble trying to organise his visit but I think all has been settled now.'

'He didn't want to come?'

'Quite the opposite,' said Lily. 'You may have read about his interest in the afterlife. He's writing a book on the history of spiritualism and has said he'd welcome a few days to work on it while attending the séance.'

'But you mentioned a difficulty in organising his visit.'

Helene leant forward. 'When he visited here in 1896 he was married to his first wife; she was an invalid, so he came alone. Jean is a completely different character. She's as much a believer in the spirits as he is, so naturally she wants to attend the séance.'

'Will she be there?'

Ada, who had been talking to an unenthusiastic Felix, picked up the threads of our conversation. 'She can't join in as we want to recreate the evening as it was. The same people, where possible. Certainly, the original number of participants.'

'Everyone is still alive?'

It seemed alcohol was finally having its effect on Sir Thomas, who regarded me with bright eyes. 'Henry Storey, a decent journalist and honourable man, died years ago. His son will be attending in his place.'

So the group were happy for substitutes but not additions. I wondered at the contradictions that maintaining a link with the dead entailed but didn't dare ask, noticing the atmosphere of the room had changed. Felix was picking over the bones of his cutlet, the meat long gone, avoiding being brought into the conversation. Lily had become tense, the veins on her neck standing out as she tried to catch Horwick's eye.

Only Ada was unperturbed. She had drunk two full glasses of wine – I had been counting – and clearly had the stomach for it. 'Perhaps Louisa had plans to join us on Wednesday evening and is a little disappointed?'

I didn't rise to the bait. 'I'll keep out of your way, of course. My photographs of the house might even be finished by then.'

Helene's voice rose as she gestured around the table. 'This séance is important to me and I don't want anything to go wrong.'

'Mother!' Lily flushed. 'Louisa is here to do a job, as well you know.'

'I'm not photographing the séance, surely?' I nearly knocked over my wine glass in my temper. If this was the purpose of inviting me here they were in for a disappointment. I had heard of spirit photographers, clear fakes manipulating cheesecloth disguised as ectoplasm onto plates to extract money from the gullible.

'Of course you're not,' said Lily, glancing across at her mother. 'You're very welcome here, Louisa, and I don't want you to get any impression otherwise.'

I thought of Helene's expression as she'd regarded me at the bottom of the stairs. 'Where did you find out about my work?'

Lily wouldn't meet my eyes. 'I'm afraid I don't remember.'

Chapter Thirteen

I turned down the family's invitation to accompany them to church the following day. I had quite enough of that at home with Dorothy, who would purse her lips when I refused to join her and Edwin on their Sunday excursions. I realised I'd forgotten to telephone Edwin the previous day. He wouldn't be at his place of work at the gentleman's outfitters on a Sunday and we had no phone in our house, so I would have to make the effort tomorrow and see what his mood was. If I could placate him about the financial benefits of this job, perhaps going home might be easier. The thought of Edwin, as ever, induced a wave of confusion. I shouldn't be afraid to speak to my husband. I'd never been like this with Bertie, so I knew what a happy marriage was.

Felix stayed behind while the three women, Helene, Lily and, to my surprise, Ada, walked side by side along the cinder path towards the church tower just visible over the eastern wall. I watched the three women walk briskly along the path, Ada struggling to keep up with the other two. Ada and Lily stopped to retrieve something from a large cat's mouth. He'd been attempting to skulk past the three of them, trying to hide his spoils. A bird, probably, as I'm not sure they would have made such a fuss over a rodent. I watched as Helene, taking advantage of the women fussing over the feline, broke away from the pair.

Helene was ankle-deep in the grass as she headed towards a cottage just visible at the end of the garden. Only the tip of the chimney and the ridge of tiled roof could be seen. A gamekeeper's house, perhaps. The incident would have been unremarkable if it hadn't been for Lily and Ada's reaction when they saw where she was going.

'Mama!' I heard Lily's anxious shout through the draughty window. I craned my head to watch as she chased her mother across the grass, pulling her by the arm back onto the path before the three of them continued their procession to the church. I looked across to the house, wondering who lived there that Helene was so keen to visit.

The Adelaide Room was silent that morning, the air a little musty, but the temperature was more comfortable than the previous day's freeze. As I was setting up my camera, I noticed the lid of the cabinet containing the children's limbs was slightly raised. The contents looked untouched, but as I counted the little arms I saw there were six, not seven, the remaining limbs rearranged to cover the loss. I counted them again in case I was mistaken but I was certain there had been seven limbs. The four Clewer children and the other three whose servant parents had, perhaps, been too afraid to refuse Felix's request for a memento of their children.

I hurried up to Janet who was closing the door of Ada's room.

'Have you taken one of the marble arms from the cabinet in the Adelaide Room?'

She frowned at my tone but softened when she saw the panic in my face. 'I haven't been in there this morning except to draw the curtains.'

'And you didn't notice anything missing from the cabinet?'

'I didn't even look at it. I was in and out in a minute. Let me see.'

Together we descended the stairs. Horwick, with his uncanny nose for anything awry, followed us into the room and peered over the cabinet.

'Yesterday there were seven limbs and now there are only six.'

'Are you sure?' asked Janet.

'Mrs Drew is correct. There are usually seven arms in the cabinet.' Horwick's tone was firm as he looked at the marble limbs. 'One of them is missing.'

'Does someone occasionally remove them?' I was thinking of Helene Clewer. Perhaps Felix's assertion that she couldn't bear to look at them was wrong. Men, as I well knew, were not necessarily experts on their wives' emotions.

'Not to my knowledge,' answered Horwick, an air of satisfaction in his voice.

I had no way of knowing which of the arms was missing. The worst outcome would be if it was one of the three Clewer sons'. I wondered how I would feel if a precious memento of Hugh and Pip was lost. As I felt a wave of sorrow, I was aware of two pairs of eyes assessing me. Their accusing glances brought me to my senses. I had nothing to do with the loss and I wouldn't take the blame.

'Someone has taken a limb since I was here yesterday. I'll talk to Colonel Clewer now.'

Janet took me to his study, a small room at the back of the house. The thick oak door was shut and I felt sick as I rapped on the panelling. I detected an air of sympathy emanating from Janet as I heard the muffled sound of Felix telling me to enter.

'Don't take the blame for this,' she whispered.

Felix was sitting behind his desk sorting through a mountain of paper. He looked up at me and noticed my expression. 'Is everything all right?'

'Yesterday I made a start on the Adelaide Room and its collection. I photographed all the children's hands and today one is missing.'

'Missing? What do you mean, missing?'

I took him to the cabinet and lifted the lid. 'They have been moved to hide the fact that there would be a space where the hand was.'

Although I'd resolved not to do it, I could feel the threat of tears behind my eyes. 'Will you be able to tell which are your children's now they're out of order?'

Felix reached into his pocket and pulled out a handkerchief, handing it to me. 'Of course I know my children's hands. They're all still here. The other limb will turn up. This isn't a museum, Louisa. Someone has taken it and, no doubt, will replace it soon enough.' He tapped my arm lightly. 'Just carry on and don't worry about it.'

After he'd left the room, I picked up one of the arms from the case, fat fingers extending from a chubby hand, the thumb and forefinger touching to make an arc. The marble was cold and heavier than a child even when they're tired and insist on being carried. I pressed my fingers over the child's fist, willing the fingers to warm back into life, but the marble remained cold and lifeless.

It came again, the tightening band of pressure in my head followed by complete silence. How I wish it had started in London so I could have had it checked out by Dr Smart. Pregnancy brings with it a heightened state and I'm sure there was a rational explanation to these ailments. I stood firm, riding out my sinking mood and crossed to the window, wondering if I would get the strange absence of my reflection I'd experienced on my first day here. I pressed against the glass and saw a movement near a small copse of trees, a shadow flitting across the grass similar to the one I had seen that first night in the Hall. I stared at the shape for a moment and, abandoning my camera, rushed to investigate.

Chapter Fourteen

I hurried into the middle of the lawn where I spun in a circle, my eyes sweeping the outline of the house, the spindly, leafless shrubs and, just beyond the dip, the chimney of the house Helene had been striding towards that morning. There was not a soul to be seen. I made my way towards the house; perhaps I'd seen a child of the cottage, which would explain the brief sighting. Children are like cats; they move faster than you think possible. It might also explain why Lily had been so keen Helene didn't make a detour to the cottage. Small children, with her loss, would surely be an upsetting reminder of happier times. When I reached the small house, however, I could see it was derelict, a rural hovel with one or two rooms downstairs, the same on the upper floor and a tiny window, little more than the size of a porthole, peeping through the tiles of the roof.

I stepped into the front garden, overrun with a tangle of briars whose small thorns tugged at my skirt. When I pushed at the front door, part of it detached itself from the frame.

'Is anyone there?'

'It was the head gardener's cottage.'

I turned at the voice and saw Lily Clewer in her church clothes, standing on the bank looking down at me. 'It's empty, as you can see. You mustn't go inside, I'm sure it's not safe.'

She climbed down towards me, clad in a thick tweed coat which hid her slim figure but emphasised her broad shoulders. I saw that one of her stockings had a ladder in it, so different from the care Helene clearly took with her outfits.

'You had gardeners?'

'Of course we did. There were many more servants at the Hall once. Jessop, the head gardener, lived in this house with his wife. The place is known as Old Jessop's cottage.' She paused. 'Did you come for a walk?'

She had her eyes on my thin dress and flimsy shoes.

'I saw a shadow in the garden. A child, possibly.'

'A child?' Her eyes flickered. 'There aren't any children at the Hall.'

'A visitor, then.'

'I don't think so. There haven't been children here for a long while.' She took in my appearance. 'You shouldn't be out here in this weather.'

At once, I felt the cold; the bite of the frosty morning and the glittering brightness of the garden adding to it. Those who say winter is devoid of colour aren't gardeners. This garden, in its icy frostiness, was a riot of red berries and yew-green leaves. Lily gave me her hand to pull me up the slope and, as I grasped it, I became aware of the woman's strength and the smell of something I hadn't noticed before. A salty tang to the air.

'Are we near the sea here?'

'The sea?' Lily indicated with her head the direction towards the jumble of firs which marked the edges of the property. 'Less than two miles to the cliffs at Saltdean. On a clear night you can hear the waves.'

Of course. Alice had said that the youngest Clewer had loved the sea and it was no surprise, given he had grown up with the sound in his ears.

Lily steered me away from the house, as I'd seen her do with her mother earlier that morning, her clasp firm. We walked back towards the Hall with Helene Clewer watching us from the terrace. She didn't turn to look at us as we passed but I could see under the brim of her hat that her eyes were rimmed red. Once more, I had the impression Lily was hurrying me past Helene as if she were determined we shouldn't speak. Her grip on my arm tightened as she steered me into the Hall.

'Mrs Clewer looks upset.'

'Mother is always this way after church. Our pew is beneath the war memorial and near the top are my brothers' names. It's impossible to ignore and it upsets her. Always.'

The final word was accompanied by a change of tone. A waspish note I hadn't heard before.

'A change from how she was when you were growing up?'

'Well, maybe, although Mother did always insist on having her own way. What she said went.'

There it was again, a blurt of resentment. A niggle of discontent in Lily's usual demeanour of a dutiful daughter. I wondered if the narrow world of this house was the cause of her bitterness. Despite changes after the war, it was still the common lot of single women to be left in charge of elderly parents. I swallowed my pity and concentrated instead on sounding a positive note.

'Perhaps India will help you all put the past behind you.'

I saw at once I'd said the wrong thing as her expression hardened.

'I don't think that's going to be possible, do you? Not everything can be forgotten, although I appreciate some deal with grief better than others.'

I stood there nonplussed, indignation battling with embarrassment.

'There's no shame in wanting to make a new life for yourself.'

'And have you made a new life for yourself?' I saw her eyes on my stomach and felt the urge to defend myself.

'It's an ongoing endeavour.'

'But worth it?' Her gaze was intense and I felt my anger gaining the upper hand.

'What other choice do we have? It's no disrespect to the dead to keep our eyes forward.'

I hadn't satisfied her, and I think she was as angry as I was. 'Well, we all have our ways of coping.'

'Like your mother's séances.'

She inclined her head.

'And do they help?'

Lily kept her eyes on the ground. 'Do they help? It depends on how you view these things. Ada has an uncanny nose for wheedling out our greatest fears. The fact that she struck lucky that night in 1896 was due to the force of two Empires coming together and unleashing their horrors.'

Lily turned to me, her eyes seeking mine. 'Don't forget that. She struck lucky, nothing more.'

Chapter Fifteen

The episode left me unsettled. There was a child roaming the garden, I was sure. First the shove in the garden on the night of my arrival, and now, the faint outline amongst the trees. A little boy, I thought. Lily had been adamant no child could be in the garden, the forcefulness of her claim sitting oddly with her usual manner. I couldn't bear the thought of a poor child darting around the grounds, occasionally creeping into the house, avoiding detection. Despite the care of philanthropists such as Octavia Hill and Charles Booth in the cities, I knew rural poverty was still rife. Perhaps it was my own grief, but I would not stand by while a child suffered from neglect, for surely no caring parent would let a child run wild in this manner?

To calm my fears, I did what I do best when I'm anxious: I got down to work to develop the images I'd taken over the last two days. I found Quinlivan washing the car and he outright refused to show me the cellars.

'Lily said they were damp.'

'That's an understatement,' he muttered, polishing one of the saucer lights with a chamois leather. 'They're also full of vermin. I can hear them clattering around late at night. What do you need for your photos?'

'A room, it doesn't need to be large, but without windows would be best. Blocking them with brown paper might be all right but I need complete dark for the best image.'

'There's the coal house. It's not full as we've been running down the fuel, but it's filthy, as you can imagine. Then there are the stables. There haven't been horses for a while but they're light and airy. The windows are high up and I can't see us getting the place dark enough for you. There are various outbuildings, but they're all pretty dilapidated.' He hesitated. 'Then there's the old icehouse . . .'

An icehouse. I'd heard of these buildings but never stepped inside one. Most city families had to rely on either buying in the ice from sellers who delivered it by cart, as my mother had done, or on a cold cupboard in the kitchen where you hoped for the best when temperatures rose.

'It's not in use?'

'We use the cold store near the tradesmen's entrance. It's far enough away from the kitchen fire to keep food cool.'

'Won't it be freezing?' I thought of my meagre Holland jacket which, although precious, provided little warmth.

'It would be if there was any ice in it. It hasn't been used for years. It won't be warm, though. You can stand full height but it's a bit, well, earthy. I could brush it out for you. It doesn't have a deep well like some.'

'Show me.'

He led me around the back of the house into a clump of trees where a small hedgehog-shaped structure was partially submerged in the clay soil. At the front there was a barred gate and, behind it, a wooden door. Neither was locked, and as we entered the cold, dark space, I heard the strike of a match and the smell of sulphur from the tip.

'I'll go first. Be careful as the floor slopes downwards.'

I heard a curse as the match burned Quinlivan's fingers, and the sound of another being struck. He fumbled on a ledge and found an old tallow candle to light, the foul odour choking the space.

I followed him closely, aware again of that smell of whisky on his skin. When we reached the end of the structure, I could see that the well where the ice would have been kept was little more than a hollow at the end of the chamber with no significant drop. If I set up my equipment this deep into the hut, I could leave the door slightly ajar once night fell. Quinlivan was wrong about the smell, though. The place stank of mouse droppings and rotted leaves.

'I'll need a supply of fresh water – a large pail will do. And then two glass beakers or jars, something you can spare as I need to mix chemicals in them.'

'That shouldn't be a problem. Anything else?'

'Is there a key?'

'I can try the ones on the bunch that's hung in the scullery – it has keys that no one knows where they fitted – but the lock will need oiling if I find the right one.'

'Will you check for me?' I looked around and spotted a small rough-hewn table and chair in one corner. Obviously a gardener or servant had also once used this place, freezing as it must have been, as a refuge.

'Once I've swept up. I'll go through them this afternoon, and if I find the key, I'll leave it on the mantelpiece over the kitchen fire.'

'I'll keep it with me once I've collected it. My developing equipment is precious and it would help if I could leave it here overnight.'

We emerged into the bracken. The fat ginger tom I'd seen earlier with Lily and Ada came streaking across the grass, sensing perhaps a new source of food, and shot past us into the icehouse.

'Gideon will sort out any stray rodents,' Quinlivan said. 'I'll see what I can do about the key.'

He left me, slipping through the trees. I followed him to the edge of the copse looking at the facade of Clewer Hall. It was a house of mystery. The contents were pristine; Felix would have no problem getting a decent price for his collection. That the estate had been left to run to ruin made me wonder about the tragedy that seeped into every pore of the building, for the decline in front of me wasn't the result of ten or so years of neglect. The rot must have happened much earlier.

As if aware of my scrutiny, as I stared across the grass the shadow I'd seen before began to creep across the Hall, beginning at the far end of the east wing until it became a charcoal-grey scar on one side of the house. There was no explanation for the phenomenon. The sun was hidden behind heavy clouds which opened for the promised shower. As I continued to watch, spats of rain fell on my head, slapping my clothes to my skin and my hair across my face.

Gathering my courage, I strode across the lawn and passed through the tradesmen's entrance, climbing the backstairs to the ground floor. From one of these rooms I'd heard the sound of falling plaster on my first night in the Hall and I pushed at the nearest door, of the room directly under mine, and stared at the sight. Strips of paper hung suspended from the wall, their rotten curls mouldering. In the middle was an old grand piano, its lid open, the teeth a gaping wound of ebony and off-white. It could not be this instrument I'd twice heard playing since my arrival.

The next room was in a similar state with the smell, possibly settled in the stained rug, suggesting it had once been the smoking room. Felix had remarked that the annexe had been shut up, not left to putrefy. Perhaps there had been a flood, not uncommon in houses with old pipes, and the family had simply shut off the far wing of the house.

I looked up at the ceiling and saw scars where plaster had fallen, scattering white gypsum across the carpet. *It's merely an old house, all groans and creaks*, I reassured myself, and left the room before more of the ceiling could fall. In the passage, I caught the sound of someone in the Adelaide Room, their feet tapping on the parquet floor.

The door was ajar and, as I put an eye to the opening, I saw Lily leaning over the cabinet with the marble hands. I held my breath, watching as she lifted the lid and carefully replaced one of the white limbs.

Chapter Sixteen

I finally got a tour of the house that afternoon. Janet came to find me in my room where I was dozing. My dream had led me into the past. Perhaps it was this grief-laden house, or Lily's accusing manner in the garden, but I was transported to the time after I'd had my boys and was staying with my mother. All four of us were on our knees in front of the hearth. My father had bought the twins a tin train, his present to them before departing to the front. They were a little young for it, a year old at most, but they liked pushing it between each other as its wheels squealed on the rug. It was the moment before the knock at the door which changed everything. We knew as soon as we saw the maid's face. The question was, which one of us was to be plunged into grief?

The rap on the door at Clewer Hall shook me from my slumber, saving me from revisiting the final moments of that scene. Janet stood before me, her manner apologetic.

'I've an hour free now. After the guests arrive tomorrow, I'm not sure when I'll next be available to give you a tour.'

I sat up, trying to shake off my dreams. The sorrow lingered as I stuffed my feet, swollen from the last few days of standing, into my thick-soled shoes and tied the laces. I found the itinerary Leo had given me and limped after the maid.

'We should start in the north-west bedroom.'

She pushed at a door which opened onto a room overlooking the front garden.

'Whose room is this?'

'Colonel Clewer's. The mistress's is along the passage.'

I crossed to the window, my mind on the figure I had seen heading towards the gardener's cottage. The damp lawn looked almost black in the dusk but, apart from two ducks heading towards the ornamental pond, not a soul was in view.

'What are you looking at?' asked Janet, joining me at the window.

'Nothing in particular. I was admiring the garden.' I gazed through the mottled glass, taking in the crumbling statues and scraggy planting. 'Is there anything special about the ruined house in the distance?'

'Old Jessop's cottage? I don't think so. Why do you ask?'

I kept my eyes on the garden. 'I got the impression Lily didn't want me to go near the place earlier today. Is there a reason for that?'

'I've heard it's rotten inside. You surely won't be wanting to photograph it? It won't attract any buyers for the house. The whole place needs pulling down.'

'No, I wasn't intending to photograph it.'

Janet was no fool and peered at me. 'You seem to be searching for something.'

I sighed. 'It's nothing. I thought I saw a child playing around there earlier.'

'A child? Quinlivan hasn't been filling your head with nonsense, has he?'

'What do you mean?'

I'd put her in a spot and she shifted, embarrassed. 'I thought . . . oh, old tales. Never mind.'

'What tales?' I stopped, aware of the force of my tone. 'Sorry. You make it sound mysterious, that's all.'

Janet hesitated, clearly wishing she'd never raised the subject.

'I don't know much, but there are rumours of a child who is sometimes seen in the garden. The family don't like talk of it – but then, the child never appears to them. It's only servants and visitors who claim to have seen the little boy.'

'And Quinlivan told you the story?'

'Yes, but I already knew of it from my mother. She says a maid left because she saw him and one of the valets before that, but I heard they blamed the drink for *his* disappearance. You sure Quinlivan hasn't already told you this?'

'It's the first I've heard of it. Do they know who the child is?'

'Only that it's a spirit from the past, nothing more.'

'He's not related to the ruined house?'

'I've never heard any mention of it.'

And yet Lily hadn't wanted me near there, I was sure. Perhaps she had seen one of the village children playing in the grounds and had been perturbed by his presence. There had been nothing supernatural about my sighting. I had briefly glimpsed a real human child.

'I saw a living thing but I'm glad you told me the story. I dare say most old houses have their tales of ghosts.'

Janet touched my arm. 'If it was the ghost child, I don't think it's a good thing for you to have seen him. Servants never stayed long afterwards. Please, be careful.'

Janet left me alone so she could return to help Alice. As I listened to her footsteps recede into the distance, I spotted Ada entering the garden and hurried to join her. My feet sank into the damp ground but Ada was aware of my presence before I reached her.

'Come to enjoy the afternoon air, Louisa?'

'It's almost dark. I thought I'd take a walk while I can. How did you know it was me?'

Only now did she turn, taking in my dishevelled appearance

after my nap. 'Everyone has an aura about them. Some claim to see a colour surrounding people. I simply feel the essence of each individual.'

Away from the Hall, she was softer, her defences down a little. 'Auras?' I asked. 'I've heard of the spirit world but never of auras.'

Ada looked around the garden. 'It's always been the same for me, even as a child. There were shadows to begin with but I was never frightened. When I was thirteen one of them spoke to me and they've been with me ever since.'

'And provided you with a livelihood.'

She frowned. 'When we go out to work, we look to where our talents lie. You understand that, don't you?'

'I understand the need to make a living, certainly.' I paused, feeling a rush of compassion for this woman trying, like me, to make ends meet. 'Are you from this area? There's the trace of the north in your accent. Manchester, perhaps?'

'Further north than that. Have you heard of Morecambe?'

I shook my head.

'It's a small town by the sea. A long way from this life.'

'You don't go back?'

She smiled. 'I have no one to go back to.'

'You *are* a widow, though.'

I watched her closely. Many a woman of dubious respectability had pretended to be bereaved with no evidence of a former husband.

'Isaac Watkins is buried in my home town. I never fancied another go – unlike yourself.'

Her words stung. 'That's hardly fair. Plenty of women remarry.'

'I'm aware of that. It's just that you appear to be a woman carrying her grief around with her.'

Her words stopped the retort I was about to deliver. She wasn't a woman I'd have naturally confided in, but underneath her predictions and card-turning, I sensed a woman who'd known loneliness and hardship too.

I took a breath. 'When Bertie died, I carried on for the children's sake. When they went too, I thought it was the end of me. The thing about grief, though, is that its edges begin to blunt. Not immediately. But, gradually, you start to remember the joy your lost ones brought. I wanted that again. It took me years to feel like it, but one day, on a busy Camden Street, I realised I wanted another child. Naturally, I needed a husband for that.'

'You can have them without.'

I was shocked, not at Ada's comment but at the fact she thought times had changed that much. Women, of course, had children out of wedlock but these poor illegitimate creatures were rarely brought up by their mothers. If they were lucky, they might be farmed out to willing relatives.

'I prefer to give my children a decent start in life.'

'And your second husband. Is he like the first?'

I turned away, cross that I'd allowed myself to be drawn into discussing my marriage. I'd come out into the garden to question Ada and now I was defending my own choices for my future.

'Bertie, my first husband, was young, carefree. We thought we had the world at our feet. That the war would be over by Christmas. You remember those days, don't you?'

Ada came closer and I felt again the fragile bond between us. 'I remember.'

'You know, then, that those times of optimism have gone. This is a new world. Edwin is reliable and trustworthy. He's been through the war and he says it made him a better man.'

Ada snorted behind me. Perhaps she sensed my omissions. That battle had left him plagued by insecurities, although I couldn't convince myself he had been a kinder man before the war. I'd allowed myself to be wooed by Edwin because he represented something I thought I'd never have again: stability and a family. I'd been a fool, of course. Edwin and I hadn't talked about the essentials before our marriage. I'd blinded myself to the fact that he resented my work. Men coming back from the war had been shocked that women could do some of their jobs as well as their husbands. They preferred their wives in the home, which is where Edwin would have me if I let him.

'Reliable and trustworthy don't strike me as the basis of a passionate union. How did the man you describe woo an independent woman like you, Louisa?'

I sighed. Ada was perceptive and I forced myself to look back on the early days of our courtship. 'Edwin was kind and that, most of all, was what I craved. We walked through Regent's Park, listened to the band playing on Saturday afternoons. I found him a calming presence.'

'That's all?' Ada sniffed. 'He sounds more like a father figure.'

'He's nothing like my father. He was . . .' I paused, trying to capture my father in a few words. 'He was funny, irreverent, passionate. Edwin is none of these things.'

'So *why* did you marry him?'

'All right,' I said, crossing my arms. 'He was charming, too, and I was physically attracted to him.'

'And now?'

'I feel like I'm in a cage.'

Ada smiled, satisfied. I should have felt resentful that she'd pushed me into recognising my own complicity in my relationship with Edwin. I had, after all, got what I wanted – a second chance at family life.

'And the baby? How do you feel about the new child?'

'The thought of the new baby is wonderful. I can assure you, I have no regrets about that.'

Ada nodded. In the darkening garden, it felt like a time for confidences.

'Ada, why am I here? Who specifically asked for me?'

I felt a splat of rain on my head and looked up at the grey clouds moving fast across the sky.

'I saw your name in a journal,' Ada answered, ignoring the raindrops which were now falling steadily onto her bare head. 'There is a pile of them behind a chair in the drawing room.'

'The *Lady's Realm*?'

'I think that was its name. It's of no importance. It's you who matters.'

I took a step towards her. 'Why do I matter?'

She ignored the urgency of my tone. 'Helene told me the auctioneers were sending someone down to photograph Colonel Clewer's collection. I believe an appointment had been made. Helene was a little apprehensive about having a stranger in the house, so we consulted the cards.'

'The tarot?'

'Of course. I saw, at once, that it would be a young woman, one who would be a catalyst for change over the coming weeks. A young woman, remember. The only person who that could possibly be was the photographer arriving to catalogue the Colonel's collection. Everyone else was a known quantity: Mrs Conan Doyle, even Mr Storey who was replacing his father.'

'But why me specifically? There are other women photographers.'

'As I told you.' Ada's gaze became more fixed and she looked as if she were in some kind of trance. 'I'd seen your name in a journal. There is no such thing as a coincidence in the spirit world. I showed your picture to Helene and she agreed at once. It must be you that came to take the photographs.'

Which was why I wasn't given much notice of my commission.

'I still don't understand what you mean by catalyst for change.'

I'd disconcerted her. She hesitated, the usual pomp with which she spoke replaced by a slight tremor.

'The cards don't reveal everything. I didn't know about the baby, for example. I don't know the role you will play in the coming days, but you will be important, Louisa.'

I saw her hesitate again. 'What's the matter?'

Ada rubbed her plump hand across her face. 'This is a house in mourning and you're so full of life. I'm not sure this is the right place for you.'

'I don't have anything to fear from here, surely.'

'I'm not so sure about that. I saw what I saw in the cards.'

'You can change destiny, I'm positive.'

I touched the life inside me. The child had kicked me thirty times that morning. I'd counted every push of pressure on my hand.

'That's not how fate works, Louisa.' She took me by the arm as the rain ceased and steered me towards the Hall. 'I'm not clear what's coming next, but I fear and loathe it with my very being.'

Chapter Seventeen

In the kitchen, Alice was busy chopping vegetables, her brow furrowed in concentration. She looked up at me briefly, my swollen form reflected in the polished blade of the knife as it glinted from the light thrown by the oil lamp.

'Has Quinlivan had time to clear the icehouse yet?'

She nodded to the mantelpiece and I reached up to skim my hand along its dusty wood. I found the key, a huge brass object bigger than the palm of my hand.

'Mind you don't slip,' Alice shouted after me as I passed outside again, bracing myself against the cold. The recently oiled door opened easily into the icehouse and I saw Quinlivan had left some fresh water in a stone jar once used for beer with a useful tap at the bottom. He'd also provided me with a storm lantern which hung from an iron ring near the roof. From my supply bag I retrieved my collapsible zinc washing trough, the roughened metal bringing back a flurry of memories.

This tray had been with me from the start of my life as a photographer. I'd wandered into Zimmermann's in Holborn Circus, seeking help as to what I needed to develop the handful of plates I'd been given with the camera. I wasn't sure if this was before or after my first meeting with Bertie at my friend Emily's house. Just before, I thought, although one of my early images had been of Bertie laughing at the camera, his muscular arms raised in imitation of a circus strongman.

I placed the trough and my bottles of chemicals on the small table, along with seven used plates. Lighting the lamp, I carried it to the entrance so there would be just enough light for my work. Everything in place, with shaking hands, I dissolved two grains of pyrogallic acid in one of the chipped vases left by Quinlivan and began to develop the plates. I was rusty – that was no surprise – but slowly my memory of the process began to unfurl.

I laid the first plate face upwards in the tray and poured over the liquid. One of the joys of photography is seeing the image you've painstakingly prepared come to life on the glass. The first image I'd taken was of the Adelaide Room. I'd taken care to set up the shot so it showed off the wallpaper with its images of chimpanzees amidst lush vegetation. Not to my taste, but an important room to attract buyers to the house. I waited, not daring to exhale, but grew light-headed from holding my breath for so long.

The image in front of me remained resolutely black, a square of dark nothingness. Panic is the enemy of accuracy and I stood back for a moment, taking deep breaths. I added a couple of drops of ammonia into the liquid and tried again, the chemical usually a godsend at teasing out reluctant images, but the plate remained black, the cold glass dull as soot.

It wasn't that the photo had failed to take. The odd thing was that the gelatin coating had turned a shade darker. This made no sense. The plate should have been turning white in places where the object I'd photographed was dark, that was the point of a negative. The mahogany table, for example, the brown swirls in the wallpaper. These should have all appeared as white shapes in the negative. Instead I was left with a black square of glass. I had taken the photo exactly as I had done countless times before and I was left with a ruined plate.

Doubting my sanity, I repeated the developing process with my next plate – and my racing heart slowed when the collection of Chinese ornamental vases slowly appeared, then I saw there was a slight blemish near the top of the image. Transparent spots are usually simply a defect in the gelatin; the image is there but it hasn't yet been coaxed to appear on the plate. This, however, wasn't an absence but a presence. A pale light, and much more serious. If there was an area where light was getting in, it suggested either a problem with the plate or, worse, an issue with my camera. If this were the case, given I would never find the funds for another, my career would be ruined.

I was mad with impatience as I waited for the rest of the images to develop. The next three were perfect and it was only on the last that the light could again be seen, this time to the left of the plate. This was some relief. It was unlikely to be an issue with my camera lens if the light was appearing in a different part of the shot. There might, however, be a problem with the plates. I had taken the boxes with me from Marsham and Clive's offices and Leo had told me they were new. Perhaps he had been sold a flawed lot. Oddly enough, it wasn't the two with the errant light, but the completely black image that disturbed me as I could think of no explanation to account for the grainy square.

It had begun to rain again; I could hear the low slap of water on the tiled roof as I leant against the wall to consider the strange sequence of events at Clewer Hall. I was a rationalist, and I had been brought up to be so. My father, despite a rapid rise in the shipping company where he worked, had been no desk man. He'd loved the feats of Victorian engineering and he had passed the wonder of science onto me. The light in my plates was unusual, but there would be a commonplace explanation. I simply hadn't found it yet. The house was less easy for me to rationalise. The shadow over the Hall and the occasional sense of pressure dropping were bewildering, but they didn't add up to much and I have always been sensitive to my surroundings. It might be that I was simply unsettled by talk of the forthcoming séance.

I felt a movement against my legs. Gideon the cat was making himself felt and I reached down to pat his damp fur. He let out a surprisingly loud purr. I suspected affection might be in short supply in this house and bent to lift him. He tensed his legs and then allowed me to pick him up, his purr turning into a short chirrup.

'You're a handsome devil, you know.'

He answered me by rolling in delight in my arms, rubbing his chin into my chest until he froze and, twisting in my arms, stared at the entrance to the icehouse.

'What is it, Gideon?'

The cat let out a yowl and, gouging my arms with scratches, streaked out of the building.

I ran to the door as a gust of wind blew across the garden, now plunged into darkness in the late afternoon. 'Is anyone out there?' I called.

There was no reply but a hot dart of pain coursed up my arm. It was as if a small child had put his mouth around my hand and sunk his teeth hard into my flesh. I reached out to grab the offender. My own children had never bitten me but it must be some feral thing to be out on a wild evening such as this. I moved too quickly. The ground was slippery and I lost my footing, landing on my knees as my head knocked against the doorjamb. Disorientated, I scanned the darkness for my assailant but whoever, or whatever, had injured me had vanished.

Chapter Eighteen

I marched into the kitchen, the pain from my throbbing hand spurring me into action. I wanted to speak to a member of the household who would take me seriously and answer my questions without exaggeration. I had settled on Alice. Her sensible attitude was what I needed now, but she had disappeared from the kitchen. There was the smell of a roasting bird in the oven and the pans of vegetables which she'd been preparing earlier rested on the table, ready to be transferred to the stove. Janet was removing a jelly from its mould when I entered, its emerald-green hue sparkling in the firelight.

'Where's Alice?'

'Gone to change. She spilt fat from the bird down her front. She'll be back down in a minute.'

I hesitated. Janet was flushed, her concentration on the evening's pudding and, in any case, she had been quick to pass on the story of the ghost child. Not Janet, I thought, pulling myself up the servants' stairs, up beyond the east wing until I reached the first floor. I passed my bedroom, then hesitated outside Ada's chamber. I was desperately in need of reassurance, but while Ada might give that, she was too full of cryptic warnings to soothe my frayed nerves. I moved on, crossing the landing to the family wing.

I felt a hand on my arm and cried out in alarm.

'Don't be frightened, it's only me.'

Helene. She looked more pallid than usual, her grey hair falling in wispy fronds onto her shoulders.

'Is there something you want?'

'Have you seen Ada? It's time for my reading and she's not in her room.' She wore her desperation so plainly that it was impossible not to feel sorry for her. We turned at the sound of a tread on the stairs and Ada appeared on the landing.

'Is everything all right?'

She'd picked up on my agitation but before I could speak, Helene hurried to her, clutching at Ada's arm. I watched as the pair retreated down into a dark corner of the drawing room, both oblivious of my swollen hand.

'Lily?' I called out.

'I'm in my room. Can you give me a minute?'

I was so relieved by her calm voice that I stumbled towards it, pushing open the door to reveal a startled Lily in her underclothes.

'I'm so sorry!'

'I won't be a moment.' She slipped a dress over her angular frame but not before I caught a glimpse of her stomach, flaccid compared to her lean limbs. She began to button up the front. 'What was it that couldn't wait?'

She'd calmed down since our earlier meeting in the garden. I held my hand out to her, the wound pulsating red then white, and her eyes dropped to my raw flesh.

'You've been bitten.'

I began to sway and held on to the bedstead to steady myself. 'I've certainly been bitten. The question is, who or what has sunk their teeth into my hand?'

'Let me see.' She reached out and studied the gash. It was the most painful at the fleshy part between my thumb and forefinger.

'Gideon?'

I laughed without mirth, causing Lily to grasp my hand tighter.

'Gideon was long gone when I was attacked. Cats have plenty of sense.'

'I have iodine in my drawer. That will help.'

She crossed to a stand and pulled out a bottle, the metallic reek filling the room.

'Keep your hand steady. If it spills on your clothes, it will stain.'

Using a piece of gauze, she dabbed at my hand.

'What's going on, Lily?' I blurted out, wincing as the cold liquid splashed onto my skin.

'Going on? What do you mean?'

The question drew me up short. My time here had been marked by a series of odd happenings and cool responses to my presence. Taken individually, they didn't add up to much. I groped for a question I could ask without antagonising Lily.

'Why doesn't anyone want to talk about the forthcoming séance?'

Lily kept her head bowed over me, revealing her scalp, visible through her thin blonde hair.

'Tell me, please. Is it to do with me? My pregnancy has caused reactions from curiosity to distress. Am I not welcome here?'

I watched as she poured water from the jug into a bowl, dipping her hands in to remove the iodine which had stained her fingers.

She sighed and reached for a hand towel. 'Of course you're welcome here. I've told you this already, and nothing has changed. Everyone is nervous, that's all. Ada's presence here, along with our expected guests, is reviving a lot of memories.'

'Because of what was said during the original séance?'

'Exactly that.' Lily must have seen the look of expectancy on my face and she relented. She closed the door, leaning back against it as she faced me. 'During the séance, Ada mentioned a curse. Well, it was nonsense, of course. This is my home and I'd never heard any mention of it before. Nevertheless, Ada told those assembled around the table that the house was under an evil prophecy.'

'Of what kind?'

Lily took a breath. 'She said that any male child born of the house would die young.'

A rush of heartburn stung my chest as the baby kicked me in protest. 'But that's horrible.'

'Of course it was. The thing is, although the séance became famous after Henry Storey's newspaper report, Ada's predictions weren't really given any weight. It's the sort of thing you'd expect a medium to say. It would have remained that way except for—'

'The war.'

'Exactly. The war meant the supposed curse came true. All three sons of the house did die. So now my mother, Quinlivan and anyone else of a gullible nature thinks that Ada is some kind of prophetess.'

'But there must have been male children who were born in your family who haven't died young.'

'Of course. My father was born here, for instance, and my grandfather – who certainly didn't die young. And, as I said, I'd never heard of any such curse before that evening.'

'But because of the war, everyone thinks it came true? Oh, Lily, that's terrible. Is that why you looked astounded when you saw I was expecting?'

'We thought you'd be older and, well, the child you're having was a surprise too. I don't believe in Ada's prophecies but I was worried about the effect you might have on my mother, who *does* take notice of them.'

I wasn't sure if I believed her. I was positive my pregnancy had caused her more consternation than Lily was prepared to admit. She had looked at my stomach and had been moved by it.

'Janet told me a story about a haunting at Clewer Hall. Is it connected to Ada's curse?'

'A haunting?' Lily paused. 'That old tale. Don't fill your head with Janet's nonsense. Nor Ada's, for that matter.'

'So what bit me?' I looked to the yellow splash covering up the teeth marks on my hand.

'Gideon's faster than you think, and he can definitely bite. Either that or you disturbed a rodent. There are other abrasions on your skin. Did you fall?'

'The surprise made me stumble.'

'A mixture of your fall and Gideon, then,' said Lily, the matter, in her eyes, concluded.

I remembered how Gideon had purred in my arms a moment before fleeing. It was possible he had remained at the doorway and jumped up to bite me. I studied my hand, the puncture marks in my skin beginning to blur.

'That's all there is to it?'

'That's all,' said Lily, her voice firm. 'We need to keep an eye on the bite over the next few days.' She hesitated. 'I'd prefer you didn't mention any of our conversation to my mother.'

Chapter Nineteen

25 June 1896
8.02 p.m.

Lily mouthed the words of the Lord's Prayer, convinced that her
maternal grandfather, the vicar of St Wystan's in Derbyshire,
must be turning in his grave. She wasn't sure how she'd expected
the séance to start but it wasn't with a prayer. She was surprised
to see that it had the effect of putting at least two of the occu-
pants of the table at their ease. Sir Thomas was a churchgoer,
filling the pew opposite theirs with his sickly wife every Sunday.
Lily watched him recite the long-remembered phrases and imper-
ceptibly relax. Conan Doyle had clearly anticipated this opening
of proceedings and his melodic voice boomed across the room.
Only Henry Storey was unsure of the wording, the vocabulary of
the Book of Common Prayer a mystery to him. He caught her
eye and winked. Lily, blushing, tightened her grip on her mother's
hand.

It had taken a while to work out the formation of the circle.
Henry had come down from the *Telegraph* specifically to tran-
scribe the séance and needed a free hand to write his notes. Ada
was adamant that the spirits would not appear unless there was
a closed circle. There had been talk of putting Henry on a small
card table, but he'd refused. He wanted to be part of the séance,
not excluded from it. In the end, he leant back, scribbling on the

ledge of the table while Lily stretched her arm in front of his to reach Sir Thomas's on the other side of him.

At the end of the prayer, there was a brief silence and then Ada's voice, 'The Lord giveth and the Lord taketh away.'

The table moved a little, just enough to make Henry shift his notebook an inch or so. The fire spat a nasty spark which hopped over the grate and landed on the carpet, sending the smell of singed wool around the room.

'I see a woman in a white nightshift. She's waving at one of you.' Ada closed her eyes. 'Who do you have a message for?'

The medium's voice changed to one of simpering coyness. 'You're my lovely girlie, aren't you? Let me give you a kiss on that apple cheek.'

Lily saw her mother's eyes open in adoration while she cringed as Ada made two kisses into the air with a loud smack.

'Haven't you grown up beautiful like I always said you would?'

The table moved again, this time with a loud scrape. Although there was a bright lamp on the table, the room was growing hazy, as if a London Particular, as its smog was called, had crept down the county from the capital. Their hands were still grasped tightly together but Lily could see Conan Doyle's eyes on Ada's arms.

'Is that you, Nanny Partridge?' called out Helene. 'It's me, your little Bee.'

'She says she misses you sitting on her knee. Do you remember?'

'Yes. I miss you too, Nanny.'

But Ada was moving on. Her face contorted into a ball of fury. 'I never said you could come here. Who do you think you are, you little bastard?'

Was it a snort of laughter she heard from Henry next to her? His head was bent over his notebook and she could hear the scratch of his pen on the paper.

Ada's voice was coarse, the tone both mocking and with an

undercurrent of violence. Helene was looking alarmed, although Conan Doyle was interested. He leant forward.

'Can you tell me your name?' he asked. 'Who are you?'

Ada's face was still working. 'Never mind my name. Who said you could come in this room? Oh, you like the wallpaper, do you? I'm not surprised. It's like you, smelly and dirty.'

Lily froze and looked at her mother, trying to catch her eye. Helene returned her gaze, her expression difficult to read.

'This is a house full of secrets. Don't think I don't know. There's not much you can hide from me. Some families are too inter-woven, the evil just gets deeper. *"And thou shalt not let any of thy seed pass through the fire to Molech, neither shalt thou profane the name of thy God."* She returned to her first voice. 'Oh my little egg. Oh my little egg.'

For the first time, Lily felt the twinge of a primeval fear. She felt Ada's eyes boring into her. 'We all have secrets here. Slipping and tripping around the garden away from prying eyes. Not the first one to do it, either. Little extras popping up. A child. Here today, gone tomorrow.'

I'm going to get up soon, she thought. *Forget trying to please Mr Conan Doyle. I need to stand and leave.*

Ada adopted a Midlands accent, all flat vowels, and turned to Conan Doyle. 'Hello Arthur, me duck. I wasn't expecting you here. It's your old friend, Billy.'

To Lily's surprise, Conan Doyle smiled. 'Billy.'

'You'll have to excuse me. I've had a drink or two – been at the mother's ruin.'

Was it her imagination or could she smell the faint tang of juniper berries? Lily wasn't sure, but Conan Doyle continued to smile and this was soon joined by a beautiful beam on Ada's face.

'Ah, hello. We have another person joining us in the room. I've been waiting for you to come to me.'

'Who is it?' breathed Helene.

'It's my spirit guide, Black Hawk. He's a huge Red Indian.'

Henry's pen wobbled for a moment. The table moved again and Lily followed Conan Doyle's eyes and saw, at the same time as he, the stick of metal poking out of Ada's arm, the brass catching the light of the lamp.

She's a fraud, thought Lily. She's nothing more than a common fraud and we've invited her into our home so she can make fools of us all.

The temperature of the room dropped. Ada must have raided the icehouse and found a way of letting it loose in the room. Lily felt her mother shiver but couldn't free her hand to pull Helene's shawl around her.

'No,' moaned Ada, clearly enjoying herself. 'You don't mean that. I don't want to be the one to tell them.' She had closed her eyes, her round face still working.

'What?' asked Helene. 'What is he saying?'

Ada's eyes flew open, her expression glazed. 'This house is caught between the balance of good and evil and the devil will prevail. Its eyes are on your sons. *Vengeance is mine; I will repay, saith the Lord*. And you will be sorry. All of the sons of this house will be mine. Every single one. Death is their dominion. They cannot survive.'

Lily felt her mother's fingernails dig into her skin and a trickle of blood run down her hand as the room was filled with a vegetal smell, of horse manure and brown mulch.

Chapter Twenty

The next morning, the house was stirring early, in a state of anticipation for the arrival of Sir Arthur and Lady Conan Doyle. Despite the energy of the footsteps along the corridor, I couldn't match them with my movements, listlessly dragging on my clothes after a hot wash. My Holland jacket hid my arms which were covered with scratches from Gideon and the wound which pulsated on my hand. In the night, I had nearly knocked on Ada's door and asked for a glass of her laudanum, which would surely have dulled the pain. However, I was worried about the effect on the baby and instead gritted my teeth until sleep finally overtook me in the early hours of the morning.

At breakfast I asked Horwick if the Hall had a telephone I might use. I'd begun to feel guilty about Edwin. Not a terrible man; just, like many of his generation, crushed by his experience of war. Everything about our life – its ordered routine, his insistence on everything being just so – was a reaction to his life in the trenches where nothing had been certain, especially his likelihood of survival.

'There's a phone in the post office in the village. I could ask Quinlivan to give you a lift there.'

'It doesn't matter.' Quinlivan was likely to be busy with the arriving guests. I could walk there in the afternoon when I had finished my day's work. I would then have a clearer idea of when

I might be able to return home, something specific to placate Edwin with.

I retook the shot of the Adelaide Room, carrying the plate straight to the icehouse to develop. This time the negative appeared sharp as a pin, the image grotesque but undamaged. The morning was marked only by my discovery of Horwick studying the glass cabinet of marble hands when I returned to the room. I coughed to make him aware of my presence and he straightened, unembarrassed.

'There are seven once more.'

I placed the camera on the table and unfastened the clasps. 'Whoever took the limb appears to have replaced it. I wonder which one went missing? They all looked alike to me although Colonel Clewer said he could distinguish those of his own children.' I spun round when Horwick remained silent. 'Do you know which was taken?'

'As you say, ma'am, they all look alike.'

I forgot the butler as I turned to my work, concentrating on the plates until Lily, putting her head round the door, asked me to join the family and guests for afternoon tea.

Sir Arthur was older than I expected. He had the ruddy complexion and luxuriant moustache of a man used to fine living. His tweed suit gave off a whiff of lanolin and pipe smoke. Jean, his wife, was thickset, with a heavy face and shrewd green eyes. Taller than her husband, she reminded me a little of Ada although I couldn't immediately identify why.

I joined her on the sofa and looked at the spread Alice had prepared: scones with thick cream and jam with lumps of strawberries, little round buns cheerily iced . . . not a seed cake in sight. I took one of the buns and bit into it.

'Louisa is taking photos of the Hall for the auction catalogue,' said Lily.

'Then you can keep me company the night of the séance,' said Jean, smoothing her skirt. 'I can tell you some of my own stories of meeting the spirits.'

'I heard you're a believer too,' I said, taking another bite, enjoying the coating of sugar over my lips. How my boys would have loved these buns . . .

'Jean's specialism is handwriting.' Sir Arthur reached out for his wife's hand.

'Automatic handwriting?' I asked, feeling foolish. I looked for clarification to Ada, who had a scornful look on her face. Either it wasn't part of her repertoire or she held it in poor regard. Possibly she simply resented the presence of a rival in the room.

'The spirit channels his energy through me, and I write the words down,' said Jean. 'I've recently corresponded with my brother Malcolm and Arthur's nephew, Oscar, both now on the other side.'

I finished the bun, hoping I wasn't going to be asked for my own view on the chances of an afterlife.

'You're not a believer?' asked Conan Doyle.

Reluctantly, I forced myself to consider the possibility of one day seeing my children again. Bertie too. It was a tempting prospect, but one I'd pushed to the back of my mind. If I followed that train of thought, in which by dying I might myself be reunited with my family, it might lead me to a dark place. I could not think of them now. I was a survivor and a rationalist, which left me at a disadvantage in this company.

'I suppose my view is, if the time is right, anyone can conjure up a person they desperately want to see.'

But was that right? Bertie had never appeared to me, no matter how much I wanted him to.

I was feeling ill once more and the baby was pressing against my bladder, a common complaint, forcing me to make my excuses and hurry to the water closet. On the gallery, I could hear the start of a piano and the thin voice singing again.

'But the pale, pale face in the garden shone through her restless dream.'

Again, that tune which echoed in my memory. A parlour song, certainly. Both lyrics and melody were imbued with wistfulness and melancholy. Not the song of a child, but that of an adult looking back on a past event. I wished I could remember how the tale continued. The words stayed in my head as I used the pan, realising everyone except Felix was in the sitting room and this was no voice of a grown man.

When I returned to the passageway, the music had stopped and I hurried down the stairs, reeling slightly, my eyes trying to focus after the day of photographs. I reached out to steady myself, my hand brushing the gilt frame of one of the paintings on the wall. The family had been talking about me in my absence, for the room became unnaturally silent when I returned to my seat. I didn't do anything to help their discomfort but picked up my cup, wondering if the Darjeeling would have a similar soporific effect as the first time I had drunk it.

I had just put the cup to my lips when there came a crash of such magnitude that my tired brain thought the roof had caved in. I struggled to my feet, following the rush of people streaming out through the door. In the drawing room, at first all I could see was glass and blood, then, as the scene coalesced, I saw Horwick on the floor.

'What's happened?' cried Jean.

I expected histrionics from Helene but she was the first to speak, her voice calm. 'The painting of the faun has fallen from the wall.'

Amongst the shards of canvas, smashed gilt frame and Horwick's stunned form, I saw the gradual spread of vermilion.

'He's bleeding!'

Lily rushed forward and began to pull the frame off Horwick while Sir Arthur, a qualified medical man, I remembered, tended to the stricken butler. I'd never felt so inadequate. I had no medical training; my contribution in the war had been to work to support my sons, and I could not even get on my knees to help soothe Horwick, who was moaning in pain. He caught my eye and tried to speak. 'The ch-child,' he mouthed. 'G-go away.'

I stared at Horwick, trying to make sense of his words. I moved closer to him but he shrank from me as the others bustled around him. I felt my baby kick at that moment and looked again at Horwick, afraid of the possibility that he might mean my own child.

I looked up to the space where the painting had hung, the same picture I'd touched when steadying myself on the stairs moments earlier. A huge chunk of plaster had fallen from the wall, and had taken the fixings with it, bringing the painting crashing down onto Horwick.

'Will he be all right?' asked Helene, her already pale skin ashen.

'His leg is broken,' said Conan Doyle. 'Possibly his collarbone too. The blood is from a wound to his head. Is there someone who can help me lift the man onto the table?'

'I'll find Quinlivan.' I spotted Alice standing at the entrance to the drawing room, grey hair escaping from her cap, her eyes wide in shock. 'Is he downstairs?'

She shook her head, her eyes still on the widening pool of blood. I brushed past the group and ran into the garden and down to the coach house. I could hear raised voices, Quinlivan's Sussex burr and a woman's, harder to discern. Turning into the light, I saw Janet standing close to Quinlivan. Despite drawing away from each other immediately, there was no hiding their intimacy.

'Is everything all right?' asked Janet.

'There's been an accident. We need your help.'

Quinlivan was gentle with the old man as he lifted him onto

the drawing room table. Although he walked with a limp, there was no mistaking his strength. Sir Arthur effortlessly took charge and I watched in admiration as he carefully examined Horwick.

'The left side of his body took most of the impact. He has a nasty break in his leg, probably happened when he fell to the floor. We need to call for a doctor. I don't have the equipment to set the bone. Where's the telephone?'

'We don't have one,' said Helene, still grey with shock. 'The nearest is in the post office, which might be closed.'

'We can knock on Mrs Ellis's door and tell her it's an emergency,' said Lily. 'She won't mind.'

'I'll go,' Quinlivan said, glancing at Janet as he left.

Felix, I saw, was pouring brandy into glasses and handing them round the group. He offered me one; I hesitated, and took it, savouring the trickle of the fiery liquid down my throat. Ada didn't, as I'd have expected, accept her glass.

'I'm feeling rather tired,' she said. 'I think I might have a lie-down.'

I realised she too was quite pale. The injuries of the old man appeared to have shaken her.

'I'll help you to your room,' I said, putting my glass down onto a table. We must have made a strange pair, climbing the stairs, both a similar size but our stomachs distended for different reasons.

When we reached the gallery, Ada looked over the balustrade at the scene below. It reminded me of a drawing I'd once seen of a post-mortem. Horwick was lying spread out on the table, with everyone gathered around.

'I passed the painting earlier and used it to steady myself.' I wanted to make a confession to this woman. I thought she might understand but I stopped when I saw my words had made her turn ashen. 'Is everything all right?'

She'd lost her composure and some of her wits. 'I didn't foresee this,' she said. 'Did you hear him mention a child?'

I nodded. 'What did he mean?'

'The child,' she repeated. 'I should have realised. I hope I haven't been wrong about everything.'

Chapter Twenty-One

I rose early after abandoning any attempt at sleep and lit the kindling which Janet had laid in the grate. I added in some sprigs of rosemary I'd gathered in the frost the previous morning and soon the room was infused with the smell of flowers and burning pine. Although it was still dark outside, I drew back the curtains and pulled the small table beside my bed in front of the window. While the room warmed, I crossed to the nursery and pushed open the door, my eyes watering at the sudden blaze of light when I flicked the switch.

Two of the chairs at the scarred table were unsuitable for use but the third, although missing a spoke on its back, was sturdy enough. I took it through to my room and sat down to compose my letter.

> *Dear Edwin*
> *I'm sorry that I had to leave so suddenly for Clewer Hall. I hope Dorothy explained the situation to you and the financial reward it will bring. When my task is completed I'll be back in touch with a telegram to inform you of my arrival. The baby and I are fine.*
> *Yours, Louisa.*

After my four days' absence, a brief telephone call, however expensive, would have been preferable to a letter but it had constantly slipped my mind. I wondered how I would feel if I got such an impersonal note. Hurt and melancholic, I suspected but I wasn't sure that would be Edwin's reaction. I had rarely seen any unguarded emotion since our first meeting when I had accompanied my uncle to purchase a waistcoat at Edwin's workplace. Edwin had taken charge of the fitting and I'd admired, first, his deference towards my uncle, and then his discretion as he looped the tape measure around my relative's gigantic girth. It was this suppression of emotion, which I had mistaken for maturity, which had first attracted me to him. I had loved Bertie, but our marriage had been young and ultimately tragic. For my second marriage I had wanted a union based on stability rather than romance. Be careful what you wish for, I now knew too well. Every marriage needs a little turbulence. Anything to prevent the inertia which can accompany routine and stifled hurt.

I had an envelope in my bag, but no stamp, which meant a trip to the village. I heard a step outside my room and opened the door to meet a startled Janet.

'Goodness, you're up early.'

She was carrying a lidded tin pail of hot water from which steam was seeping around the edges.

'Is that for me?'

'Watch it, it's only just come off the fire. Cook thought that if we put them out now it would be done by the time everyone got up.'

'You're doing all the rooms? I thought the other wing had a bathroom.'

'Mrs Clewer thought that was best left for the guests. The family will wash from jugs like in the old days.'

I tried to take the steaming pail from her but she insisted on carrying it in for me and tipping the bubbling water into my ewer.

'How's Horwick?'

'According to cook, he's had a terrible night. So has she, by the look of it.'

'Where's his room, in the attic?'

'Near the kitchen – a hark back to the days when he ruled the roost in the servants' quarters. It's just as well it wasn't far to carry him last night.'

'Will he be all right? There was a lot of blood yesterday.'

'Physically, they think so. I'm not so sure about his nerves. According to Alice, he asked her to write to his sister. He wants to recuperate there. Near on fifty years he's been here and now he can't wait to go.'

I remembered the words he had mouthed at me after the accident. *The child. Go away.* 'Has he said why he wants to leave so quickly?'

'Perhaps he thinks there's unfinished business from the last séance? I'm not sure.'

'You mean the curse on the house Ada mentioned?'

Janet looked across at me. 'I'm just guessing. He hates Ada. He thinks she brings bad luck with her.'

'Will he be able to leave before the séance?'

Janet began folding my clothes. 'Probably not. We need to wait for a reply before he can go anywhere. Don't worry about his ramblings.'

'What will you do for staff? There's another guest arriving today, isn't there?'

'George Storey from the *Daily Herald*. He was due tomorrow but there's snow coming and he doesn't want to miss the gathering, so he's arriving a day early.'

'But how will you cope, just you and Alice?'

'Miss Lily will help. Quinlivan too.' She hesitated and I remembered the pair of them yesterday. I decided to say nothing, remembering the letter sitting on the table and anyway, I could never bear the sickly coyness that people adopt when talking to those in blossoming love affairs.

'Can't you ring an agency in Brighton? Is there money to stretch to paying for extra help for a few days?'

Janet looked amused. 'They're a week behind with staff wages, so I'll say not. I might be able to find someone a bit closer to help me, though.'

Gunmetal-coloured clouds dominated the sky as I walked to the village. January had been cold but I could feel the air cooling in preparation for the forthcoming snow. The drive was easier to navigate on foot than in the car, and I felt my spirits lift as I left the Clewer grounds and walked along the narrow road. I could see the outline of the village in front of me, the buildings constructed in flinty pebbles which must be a feature of the Sussex Downs. The scent of the sea was stronger here too, the wind bringing the smell of brine and seaweed and, in the distance, the cry of screeching gulls.

The post office was run by a woman built on the same lines as Ada. Unlike the medium, however, she had a brisk, no-nonsense manner, selling me a stamp and taking the letter from me to catch the midday post.

'Staying up at the Hall?' The question was innocuous enough but she paused, waiting for my reply.

'Just for this week. I'm taking some photographs.' At the woman's blank face, I hurried on. 'For the sale.'

'Of course. How's Mr Horwick?'

'I think he had a difficult night. Quinlivan phoned from here, didn't he?'

'I was shutting up when he arrived. I knew something was wrong as soon as I saw his face. A picture falling from the wall, wasn't it? I'm surprised it hasn't happened before. I bet the whole house is riddled with damp.'

'Do you know the family?'

'Miss Lily comes here most weeks. I haven't seen the Colonel and his wife for a long while.'

I thought about the isolation of the Clewers, so near the village and yet only, it seemed, on friendly terms with their neighbour, Sir Thomas Jensen.

She looked me up and down, taking in my form. 'Are you comfortable there?'

I caught her eye and we shared a moment of complicity. 'Comfortable enough. There are strange creaks and the rooms are suffused with cold, but I shan't be there long enough for it to affect me.'

'Ah.' She would have left it at that and perhaps I shouldn't have pressed the matter. It wouldn't do me any good to be seen gossiping with the village postmistress, surely the hub of all local news. But curiosity is stronger than discretion and I plunged on.

'I've already been told the story of the child said to haunt the gardens,' I said, watching for the woman's reaction.

'Oh, there have been plenty of stories over the years. Don't bother yourself about those tales.'

'You know of the séance too? The suggestion of a curse on children of the family? The Clewer family lost all three sons, didn't they?'

Her manner altered, dismissal turning to disapproval. 'Pay no attention to any of that nonsense.'

I hurried to placate her. 'I'm only here to take my photographs. I'll be busy with those. I was simply curious because the Hall feels as if it's a shadow of its former self. Do children use the garden at all? Perhaps from the village?'

'The Simmons children do. There are about five or six of them who run wild around here. They use the Clewer gardens as a cut-through from the village down to the sea. They wouldn't dare use Sir Thomas's land. He's got his own grandchildren but wouldn't want them mixing with those ragamuffins. He'd use his cane on them if he caught one in his gardens. The gamekeeper's been told to do the same.'

So the culprit was a village child. As I'd thought, a rational explanation, although the knowledge brought a sense of relief. I, too, had been affected by the decrepit house.

I bought myself a bar of chocolate, a rare luxury, but given that I had spent nothing for four days, I thought my hard work justi-fied it. I ate the bar as I hurried back to Clewer Hall, savouring the juxtaposition of the sweet chocolate and the fight against the elements. I was halfway up the driveway when I heard the sounds of the motor car behind me. Quinlivan tipped his hat at me and I moved out of the way to let him pass, but the car halted and the back door opened.

'Care for a lift?'

Chapter Twenty-Two

The man in the car could only be George Storey. I remembered his father, Henry, from his articles in the *Telegraph* which my father had enjoyed reading out loud. His origins might have been in the society section of the paper but he became a heavyweight commentator on the shift from Victorian buoyancy to Edwardian self-doubt. I knew little about his son other than he was a journalist with the left-leaning *Daily Herald*. Different politics from his father, then, although still successful. Clearly his principles didn't preclude him from arriving in a chauffeur-driven car. I ducked under the hood.

'I'm happy to walk.'

He laughed. 'Are you sure? You look like a goose about to lay an egg.'

I moved to shut the door but he put out his hand to stop it closing.

'I'm sorry, poor attempt at humour. My guess it's a long walk to the house. Why don't you climb in?'

I wanted to refuse but the relative warmth of the car was a relief as I settled myself next to him. I wondered if he could smell the chocolate bar which I hoped I hadn't smeared onto my face. He turned slightly to look at me.

'Are you a member of the Clewer family?'

'I'm a visitor here.'

He twisted further towards me. 'You're here for the séance?'

'I'm here to take photographs in advance of the house sale.'

'A professional photographer? I rather wish the people I have to deal with at the paper were like you.'

'What? Pregnant?'

He laughed. 'No, of course not.'

'A woman, then?'

He shifted, uncomfortable, and not just from the movement of the car. I relented. 'I'm sorry, I didn't sleep very well. There was an accident here yesterday.'

'Quinlivan told me. What happened to your hand?'

I looked down and saw that although the pain had eased a little, the bruise was now reddish-purple and the pattern of teeth easily distinguishable.

'I was bitten while holding Gideon the cat,' I said, keeping my eyes on Quinlivan, who briefly glanced in the side mirror at me.

'I hope it's not a bad omen for tomorrow.'

'I won't be attending the séance.'

George clasped his knee. 'Lucky you.'

'You don't approve?' I asked. I still hadn't managed to get a proper look at him. I could feel his heat as I inhaled the scent of the city on him.

He took a moment to answer which, I'd discovered, was a common response when anyone spoke about the séance.

'It's neither here nor there whether I approve. The fact is, I didn't feel I had any choice when it came to my being here. I'm as curious as the next person, especially as my father attended the previous gathering and, in any case, my editor thought it an excellent idea for a newspaper article.'

We had arrived at the front door and, unlike on my first day, Horwick wasn't there to make a decision as to which entrance

George should use. As the car came to a standstill, instead of waiting for Quinlivan to open the door, George sprang out and came around to my side, helping me out with an inelegant pull. Quinlivan glanced across at me and smirked. George didn't wait for us but headed towards the open door where Janet stood on the threshold, ready to usher him into the drawing room.

'What really happened to your hand?' asked Quinlivan as he pulled George's luggage from the trunk.

'I was bitten, as I said. Lily thought it must have been the cat.'

'May I see?'

I held out my hand, which still bore traces of the yellow iodine despite my morning wash.

'The creature that bit you had sharp teeth, certainly.' Quinlivan followed me into the central drawing room, handing George's coat to Janet. George, I saw, was looking around him, taking in the shabby furnishings and chipped walls.

'Is there much for you to photograph?'

I nodded towards the far end of the hallway. 'There are some wonderful pieces in the cabinets. In the Adelaide Room too.'

'The location of the séance? Perhaps you could show me sometime. I'd be interested in seeing them with your photographer's eye.'

I flushed as I felt his eyes on me. 'You have an interest in photography?'

'Only a layman's, but the world can look a different place through a lens.'

I thought of my ruined plates and grimaced. 'When I get it right, certainly. I'll be happy to show you the curios.'

I climbed the stairs, using the opportunity to look down and study the newcomer. He was tall, taller than my Bertie, and with a head of curly brown hair. He was dressed for the London street

– those shoes wouldn't last five minutes in the country – but there was nothing foppish about him. Rather, he had the air of someone with business to conduct. Our eyes met for a moment before I continued up the steps.

Chapter Twenty-Three

I resumed work, conscious of the dark clouds which were gathering over the sea. It was to be my final day in the Adelaide Room. I would need to get everything photographed and then vacate the space in readiness for the next day's séance. It was a worry. If the snow came, then the sky would be overcast and unlikely to give me enough light for the photographs. This meant I needed a day with no distractions. No talk of ghost children or curses. It was a time to focus.

The final cabinet to photograph was unusual in that it wasn't a collection of objects amassed for their aesthetic value like all the others in the room. At some point in the last twenty years or so, Felix had begun to collect phonograph records. Some singers I recognised. Nellie Melba, of course, and the great Caruso. Others were unknown to me. Eleanora de Cisneros and Victor Maurel singing arias from Verdi and Rossini. They were included in the list for sale; I had checked, and could well imagine why. I found music impossible to listen to these days too, grief finding a way of choking past pleasures.

I'd learnt to dance with my brother. He had two left feet, lumpenly guiding me around the dance floor of Mrs Whittaker's dance establishment. Bertie hadn't been much more accomplished but he had a natural rhythm and we'd attended a few tea dances during our courtship, laughing at our ineptitude. After he'd died, even the sound bashed out on the twins' toy piano had been painful to listen to and after their deaths, I'd banished music from my life.

'To your taste?'

I swung round to see George standing in the doorway, a cigarette in hand.

'I'm no opera expert.'

He entered the room, his eyes on the wallpaper. 'Me neither. A seat at Covent Garden currently goes for eight shillings – meanwhile, the residents of nearby Farringdon starve.'

'You disapprove of people enjoying themselves?' I put the discs back and set up my camera to take an image of the gramophone cabinet. J. C. Stephens would be selling the items as a single job lot.

'No, I don't disapprove of pleasure. I just prefer it to be proportionate.'

'There have always been rich and poor.' I took out a plate and slotted it into the camera. 'The war may have democratised some aspects of society, but not wealth.'

'Well, perhaps this will change under Mr MacDonald if he can get back into power.'

I put my eye against the camera's viewer. Ramsay MacDonald had ruined his chance last year but he might still get another try at becoming Prime Minister. I'd heard the murmurings of dissent on the streets: men returned from war and with no work, blaming women and the young for their unemployed status. George was right, though. Set against this discord, the new rich were getting wealthier. Ten years earlier I might have been the one with short hair dancing the Black Bottom.

'Can I help?' he asked, extinguishing his cigarette in the ashtray.

I straightened, rubbing my back. 'I'd rather you didn't. I can't afford to make any mistakes.'

'Do you? Make mistakes, I mean? I often think making errors is the only way to learn.'

I thought of the black glass plate. 'We all make mistakes.'

'I've heard of you, you know. You didn't tell me your name in the car, I had to ask Quinlivan. I remember you were one of the photographers employed by that magazine which folded during the war.'

I flushed at the thought that this man knew of my work. Up to now, I felt as if I were here only due to Ada's interference. Here was a reminder that I had a reputation, of sorts, within the industry where I worked. 'You don't strike me as the typical reader of the *Lady's Realm*.'

'True, but I have three sisters and I used to read their copies. Well, why not? You can find out about the world as much through women's activities as those of men.'

I raised my head in surprise. 'You truly think that?'

'I do.' George began to flick through the records, whistling a tune under his breath. He selected one and put it on the player, turning the handle until it spun at a dizzying speed. The music swung around the room. Not opera, but a big band tune. For a moment I thought George was going to ask me to dance – I might even have said yes – but he had his eyes on my camera.

'That belongs in a museum.'

I bristled. 'It's one of the best. A Butcher's Cameo. They don't make them like this now.'

'Of course not. Kodak has invested in celluloid film.' He didn't try to keep the amusement from his voice.

'It doesn't produce images with the clarity of dry plates, I can assure you.'

I'd seen some of the substandard images taken on film which was still in its infancy. Glass plate photography would be around for a little while longer, although I'd have dearly loved one of those little cameras being made in America which you could carry around with ease.

'In any case, I can't afford a new one.'

His face fell. 'Of course, I'm sorry. It wasn't a criticism. You've a fine reputation as a photographer. I was simply making an observation.'

His change of mood put me off balance. 'This is the room where the séance will take place.'

He grimaced. 'I'd never have agreed to come if my father hadn't done so before me. These things are a good way of parting people from their money. It's the landed gentry who make the news, but I've seen mediums in packed assembly rooms and public community halls, and even a sixpence entry fee can be the difference between someone feeding their family or not.'

'I suppose it's the most natural thing in the world to want to contact someone who has died suddenly.'

'Which means most of the population of this country. I'm not denying Ada Watkins has a captive audience, but I don't want to be seen to be agreeing with it.'

'You couldn't have declined, despite your editor's enthusiasm for the idea?' I thought back to the discussion which had taken place in the drawing room and the flawed thinking behind the invites. Perhaps if George had refused the invitation then Jean Conan Doyle would have got her place.

George lifted the needle off the record, the cheerful tune suddenly an irritant. 'I have to admit I was curious. My father died when I was thirteen. My sisters have the advantage over me in that they knew him better than I did. I remember him working hard and seeing him only at weekends. Sometimes not even then.'

'But he was a young man in the 1890s.'

'A little younger than I am now. When Pa was dying, I got to know him better. I was sitting on his bed one evening near the end. Edith, the eldest of my sisters, was having her first child and the women of the house had gone to keep her company. I was left alone with Father and he told me about the night of the séance.'

'He left an excellent account of the evening, I believe.'

'You've read it?'

I shook my head. 'I had no idea about the séance before I arrived at the Hall.'

'I should have brought a copy with me. Perhaps there's one in the house. It caused a bit of a stir at the time but it was long in the past by 1911. That evening my father wanted to talk about the séance. He was disparaging of Ada Watkins, convinced she was a fraud, but he was shocked about her predictions. That there was a curse on all the Clewer sons.'

'The prophecy made it into the paper?'

'Of course. It was a terrible thing to predict. But funnily enough that wasn't what worried him. Remember, when he spoke to me, the three Clewer heirs were still alive. The war hadn't happened but he was still perturbed.'

'What worried him?'

'He was shocked at the distress the prediction had caused. We all know how these so-called spiritualists behave. There's usually a bit of biblical spouting followed by communing with various dead friends and relations. The curse revelation came as a surprise, of course, but the family were devastated by it.'

'By family, you mean Helene and Lily? Felix wasn't present.'

'Yes, exactly. Helene had to be helped from the table but Lily was equally perturbed. Their reaction was a bit extreme.'

'The curse was a terrible thing to reveal. No wonder they were upset.'

'He said the séance was full of hints and half-revelations. I appreciate that's how mediums operate but it was more than that. Ada talked of a child here one day and gone the next.'

'A child? What did she mean by that?'

'I've no idea. Perhaps one of the guests had a baby who died. The family were certainly upset. It affected my father. He didn't like Ada, that much was clear, but this was something else. He said the house was imbued with a sense of malice and spite. I mean, I may not share my father's politics but I'm his son. We're one of a kind. Not given to flights of fancy.'

'Your father thought this house malevolent?'

George looked at me. 'Not thought. He was convinced of it.'

Chapter Twenty-Four

The atmosphere at dinner was a peculiar mixture of bonhomie and tension. Quinlivan served, very adeptly I thought, and I spotted Conan Doyle gazing thoughtfully at his scar. All the attendees of the next day's séance were present with the exception of Sir Thomas, who had family visiting. Tired after my day of lugging the camera around, I struggled to keep track of the conversation at the table. Jean Conan Doyle, I noticed, was miserable. I'd been placed next to her husband and every time I turned to speak to him, I found her green eyes boring into mine. Lily, sitting next to Jean, spotted her wretchedness and, perhaps to appease her distinguished guest, suggested Jean give a demonstration of automatic handwriting.

'Not in the Adelaide Room,' said Ada.

The vehemence of her tone caused Felix to raise his head. 'You're most certainly not using the sitting room. The Adelaide Room will do perfectly.'

I thought Ada would be put out, affronted even, but she paled and picked up her wine glass, taking a deep gulp.

Jean cheered up considerably and even gave me a smile when I agreed to attend the sitting. Old traditions were changing. Felix rose at the same time as his wife and disappeared into his study, his socialising done for the evening. It meant I didn't have to endure the interminable coffee with the other women but could follow George into the room where a fire had been hastily lit.

This evening, the passage was still except for a faint pulse from deep within its walls.

Inside the room, Sir Arthur placed his wife near the marble chimney piece with a pencil and a block of writing paper as we settled around the table. Ada's face was puce, her lips working as if mouthing a prayer. It was Conan Doyle who appealed out loud to the Almighty, however, asking him to connect the gathering with friends who had passed over. Jean, I noticed, had her eyes closed as her husband turned to her.

'Are you ready, my dear?'

Instead of answering, she slapped on the table three times with the palm of her hand.

'It's the spirit saying yes,' Conan Doyle explained to me as Ada snorted.

Jean's eyelids had begun to flutter and I listened to her breathing become slower and more laboured. She picked up the pencil and began to write on the paper at a speed that took my breath away. I saw her agitation as she scored the sheets, surely gouging the tabletop underneath. As she completed each sheet, Sir Arthur removed it from her and put it to one side.

We looked at the pile, wondering who should pick up the message.

'Who is it for?' asked Helene, her eyes fixed on the paper. She looked at Ada. 'Perhaps you should—'

'No.' Ada's voice was firm and I remembered the pair of spectacles she'd worn for the tarot reading.

'I'll look at it.'

I took the first sheet of paper from the bottom of the pile. Jean had put a little Christian cross at the corner and had filled the writing paper with a series of disjointed sentences written in a flourishing hand. I read out loud the first sentence, my voice cracking.

I miss you Mummy more than you'll ever know. I stopped and swallowed. The message could only be for me, for this was the writing of a child, scratchy and unformed. I forced myself to carry on; unbeliever that I was, if one of my sons was trying to contact me, then I would listen. *It's . . . it's warm up here and I have lots of friends with me and my brother, of course, but I miss your smile. Do you . . . do you still have the photograph—*

I broke off, trying to still my trembling hands, and pulled the paper closer to decipher the writing through my tears. My cheeks felt taut across my face and I thought I would choke as I struggled to get the words out. George noticed my upset and, reaching across, took the sheet from my hands and continued reading.

God bless Sir Arthur, for everything he's doing. I know if I want to contact you on the earth plane I can use his knowledge of the spirit world to—

'I have to leave.' I stood and hurried from the room, surprised to find Ada close on my heels.

'Don't pay any attention to it.'

I turned to her and saw she hadn't recovered from Horwick's accident the previous afternoon. I could smell the laudanum on her breath which the peppermint she was sucking on was failing to mask.

'It was the voice of one of my children.'

'She knows your story. Lily and Lady Jean have spoken of you and the circumstances by which you find yourself here. Lily said you had lost children. It's no coincidence the message came from a child.'

'I've been tricked?' I could have hurled a painting from the wall myself. That someone would take advantage of my grief in this manner! 'Why are you telling me this? You talk to the spirits yourself. Why expose her?'

'I want you to know you don't need to be afraid of your own

children.' She paused, her gaze a little unfocused. 'How long do you have left to complete your work?'

'If the weather holds, I could be finished in two days or so.' I stopped. The piano had started again. The same tune, but this time the music was closer. I could hear, finally, that it wasn't a child but the thin reedy voice of a young woman's high soprano.

'Can you hear singing?'

Ada turned towards the east wing. 'Yes, I can hear the music. You can too?'

'I've heard it since my first day here. Except there's no one in the house who can be playing the piano. Everyone is in the Adelaide Room except the servants, of course.' I didn't dare mention that I had investigated the rooms at the end of the wing and seen the destroyed instrument.

'You have the gift, that's all. There's no need to be frightened.'

'The gift? I have no gift.'

'If you can hear the music, you have it.'

'What am I hearing?'

'It's an echo of a tune played long ago.' She winced and put her hand to her chest. 'The food is too rich here. I need to lie down.' She climbed the stairs, her gait unsteady, and abruptly the music stopped.

Chapter Twenty-Five

About five inches of snow fell that night, leaving an eiderdown of white spreading out as far as I could see. It would be a day of ennui, as all my developing was up to date and the shrouded light made it impossible to photograph anything new. I'd already decided that I would pay no attention to Ada's statement of the previous evening. I was hearing music, it was true, but the house had a gramophone and there might even be a piano I hadn't discovered. It would take more than snatches of music to convince me of anything supernatural. I dressed more carefully than usual, bringing out the dress I'd worn to travel down to Clewer Hall. My feet ached but I gamely stuffed them into my shoes, fastening the strap on the first setting. George was alone in the dining room, his mood morose.

'Is everything all right?' I asked him, inspecting the substantial feast laid on by Alice. I lifted the lid of one of the silver dishes, recoiling at the smell of kippers.

'I've just discovered there's no chance of papers today,' he said.

'Perhaps the village shop will have them.'

He shook his head. 'I've already spoken to Janet. The road to Brighton is closed.' He looked round and mock-whispered, 'There's not even a telephone here!'

I smiled. 'You really are stuck, then. You could borrow a book from Felix's study. What do you like to read?'

'I enjoy H. G. Wells, and there's something about this house which makes me want to connect to my boyhood. It must be the knowledge of my father's visit here. In any case, it's too much to expect to find anything more modern.'

'I've seen Lily reading. Perhaps you could ask to borrow a book from her.'

'It doesn't matter. Like you, I'm really here to work. I have my typewriter with me. I might bash up an article on what went on last night.' He leant back in his chair, regarding me. 'Do you read the newspapers?'

'I like the *Morning Post*.' This wasn't strictly true. It was Edwin's newspaper of choice which he bought every morning but I hardly wanted to tell George that. It wouldn't have made any difference as he looked unimpressed anyway.

'It's a little lightweight. I'd have thought you'd enjoy something more substantial.'

I was flattered and made to reply, but George had been distracted by his watch. 'This damn thing's not working. I thought I wound it up this morning, too. It's twenty past five according to this infernal dial.' George began attacking a plate of kidneys, his brows knitted in annoyance.

'Perhaps it needs looking at when you return to London.'

'I hope there's nothing wrong. It belonged to my father.'

A girl entered the room carrying a fresh teapot, a miniature Janet, looking impossibly young. She saw me staring at her. 'I'm Lizzie, ma'am, Janet's sister. I'm helping out as Mr Horwick is injured and there's a lot going on today.'

'Don't you have classes?'

'School's shut and my mother said I could come.'

George looked up and frowned. 'How old are you?'

'Nearly fourteen, sir.'

I could see some of Janet's assurance in the girl but, at thirteen, she was a child. 'You won't be here during the séance, will you?'

'I'm to go home as soon as dinner is finished. My ma is coming to collect me.'

George continued to regard her. 'Do you want to go into service when you leave school?'

'Oh no, sir. I can sew well and there's a job promised me at Hannington's in Brighton altering clothes for customers.'

She left, carrying away the empty teapot. I poured a fresh cup for myself and made a face. Lizzie needed a lesson on how to prepare a decent brew. This one was tepid, with a bitter aftertaste.

George buttered a slice of toast. 'It's the way things are going. Whoever buys this house will need deep pockets to find staff. The days of tugging your forelock and working for a pittance are thankfully receding.'

'You can end up working for a pittance, with or without the gentry.'

George looked up in approval, clearly in the mood for a political discussion. 'I'm well aware of that, Louisa. I'm simply making a comment on the loss of working people willing to take up subservient roles.'

I thought of Alice, content in the kitchen, with a peaceful retirement to look forward to. She appeared far more optimistic for the future than either Helene or her daughter. Subservient was the last word I would have used to describe Alice. I rose, desperate to get away from the smell of the kippers.

'I think I'll retrieve my developing kit from the icehouse. I'm worried about my chemicals in this freeze.'

'Will you be all right in the snow?' He turned to look up at me. 'Seriously, Louisa, the ground looks treacherous.'

I smiled down at him, my body warming in response to his concern. 'I can manage.'

*

I let myself out of the side door, my feet sinking into the drifts. I could still feel the tannin from the over-strong tea on my teeth making me a little nauseous, an effect magnified by the white glare from the snow. Disorientated, I shielded my eyes as an invisible pair of palms pushed down on my scalp, the snow-blown tree trunks blurring into serpentine waves. Dismayed at my wits disappearing again, I focused on the crystalline snow, tracking a set of small footprints running away from me across the lawn towards Old Jessop's cottage. I followed them, marvelling that a child would be running barefoot in this weather. Here was the proof that I wasn't dealing with a ghostly apparition, but a real-life child. At the threshold, I called into the empty house.

'Hello. Is anyone there?'

There was a sound, the flutter of something falling, which emboldened me to get further inside.

'Are you there?' I saw icicles hanging from the ceiling, dripping water from the roof frozen into shards.

As my foot went through a rotted board, I pulled it out with a wince, not daring to go any further.

A soft thud came from upstairs and I took a step into the room.

'What are you doing?'

I spun round and came face to face with Lily standing at the entrance.

'Why are you inside Old Jessop's cottage? I've told you that this place is lethal.'

'Someone is in one of the rooms upstairs. I've followed their footprints here.'

Lily looked around at the garden. 'I can see nothing.'

I hurried to her and looked down at the snow. The only marks were those of my own insubstantial shoes leading up to the house and the tracks of Lily's boots. Again, the astringency of the tea assailed me and I swallowed, trying to subdue the nausea.

'I saw a child's footsteps in the snow, I'm sure of it. I was worried about an unshod child out in this weather.'

Lily stared at the ground and up at me, her expression difficult to read. 'You shouldn't be here. Come inside.'

As we left, she shut the door to with a sharp pull. She gripped my elbow as she led me across the lawn and past the ornamental pond where thin pads of ice skimmed the surface.

'You can leave me here. I came out to rescue my developing equipment.'

Lily hesitated, her manner cool. 'Perhaps you could concentrate on the job you have been commissioned to do, Louisa. I have enough to worry about and, in any case, shouldn't you be thinking of your baby?'

'I'm sure—'

'You're imagining things. It's only natural given your history but, please, I'd appreciate it if you'd attend to the task in hand.'

Chapter Twenty-Six

Lily's words stung. I was here because of my baby. I needed the money to ensure it had a decent start in life and nothing I had done to date had endangered my child. Lily didn't like me near the cottage, that much was clear, but I hadn't been inside the building. I had simply followed footprints which had then disappeared. The snow was still falling; perhaps that was it. The footprints had been covered by the fresh snow. My head ached once more and, at a loss, I wandered into the sitting room where I found Helene settled on a sofa wearing a filmy sleeveless dress with only a thin cardigan draped around her shoulders. As she spoke, her frosted breath streamed across the air like a will-o'-the-wisp.

'Please stay a while, Louisa. I could do with some company.'

Surprised by her calm manner, I took the sofa opposite hers, pulling my cardigan around me in case my swollen stomach was an affront to her. One of the servants had lit a fire but the embroidered screen directed much of the heat back up the chimney. Helene might be able to live with this kind of cold but I couldn't.

'Do you mind if I remove the fireguard? It will warm up the room quickly and I can replace it if you feel your skin burning.'

She looked at me as if the thought hadn't occurred to her. 'Of course I don't mind. I'm sorry it's so cold. Are you comfortable in your room?'

'Quite comfortable.' Not exactly true, but I'd made myself as cosy as I was likely to be in this house. 'I'm glad no one is making too much of a fuss. I know my pregnancy was a shock.'

Her answer was a surprise. 'Pregnancy isn't an illness. I brought all my children into the world without much bother. It was once they were here that the trouble started. You mustn't let anyone treat you like an invalid.'

For the first time I felt an affinity with Helene. Like her, I'd had children and lived to bury them.

'It must have been a wonderful house in which to raise a family. All this space.'

'It was. Although, of course, all my boys left before I was ready to let them go.'

'Sent away to school, you mean?'

She paused. 'Felix wanted them to go to his old school, Lancing, and I think Lily was quite lonely afterwards. Now, all I have is the house and soon not even that.'

'You don't want to leave?'

'I can't bear to go.' The admission burst out of her and I flinched at her intensity. 'This is my home.' She paused, her eyes on me. 'You do understand that.'

I thought of my unloved house back in Kentish Town. 'I can understand the attraction of the familiar.'

'Then you don't understand.' Helene's tone was flat. 'It's probably because you've remarried. You were lucky, there aren't many men left. Lily left it too late.'

I detected a sliver of malice. Lily must be in her late forties. Ten years ago, at the start of the war, she would already have been a spinster in the eyes of society. The war might be responsible for most of this family's tragedies, but not all of them. Helene's mind, however, wasn't on her daughter.

'Perhaps I could look through your plates sometime.'

I frowned. 'They're negatives. I'm not sure there's much to see.'

'Nevertheless, I would like to look at them.'

It was an order and one I had no intention of complying with. Plates are for the professionals. If Helene wanted to see the printed images, then she would need to go through the auctioneers. Her insistence was a mystery to add to the layers which were settling like the snow outside. Before I could reply, the door opened and we were joined by Conan Doyle. He looked vigorously healthy, pink-cheeked and smelling of gentleman's cologne.

'Jean has a slight headache after yesterday evening. It's not unusual, but I've suggested she rest in her room for the morning.'

I was glad to see him on his own as I was still dismayed by the business of the automatic handwriting. I had overreacted, I was sure, but what mother wouldn't have? I decided to have a stab at voicing my concerns as he lowered himself into one of the ancient chairs.

'Are you looking forward to the séance?'

'Of course I am. I've been committed to advancing spiritualism for nearly forty years.'

'And your interest hasn't been dented by some of the frauds who appear to communicate with the dead but use trickery and special effects?'

I noticed Helene frowning at me.

'I've sat with a great number of mediums over the years. I've more experience, perhaps, than anyone, and no, I've not been put off by the clearly poor ones.'

'And how did you find the séance here in 1896?'

'I can't really remember. I'm sorry, my dear, but it was such a long time ago.'

'But it generated so much publicity.'

'I'm afraid that, in some respects, it was the wrong sort of publicity. I did rather want to ask a journalist from *Light* magazine to come down. I find those with an affinity with the spirit make for a more accurate report, but Henry Storey found out about my plans and beat me to the commission. He was a very bright young man.'

'His son seems clever, too.'

Sir Arthur frowned and a disloyal thought entered my mind that he might not welcome intelligence or, indeed, any type of scrutiny when it came to accounts of his séances. But when I looked at him, I saw his eyes were on Ada, who was standing in the drawing room, gazing up at the space where the painting had once hung.

'Good, bad, indifferent . . . I've seen them all. The important thing is to ensure the bad apples don't spoil the barrel.'

Chapter Twenty-Seven

25 June 1896
5.53 p.m.

Ada took stock of the room she'd been deposited in with a pot of tea and a plate of water biscuits. It was a space used by seamstresses, governesses and other respectable working women who came to the house. She'd heard that Clewer Hall was a place of treasures, but here the paintings consisted of an inferior still life and a child's sampler, inexpertly sewn. The tea tray was brought in by a healthy-looking girl with fine pale blue eyes. She stared at Ada for a moment and then lowered her gaze, clearly wishing to linger.

Ada took a sip of the tea and stretched her legs, making sure the belt attached to her thigh didn't jingle. Her outfit was heavy, largely due to the accoutrements she'd sewn into the fabric, and she was fighting off the desire to take a short nap.

The girl entered the room again, glancing behind her.

'Do you have everything you need? Have you tried a biscuit?'

'I'm not banting, you know.'

The girl flushed, embarrassed at the poor quality of the refreshments. 'There's some butter ones if you prefer. Cook told me to give you these.'

I bet she did, thought Ada, taking a bit of the tasteless cracker. 'Will you be around later?'

'Oh no. Mrs Perry, the housekeeper, has told me to stay in my room.'

'There's nothing to be worried about.'

'I'm not afraid. My ma has second sight. She talks to my gran every day and she's been in the ground eight years.'

'That's not second sight. It's reaching out to those who have passed over.'

'But she meets people and can tell when something bad's about to happen. She told old Mrs Paul that she should watch out for any stray dogs and, sure enough, she was bitten a week later.'

Ada picked up another biscuit.

'What's your name?'

'Glad. Gladys, but my friends call me Glad.'

'And, Glad, what does your mother have to say about this family?'

'Oh, nothing. Ma has to see them close for her second sight to work.'

'Don't they have garden parties where staff and villagers can mingle with the family? Most of the gentry do.'

'Yes, but Ma works on Tinley's Farm. He doesn't like the Clewers so he won't give Ma the day off to come.'

'Any reason he doesn't like them?'

'Some argument over land.' The girl sounded uninterested and Ada changed tack.

'What do you think of the family, then?'

'I don't see much of the master. He likes to go to auctions. He collects all the stuff you can see in the cabinets and the house is beginning to suffer. He needs to be here to answer questions from Mr Horwick and Mrs Perry but he's always out.'

'And Mrs Clewer?'

'She's very beautiful and likes to sit in the garden when the weather is nice, unless she's visiting Brighton or London. My friend Daisy is her lady's maid and she doesn't tattle.'

'She's Mrs Clewer's maid? Who does for the daughter?'

'Miss Lily? There's a chambermaid who looks after her and all the bedrooms. Miss Lily's easy, though.'

'And Mrs Clewer isn't?'

Gladys shrugged, picking at her dress. 'She likes her hair just so and her jewels put out so she can decide what she'll wear each evening. It's not back-breaking work, but Daisy doesn't half complain.'

The usual story, the housemaid's resentment at the easier life of a lady's maid.

'They have other children?'

'Three boys away at school.'

Not much there, thought Ada, pushing the plate of biscuits away. She'd have to rely on her usual script and hope no one had seen her perform before.

'You're going to be in the papers, aren't you?'

Ada winced at the thought of the newspaperman from London. She'd done everything to try to prevent Mrs Clewer extending the invitation, but it had been arranged and there was little she could do.

Gladys jumped at the sound of footsteps outside. 'I have to go.'

'I wouldn't mind a fresh pot.'

While Gladys, with her adenoidal voice, huffed out of the room, Ada looked around for clues to the family. From the window she could see a gardener digging in the rose garden. One of the plants had withered and he was attacking it with vigour. Across the lawn was a table laid with tea things where a young girl was reading under a parasol.

The door opened and Gladys set down a fresh pot of tea.

'Is that Miss Lily over there? She likes reading?' asked Ada.

'Oh, yes. She always has her nose buried in a book.'

'And Mrs Clewer, is she bookish?'

'Oh, no.'

'Miss Lily must take after her father.'

'Perhaps.'

'You know, Gladys – and I know I can tell you this because you told me your mother has the gift too – there's something about this house I can't put my finger on . . .'

'What do you mean?'

'Oh, nothing terrible. I'm not trying to frighten you. I just get a feeling about something. Has – forgive me . . .' Ada reached into her pocket and pulled out a handkerchief, dabbing her nose, 'has there been a death here recently?'

'Oh, no.'

'You're sure?'

'I've been here two years and no one has died.'

'But I get this sense of, I don't know . . . sadness. Do you know what I mean?'

Gladys stood in front of her chewing her lip. 'I'm not sure. I don't feel sad here.'

Good God, this girl's hard work, thought Ada.

'Perhaps it's hidden from you. Lots of houses have secrets. Maybe you're a little young to know them.'

Gladys sucked in the side of her cheek, her expression strained. Ada watched as her face cleared, a smile forming at the corners of her mouth.

'I know a secret,' said Gladys with satisfaction.

Chapter Twenty-Eight

As the snow continued to fall, I went to look for Horwick to see if he had recovered enough for me to quiz him about his cryptic words as he lay injured on the floor. Alice pointed with her wooden spatula to a door at the far end of the servants' passage, underneath the family wing.

'Don't tire him out. I've sent word to his sister and I'm waiting for a reply. He needs to be kept quiet until Quinlivan can drive him to Bournemouth.'

I winced at the discomfort Horwick would experience in the car with its uneven suspension and jolting wheels. I knocked softly on his door and was surprised to hear a female voice tell me to enter. Lily was sitting on a plain wooden chair by Horwick's side, reading a book by Elinor Glyn.

'How is he?' I whispered, taking the seat on the other side of the bed, testing it first to check it would hold my weight.

'He mainly sleeps. The doctor came again this morning and thinks the wound to his head is superficial. It's his leg that's the worry. Really, Horwick needs to be up and about as soon as possible and keep moving, although he's hardly in a position to do that now.'

All I could see of the butler's face between the bandages was a beaky nose and a section of his lower chin covered in grey stubble. His plastered leg was raised on a small wooden box. Dressed only in combinations, he looked far more elderly than I'd thought him to be.

'I wanted to check he was all right. After the accident, I had to help Ada to her room. She was quite overcome. I feel I rather neglected Horwick.'

Lily made a face. 'Ada can generally look after herself. How are you feeling?' She had her eyes on my stomach once more.

'I feel well.' Which I did, except for the continuing nausea and moments when my senses became distorted. It was a shame I'd missed the doctor. If I'd had a chance, I might have pulled him to one side and asked for an opinion on why I felt sick all the time. But perhaps it was better that I kept it to myself. Any illness, even of the mind, might be put down to my pregnancy, and I really needed to finish my work first.

We sat in peaceful companionship for a moment, listening to Horwick's breathing. Lily's words, when she broke the silence, were a shock.

'You're lucky, you know.'

'Me?' Horwick stirred as my voice rose. 'Why am I lucky?'

'You have a future. You've a husband and a child on the way. The century stretches out in front of us and you have some idea of the riches it will contain. What's left for me? A life in a foreign country looking after increasingly elderly parents.'

'If you feel like that, why don't you say something? You're entitled to a life of your own.'

'Am I? It's for the best, especially for Mother. You've seen how she is.'

'She told me she doesn't want to leave.'

'She knows there's no other choice. And I'm bound to her. My parents have been good to me and it's time for me to repay some of that debt.'

I frowned at her choice of words. She mistook my expression for disapproval.

'Not everyone has your courage, Louisa.' The tone of her voice was acerbic, an impression reinforced by Lily's clenched jaw, veins straining against her pale neck.

Her anger was matched by mine, for this woman knew nothing about my life except the bare bones of my loss. 'It's come at a price.'

'You lost your first husband in the war, I believe?'

'As many did. My children were taken from me just after. That was harder to bear.' I saw my words had no effect on her and I grew brutal. 'I buried them by myself. Just me and my mother standing over their little graves in the hard November frost.'

Her eyes sought mine, moved not by the cold burial of my two darling children, but the mention of my parent.

'You were close to your mother?'

'Very.'

'She's not here now?'

'She died two years ago.' I glanced at Lily, who was shivering a little. 'There was nothing tragic about her death. She died of cancer. Age and circumstance had taken their toll but she went peacefully.'

Lily nodded, wrenching her eyes away from mine. 'We do rely on our mothers, don't we? I'm sure yours was a comfort to you too.'

My mother had made all the difference after the death of Hugh and Pip in the winter of the war's end. I'd only been able to carry on with her help.

'Is Helene a comfort to you?'

Lily flinched, adjusting Horwick's blanket and not meeting my eye. 'She's not herself. You've noticed that, I'm sure.'

'She's still grieving for her sons.'

Lily froze. When she looked up at me, I could see by her flushed face that she was angry. 'She isn't the only person bearing a weight of loss. I, too, know how grief feels. I wish mine wasn't suffused with regrets.'

'Regret is part of all grief.' I thought of the nights I'd analysed each argument I'd ever had with Bertie and berated myself at each harsh word directed at my boys. Seven years since the twins' deaths had done little to soften the jab of pain these recollections caused.

'Of course. You're right.'

I was aware that the heat in the room was becoming unbearable, partly caused by the proximity of the kitchen range. Lily stood, stretching her back. 'Do you intend to sit with Horwick? I'd feel happier if I thought he wasn't alone if he wakes.'

I nodded. 'Of course. I'll stay with him until I need to change for dinner.'

'Thank you, Louisa,' she said, placing a hand on my shoulder.

Once she had gone, I opened the partially submerged window to let in the cold winter air for a moment. Even the short, icy blast freshened up the room, removing the sour odour of illness. I saw, however, that I would get no answers to my questions from Horwick in his present state.

The conversation with Lily had been an enigma. I frowned, trying to remember Lily's words, certain I had misinterpreted her. She had mentioned grief and she had revealed that hers was tinged with regret. An unusual phrase to use in relation to your siblings. No, not just unusual. It didn't make any sense. Somehow I had failed to grasp Lily's true meaning.

Chapter Twenty-Nine

Alice had pushed the boat out with her dinner that evening, filling the house with aromas of roast bird and spiced orange. The first course was an oxtail consommé with sherry, followed by cold poached salmon. Both courses were a little rich for me, although the next, a dish of capons sent over by Sir Thomas from his estate and served with a pear sauce, was far more palatable. I picked over my meal, listening to the conversations around me which ignited then were extinguished like a damp spill.

The table was separated into two distinct groups. It wasn't clear who had decided on the table plan but the members of the original séance had been placed together. Clockwise from my left was George, Ada, Conan Doyle, Lily, Sir Thomas Jensen and Helene sat in a tableau. If the seating had been arranged to ensure some kind of bonhomie before the séance, it had failed. Lily and Sir Thomas ignored each other and a v-shaped gap opened where on one side Sir Thomas leant towards Helene to discuss his son Samuel's chances of running for Parliament and, on the other, where Lily turned to monopolise Conan Doyle. Lily's body was taut as she inclined away from Sir Thomas, but I got the impression she was straining to hear her mother's conversation with their neighbour.

Sir Thomas, who I remembered was a widower, was courtly towards Helene, although she was distracted, her eyes constantly on Ada. I tried to join in their conversation.

'Which party is your son hoping to represent?'

Sir Thomas's mouth opened slightly and I heard George sitting next to me snort in amusement.

'Mr Baldwin's party, of course. The Jensens are Conservative to the core.'

If I hadn't turned my head at that moment, I'd have missed the glance Lily threw Sir Thomas, her face darkening with resentment. I gave up and tried to talk to George, who wasn't in the mood for small talk.

'Did your father mention the dinner before the séance in 1896? It must be strange, thinking of him sitting here as you are now.'

'He made no mention of it whatsoever. I can't say I feel very comfortable. Perhaps it's the fact that I'm wearing his dinner suit. I feel a little like the spectre at the feast.'

I had been initially embarrassed to be at the table once more in my well-worn satin, but I'd been reassured by the fact that no one's clothes were new or fashionable. The sleeves of George's jacket, I saw, were a little short.

'The evening will be over soon enough.'

'Thank God.'

I gave up and concentrated on my food. Janet kept to the background, ensuring that the dishes moved with ease from the kitchen to the dining table. Quinlivan was nowhere to be seen but I guessed he would be helping Alice, with Lizzie acting as temporary scullery maid.

To finish, Alice had made an orange soufflé, no mean feat for such a gathering, puffed up like a chef's hat with a golden crown. In a less formal setting, I'd have clapped in appreciation. Ada, a woman who clearly liked her food, ate her serving with uncharacteristic haste. With a nod to Mrs Clewer, she rose and left the table.

'Ada needs to prepare herself for this evening. She'll meet us in the Adelaide Room,' Helene said by way of explanation. She had on a set of emeralds, a choker and drop earrings which dragged down the lobes of her ears. Lily was less formally dressed, but had also made an effort, sporting a set of pearls I hadn't seen before.

'What will you do, my dear, while we're occupied?' asked Conan Doyle across the table to his wife.

His wife smiled. 'I have a book with me, and I think I'll join Felix in the sitting room until you've finished.'

'And you, Louisa?' asked Felix. 'Will we have the pleasure of your company?'

'I thought I might have an early night. I've a lot to do in the morning if I'm to finish my work this weekend. I won't join you, if you don't mind.'

I refused coffee – even the smell of it made me heave – and went down to the kitchen, which was still a hive of activity. Lizzie had disappeared; her mother was clearly taking no chances and had already collected her. Taking a tea towel from Quinlivan, I began to wipe the plates he was pulling from a sink of soapy water.

'What time does the séance start?' I asked.

'We've been told eight thirty. The room's ready and the fire has been lit for a few hours so they can start as soon as they like. I've banked it up high.'

'Will you stay?'

Quinlivan shook his head. 'I have no trouble remembering the dead. I'll be in my room. Janet knows where to find me if there's trouble.'

'Trouble?'

'If she needs help,' he amended. 'What about you? Will you be joining the others in the sitting room?'

I dipped my hand idly in the water. 'Will the warmth of the fire spread to the orangery?'

Quinlivan paused and turned to me, his face full of mischief. 'It'll be bloody freezing – but I have a horse blanket I can lend you.'

Bloody freezing was an understatement. The orangery was colder than the icehouse and that was saying something. Snow had settled on the sills of the windows, drifting up the panes to meet feathery veins of ice on the glass. The only light I had was that which seeped from the fire and the table lamp in the Adelaide Room. If I was discovered, I would have nothing to explain my presence in the darkness and I would need to brazen it out. I settled myself in one of the wicker chairs with the blanket pulled up to my chin.

The Adelaide Room was empty when I passed through, only a low fire burning in the grate despite Quinlivan's assurance that he'd stoked it up. I wondered if this was Ada's work. If she was using any tricks to spice up her séances, she would want to minimise the amount of light. A door opened and I heard the tip-tap of Ada's shoes on the parquet flooring, followed by another set of feet.

'The guests have finished dinner and are having coffee in the sitting room. Are you ready for them?'

It was Janet, her voice carefully neutral. I heard no reply. Ada must simply have nodded for, after a short interval, there was the sound of more footsteps and the scrape of chairs being pulled back from the table.

'It's chilly in here despite the fire,' I heard Lily say. She must have poked at the embers, as sparks drifted into the orangery, glittering through the air before fizzling out.

'Would you like us to sit in our original positions?' asked Sir Thomas, his voice slurred from wine.

'Everything is to be *exactly* the same.' Helene's voice was shrill, her nerves stretched. 'Mr Storey, your father sat here.'

'First, perhaps, we should make sure all the doors are fastened tightly?' George's voice grew louder as he approached the orangery door, which I knew didn't close properly. I saw him pull at it fruitlessly for a moment and then pause, his face turned in my direction. I didn't dare move but, before he returned to his seat, I saw that he had pushed the door slightly further ajar. George Storey was nobody's fool.

Ada's nasal tone drifted across the darkness. 'We're all here. We shall begin.'

Chapter Thirty

'Wait a moment.'

I recognised the faint Edinburgh accent of Conan Doyle.

'With a distinguished journalist here, and my intention to write up the details of the séance in *Light* magazine, I wonder if Mrs Watkins will indulge me in providing some proofs to our readers.'

His tone was so casual he might have been asking if she could pass the salt.

'Proofs?' Ada's voice was sharp. 'What proofs do you need?'

'Perhaps I've used the wrong turn of phrase. I was wondering if you had any objection to us tying your hands to the arms of your chair?'

I took an intake of breath, masked, I think, by the cry of alarm from Helene. Ada, to my surprise, appeared to have anticipated the request.

'I have no objection whatsoever. Have you brought cord with you? I'm sure you would prefer to use your own means of binding me.' Her words were sharp as lemons.

There was a shuffling and a moment's pause. I wondered that they hadn't also asked to bind her feet. I remembered a habit from my schooldays where I'd stick out a foot and give my poor class-mate a sharp jab in the backside. Then I recalled the circumference of the table and Ada's squat frame and suspected Conan Doyle had decided there was little she could do with her arms bound.

'I think that is perfectly satisfactory,' said Conan Doyle and I made a face. His wife might not have been able to complete her automatic handwriting with tied hands, but none of us asked any other proofs of her. I wonder how he would have felt if we'd demanded something similar?

Ada, however, sounded unconcerned. 'If we're quite finished, we'll start again. I'd like you to put your hands on the table. There's no need for them to touch as I can't complete the circle. It's simply to ensure there are no tricks from others present.'

Good for you, I thought, my allegiance unexpectedly shifting. They were expecting her to sing for her supper, and Ada and I were no different in that respect.

'We're going to start with a reading from The First Book of Ezekiel, in which the spirit appears to the Prophet. *And I looked, and, behold, a whirlwind came out of the north, a great cloud, and a fire infolding itself, and a brightness was about it, and out of the midst thereof as the colour of amber, out of the midst of the fire.*'

I wondered if Ada was using her reading glasses, which would slightly spoil the effect. More likely, I thought, she'd memorised the verse and it was a regular feature of her séances. The room became silent. Across from me, I could hear the ticking of the copper-turned-verdigris clock. Ada's breathing became more sonorous and the air stilled further.

The strained atmosphere of the assembled company wove itself around us like a thread, spooling out from the Adelaide Room to me in the orangery. It was as if we were all collectively holding our breath. The table, me, the house. Finally, Ada spoke.

'I have a young man in front of me. He's wearing a uniform and looks ever so smart, although his cap's not on straight. Can you tell me your name? There's no need to be shy.'

I was embarrassed for her. A more convincing fake would have started on a lighter note, conjured up a spirit to put the table at their ease. We all knew the losses the Clewers had experienced, and the death of Conan Doyle's soldier son was also public knowledge. I wondered which victim she would alight on first.

'He's embarrassed after I told him his hat was skew-whiff. Oh look, he's taking it off. I can see the effort he's made to make himself smart. He's even put a bit of brilliantine in his hair to flatten down that cowlick.'

There was a silence and I heard Lily's sharp comment. 'None of my brothers wore brilliantine.'

But my Bertie had.

'He's saying he's sorry he can't be with you, but it will turn out right in the end. That's his message to you. He knows you're unhappy, but it will turn out fine. He's watching out for you and he misses you.'

There was sobbing from the Adelaide Room, which was just as well as it masked my own muffled tears. Ada might be a fraud but she knew how to tug on the emotions of the grieving and even I was pulled into the story she spun.

Ada's breathing had become deeper and her voice had slowed to a drawl. 'He's fading, he's fading but someone else is coming through.'

'I can feel something cold on my forehead!' cried Helene. 'It's cool and soft, a comforting hand.'

'I can't see anything, my dear,' said Sir Thomas.

In the darkened room, I saw a light move around, creating an effect like the searchlights they used to spot Zeppelins at the end of the war.

'Who's using a torch?' asked Conan Doyle.

There was a thump on the floor and the sound of metal rolling on the carpet.

Ada began to moan louder to cover the sound. 'I can see him! He's here at last. My spirit guide, Black Hawk. He's the most reliable of messengers and he never fails to appear when there's trouble ahead.'

'What kind of trouble?'

I leant forward but couldn't make out the identity of the male speaker.

There was a long silence, the house slowly releasing its breath. Ada's already low-pitched voice deepened further, betraying for the first time her northern England origins.

'The house hasn't finished with you yet. Vengeance is mine, I will repay, saith the Lord. Four isn't enough.'

'Four?' asked George. 'What do you mean by four?'

'Four,' said Ada, her voice rising. 'Four sons have perished but there are to be more. *Come gather, ye children.*'

There was a cry, immediately stifled, and a gasp of shock. I leant forward, trying to hear the response but there was a stunned silence.

'Who is the fourth?' George asked again.

Ada began to moan. 'Black Hawk says the angry spirit hasn't finished and is looking for people to pull across the great divide. There are still more deaths to come.'

'There are no more sons!' shouted Helene. 'I've lost all my boys! What more do you want? Where else are you going to find sons to take from me?'

The baby kicked and the pain in my head grew until it threatened to subsume me. The room darkened and turned black and I remembered no more.

Chapter Thirty-One

There was a trick I'd learnt over the years which had served me well. When the night demons came to me in my sleep, I'd deliberately wake myself to face their whispers and sly pinches. It gave me courage, even in the worst hours, and had allowed me to pick up the pieces of my broken life. As I lay slumped in my chair in the orangery, I was aware that the terror wasn't inside me but pulsating from the walls of the room next door. But the old trick worked just the same. I forced myself out of my faint, into the decrepit room. Around me swirled thick vapour infused with a pungent floral scent.

'Come thick night, and pall thee in the dunnest smoke of hell,' I heard Ada proclaim.

I didn't recognise the quote but it was surely not one of Ada's own. I wondered how much of the séance I'd missed. The verdigris clock showed it was ten minutes to nine. The séance was twenty minutes into its journey and I had missed plenty of hateful revelations, I was sure. As I struggled to sit, there was the sound of fracturing glass and Sir Thomas's voice cut through the gasps.

'I, for one, have had enough of this charade! I'm sorry, Helene, but this evening has finished for me.'

'I'll join you,' came another voice. Ada must have gone completely over the top to have upset Conan Doyle.

I lay there, listening to the scrape of chairs alongside coughing and protestations, until the room fell silent and I heard George speak.

'You can come out now, Louisa. I'm just jotting down some notes before I forget.'

'You need to give me a moment.'

I heard footsteps across the wooden floor and he was beside me in an instant. 'What's wrong?'

'I think the excitement of the evening took its toll, that's all.'

'Can you stand?'

'Probably, if I do so slowly. Did the others know I was here?'

'I had the seat nearest the door. No one else had any inkling you were in this room.'

'And you were happy for me to listen in?'

'It made no difference to me – and, anyway, I thought you might not be able to keep away. I'm just surprised Jean didn't join you.'

'She's probably fuming in the sitting room.'

Standing improved things a little. It was all about balance and, on my feet, I felt more sure of myself. It was George who appeared at a loss.

'I would never have remained at the table if I'd thought you were ill. I assumed you were enjoying the histrionics.'

'There wasn't that much to enjoy. Ada seems to have upset everyone.'

'Not me.' He picked up the blanket from the floor where it had fallen and gathered it around me. 'I've spent a good part of my life wondering what my father meant, and all I saw tonight was a magic show where the star turn was past her best.'

'She's a fraud?'

'An out-and-out charlatan. That sound of breaking glass you heard was her stamping on a vial of phosphorus to produce smoke. She had her hands tied but we should have bound her legs as well.'

I felt a flash of compassion for Ada, trussed up like a partridge, while the men watched her every move.

'She allowed you to bind her. Perhaps it wasn't all show.'

'I can assure you it was. It was embarrassing to watch.'

'But she mentioned the curse again, the same warning as in 1896.'

'Of course she mentioned it. It's the only thing, as far as we know, that supposedly came true. She was going to milk it for as much as she could.'

'But George, what did she mean by four sons of the house?'

His face changed as I spoke his name and something inside me shifted as well. It was as if a stoppered bottle had been spilt and the contents were escaping across the floor. At the same time, my baby quickened, as if in response to my churning emotions.

'What's the matter?'

I clutched my stomach. 'It's nothing. A fake contraction, nothing more. It's too early for me to be in labour. Will you give me a moment?'

It happened again, a bitter twist low in my groin spreading up to my stomach. I clenched George's arm and he stood there, letting my nails dig into him until the contraction subsided.

It's the house, I thought. *The house is speaking to my baby. What evil is it pouring into its ear?* After a moment, I could stand straight again. George remained motionless, looking down on me.

'What does your husband think of you being here?'

'Edwin? I shouldn't have thought he cared in the slightest.' Inadequate and probably false words, but it was all I could say. I couldn't tell him of my foolish marriage to a man I had nothing in common with and my stupid attempts to create a new life for myself. I could barely look at myself in the mirror these days, and what would the successful George Storey know about simply hanging on?

'Then he's a fool.'

As the tension crackled around us, I was aware that George had a different set of values to those I was familiar with. It's too easy to compare people in your life. I'd measured men by my father and brother, and then against Bertie and, to some extent, Edwin. But George was like none of them. All the men I had been close to held an essential regard for convention.

But as George stood there, not attempting to break the cloak of intimacy I could feel building between us, I saw he was also a man who would be prepared to defy convention. The thought was intoxicating and, for the first time since I arrived at Clewer Hall, I considered the possibility that Ada might be right: that this house had a role to play in my destiny.

Chapter Thirty-Two

To my frustration, George wouldn't talk any more of the séance until I'd rested. I thought we might have to make an effort to slip past the guests unseen, but a tumult of angry voices reverberated around the drawing room as we emerged out of the passage. The Conan Doyles were standing to one side, Jean looking on in grim satisfaction while her husband puffed on a cigar, dropping ash onto the cracked tiles. Felix shouted orders to Quinlivan as Sir Thomas attempted to quieten the agitated dogs which had accompanied him. Only Lily and Helene were out of sight although I could hear one of them sobbing in the sitting room. Janet was for once discomposed, glancing across at me from the doorway leading to the kitchens.

'What's happened?' I asked her, slipping past George who looked cheered that other guests shared his outrage.

She kept her voice low, her eyes on the unfolding scene. 'The master has finally snapped. He's heard what was said in the séance. Sir Thomas is furious, too. He threatened to horsewhip Ada. She's to go this evening.'

'But she's only behaving as she did before. Why this reaction now?'

Janet shrugged. 'Perhaps she's finally been found out for what she is. There are things I found in her room. Wires, a vial of oil of roses which she knew Mrs Clewer's mother wore, and some bell contraption attached to a belt. It looks big enough to go round a leg. I knew she was up to no good.'

'Did you tell anyone?'

'Only Quinlivan, and it was hardly a surprise to him.'

I looked across to Sir Thomas, who met my gaze with an expression of ice.

'Was she that bad?'

'She is a foul scoundrel. I only agreed to come as a neighbourly favour to Felix and Helene. I should have stayed well away.'

His tone struck a false note. Ada had behaved exactly as I'd expected and nothing she'd said while I was listening in the orangery struck me as deliberately aimed at Sir Thomas. Perhaps I'd missed something during my faint.

'Did she refer to someone you've lost?'

My question only served to infuriate him further and he took his ire out on me. 'Does it matter who she talked about?' he shouted, rocking on his heels as George moved towards me.

'It's hardly Louisa's fault. Perhaps you should remember who you're addressing.'

Sir Thomas seized both dogs by their collars and dragged them towards the servants' stairs.

'I'm going to warm up these animals. They've got the collywobbles like everyone else. A feed will do them good.'

I saw Conan Doyle and his wife stand up.

'I think we should retire to bed. This evening has left us both shattered.' Jean looked around, pausing as the sound of sobs in the living room slowed to deep heaves. 'Please pass on our regards to Helene for an excellent dinner.'

As I watched them climb the stairs, I remembered Ada's doddery gait. 'Must she leave tonight?' I asked Janet. 'It's not a night for travelling.'

'The Colonel's asked Quinlivan to get the car ready. He's in a tizzy as he's not sure there's enough petrol to get to Brighton, let alone make the return journey, but the master is adamant.'

164

'Why don't you go with Quinlivan? It's a bitter night and he'd be glad of the company on the way back.'

'Me?'

'I saw how you were in the coach house. Keep him company, I'm sure Quinlivan will behave himself.'

Janet was regaining her composure and caught my eye with an amused expression. 'You've had two husbands and you really think that? Quinlivan's like all men. I wouldn't put it past him to pretend to run out of petrol just to spend the night with me in the car. In any case, my mother would kill me. She waits up until I get in.'

'Your house is in walking distance?'

'The other side of the village. Quinlivan usually escorts me home before locking up.'

Why did I suggest Janet accompany Ada in her night flight? I think I was more concerned about Ada than I let on and was using Quinlivan as an excuse. During the first séance, Ada had shocked everyone by mentioning a curse. This time, she had revealed that four children had died and the table had been in uproar. A woman had cried out and another had gasped, I was sure of it.

'I need to see Ada before she goes. Is she in her room?'

'She made herself scarce after the séance. You could try there.'

I hauled myself up the stairs, aware of my tired limbs, rapping hard on the door and listening to my voice echoing around the space. With a backwards glance, I saw Janet had followed me. I twisted the handle and found that the room was empty. If Ada was about to leave, she'd made no attempt to start packing. The room was as tidy as when I'd entered for my tarot reading, with Ada's washbag on the stand and her bed turned down for the night.

Janet was close behind me. 'I'll need to get her things together. She was a little unsteady on her feet after the séance and she was swaying when she went out the front door.'

'She went into the garden?'

'I assumed she needed some fresh air before packing.'

'She's no longer young. You don't think Felix will change his mind?'

Janet surveyed the room. 'He's in a fury like I've never seen before. After putting up with Ada all these years, I wouldn't have thought him capable of it, but you never really know a person, do you?'

I crossed to the window and looked out but could only see feathery flakes of snow attaching themselves to the glass.

'No, no, you don't. People always have the capacity to surprise you.'

I hurried to my room and put on my travelling coat, clumping down the servants' stairs so the family wouldn't know I was looking for Ada. I saw Sir Thomas's dogs in a corner of the kitchen, their noses in two chipped bowls, although there was no sign of their master. Alice was putting crockery on a shelf, her face set.

'I'm going to look for Ada. I should be able to follow her footprints in the snow.'

'She's leaving.' Alice's voice was flat.

'I heard.' I saw Alice's eyes were reddened from crying. 'What's the matter? You didn't like her here, did you?'

'The trouble won't go with her, though, will it? Whatever she said tonight will still haunt those left behind. I've seen it before.'

'I won't be long. I just need to speak to Ada before she leaves.'

'If you must. Take this.' Alice handed me a flashlight, small and squat with a surprisingly strong beam.

I pulled back the iron bolt and walked into the night. The snow was falling heavily and I was less sure now that Ada's tracks would be apparent. There was no wind, but the bitter cold still seeped through my winter coat and laid icy fingers on my face as I shone the torch on the virgin, powdery snow, the only tracks the ones I left behind me.

I had reached the front of the house when the weighty pressure on my head and roaring in my ears returned. I swept my flashlight around the garden but all the beam caught was the glitter of snow and, through my blurred vision, a movement near the cypress trees. I ran towards the copse as sound disappeared, to be replaced by complete silence. I became acutely aware of the danger I was in, because I could hear nothing, could feel nothing, and I was running on freshly lain snow. I looked down and, although my eyesight was wavering, I could make out footprints by Ada's dainty shoes alongside larger ones, made from a male boot. At once, my hearing returned and I recognised the thump of snow falling off the cypresses and, in the distance, Sir Thomas's dogs barking.

I shone the flashlight at the tracks and around the garden until the beam alighted on a shape on the ground.

Ada.

Chapter Thirty-Three

I ran to her, my feet sinking into marshmallow drifts until I reached the copse where the ground was ice-hard. Kneeling beside Ada, I wiped away flakes of snow which had drifted through the branches and settled on her face. I thought I was too late, but when I put my ear to her mouth, I heard a faint rasping followed by a catch in her breath. One arm was twitching, her clawed hand opening and closing. She was seriously injured, I could tell, but it was impossible to fathom what had felled her. Perhaps the arm was the sign of a stroke. She'd crawled a little along the ground, I could see, for the snow bore the imprint of where she'd dragged her heavy body until the effort had proved too much.

I wiped more snow from her dress and tried to lift her head, although I fear I hurt her doing so. At least I had on my coat which I could wrap around her, though it left me mortally cold.

'Ada,' I whispered. 'I'm going to leave you for a moment. I need go and find help.'

Her mouth moved. I put my ear to her face but her hot, irregular breathing brushed my skin, nothing more.

'I must find help.'

She found the strength to lift her hand and place it on my sleeve. 'Not . . . safe.'

The atmosphere of the copse darkened. I heard the crunch of a boot on compacted snow and the snap of twigs breaking. Talk of the supernatural over the last few days had blinded me to the fact that there was a flesh-and-blood threat. For surely ghosts don't make twigs crack?

Ada's grip tightened. 'Go . . . away. The child. Go . . .'

The same words that Horwick had mouthed to me from the hallway floor. 'Which child, Ada? Which child are you talking about?' I heard the tread again, closer this time.

'Who's there?' My voice called across the night air and the noise stopped. Not the disappearance of sound I'd experienced since my arrival at Clewer Hall, but the silence of a person holding their breath. The certainty that I was in danger propelled me to my feet, my meagre evening shoes slipping on the frozen ground.

'Come out and show yourself! We need help.' I was desperate to sound brave but my quaking voice would have fooled no one. There was a crunch of dead leaves and the glow of a lamp bouncing up and down.

'What are you doing outside again, Louisa?'

Lily. But surely I had no need to be afraid of Lily? She came out of the shadows, taking in the prone Ada and me in the wreck of my evening dress. She looked behind her; perhaps she had heard the same noise as I had, but her manner when she turned back to me was the same as always.

'What's happened?' I heard a note of accusation in her voice.

'I came looking for Ada and I found her like this.'

'Let me see.' She knelt beside me, her sickly honeysuckle perfume mingling with a thicker, visceral smell. In the glow of the lamp, I saw a thick stain creep from underneath Ada.

'She's seriously hurt, Louisa. One of us needs to stay with her.' She took in my thin satin dress. 'You can't stay out here in those clothes. You run for help.'

I hesitated, for I didn't want to leave Ada but I saw she was trying to speak again, her eyes locking with mine. Her lips formed a circle. 'Go.'

I slithered to my feet and saw my dress was covered in a dark, viscous substance which had spread up inside my sleeves. Any lower and I'd have thought the baby had come early, but this was something stickier and denser than my waters breaking.

'So much blood . . .' I said to Lily. 'This is surely not an accident.'

'The head bleeds a lot.'

'But—'

'For God's sake, Louisa! She has fallen, that's all. Go and get help. I will stay with her and try to stem the bleeding. Hurry!'

In a trance, I forced myself to put one foot in front of the other as I slid across the lawn towards the light of the drawing room. As I entered, Felix, who was speaking to Quinlivan, froze at the sight of me. Helene, sitting at the mahogany table with her head in her hands, looked up at me, her eyes widening. There was a moment when I thought I spotted Ada opposite her but my eyes cleared and I saw it was George, scribbling on notepaper.

'Ada has been attacked!'

I don't know why I spoke of my suspicions so publicly. Perhaps it was the state of my oyster satin dress, now covered in livery clots reflecting in the glass of the octagonal mirror. You don't split your head open like a pumpkin from falling on the ground, however icy.

George came to me. 'My God, what's happened to you?'

I shook my head, stuttering with cold and shock. 'N-not me, A-Ada. This-this is her blood.'

'Where is she?'

'In the c-copse near the pond. Lily is with her.'

'I'll go to her.' Felix was at George's side at once. I turned as Sir Thomas came in through the front door, his eyes narrowing as he took in my appearance.

'Tom, I need your help.' Felix steered his neighbour back

towards the garden. 'Come with me. Quinlivan, fetch Dr Gosden from the village.'

George looked at me, desperate to follow the men. 'I don't want to leave you alone here.'

'I'll look after her.' Helene reached for my hands. 'You're frozen to the bone, Louisa, and you need to keep warm for the baby's sake as much as your own. I'll take you to Alice.'

She led me away from George who took the opportunity to race outside as we descended into the warmth of the kitchen where Quinlivan was hurriedly pulling on a coat.

'Try Dr Gosden first. If there's no answer, his colleague, Preston, will help.' Alice stopped, gaping when she saw my clothes. 'Heavens above, Louisa! Let me take a look at you.'

'Why don't you ask Mr Conan Doyle to look at Ada?' I was trying to catch my breath as the warm air hit my lungs.

'He's a guest.' Helene's voice was high-pitched, her manner regal. 'He's already attended to Horwick. A village man will know what to do.'

Despite her assurance, I noticed she was plucking at the bodice of her dress, her fingers working the silk.

Alice stepped forward. 'Why don't you go back to your room, ma'am? Janet will go with you and I'll bring you up something shortly.'

Janet led Helene up the stairs and I heard her murmur soothing noises as their footsteps receded.

I had begun to tremble, the shock finally hitting me. Alice wrapped me in a blanket to cover my nakedness as she took off my dress and underclothes, examining each in turn. She washed my bloodied body as I clasped the blanket to me, finally breathing a sigh of relief.

'The blood isn't yours.'

Janet returned, carrying a huge eiderdown which smelt of flour and lavender water; she'd probably taken it from Alice's bed. I rested in a chair next to the range, a stone hot-water bottle under my feet as Alice fed me a thin broth. Spare stock, I suppose, which at first caused me to gag but gradually began to soothe my raw throat. When she'd finished spooning the liquid into my mouth, and I was sure the tremors had stopped, I got to my feet.

'I need to get back outside. I must talk to Ada again.'

Alice shook her head, wiping her hands on a cloth. 'It's deathly cold out there. They'll be bringing her in soon enough.'

'There was too much blood for an accident.' I kept my voice steady, desperate to convince, but she shook her head.

'Don't bother the family with your fancies. They've enough to be worried about.'

'You're right, Louisa.'

We both turned to stare at George who stood at the threshold of the kitchen, his face grey with strain. I glanced up at the clock. Nearly eleven o'clock, and yet the evening had felt endless.

'You're not mistaken. There *is* too much blood. I've told the doctor of what you said and he wants to speak to you. Ada is dead.'

Chapter Thirty-Four

Alice staggered into her chair at George's news, taking me by surprise given she'd just washed Ada's blood from my body. I was reminded, once more, that this was a house of grief and every death must be a reminder of other losses. I felt a cloak of calm descend over me. My mother had once complimented me that I was dependable in a crisis, as if I had much choice in the matter. Now, I would put my self-reliance to good use and my voice would be heard in relation to Ada's death.

'I want to talk to the doctor. Janet, will you go and fetch one of my day outfits? I can hardly meet the man dressed only in an eiderdown. I'll dress in front of the fire.'

George took a step back. 'I'll wait for you in Horwick's room.'

I changed quickly, adrenaline replacing shock. When I was ready, we entered the drawing room together, where a sheet of ice-cold air hit us. A young man, only a little older than me, stood with his arms folded, a little apart from the family and guests, most of whom were sitting in silence. Heads turned to acknowledge my arrival but no one moved, the reticence of the gentry classes reminding me once more how little I fitted in here.

Sir Arthur and Jean Conan Doyle were absent, although they must have heard the commotion in the house. Perhaps they thought it wise to stay away. And although Janet had been instructed to take her to her room, Helene was back at the mahogany table, reading an old copy of *Lady's Realm*, the face of the

Duchess of Devonshire gracing the cover. Lily was kneeling next to her with a consoling arm around her mother's shoulder, but she glanced at George and me, her face taut with anxiety. I saw her dress was bloodied, as mine had been, although she should have been protected by my coat which I'd used to cover Ada.

'Where's the body?' I whispered. They surely hadn't left her outside.

'She's in her bedroom, where the doctor examined her,' said George, his eyes on the room. 'She died while Lily was tending to her outside. We took her to her chamber for Dr Preston's arrival, although she was past help by that stage. He's rung for his partner to come and look at Ada's body. I don't think anyone was expecting that.'

'Because of what I said?'

George put his hands in his pockets, a gesture I was beginning to associate with times when he was unsure how to answer me. He kept his voice low. 'Possibly. He may well have his own reservations. Let's see what his colleague says. Quinlivan had to go and rouse the postmistress to use her telephone to call Dr Gosden who's staying with family in Brighton.'

I wondered what Mrs Ellis thought of being disturbed a second time in a week. It would no doubt be the talk of the village soon enough.

'He's coming to speak to you now,' said George.

The doctor approached us, glancing across to the family who kept their eyes averted from us. I might have been a leper the way they were deliberately avoiding coming over to me.

'It was you who found Mrs Watkins in the garden, wasn't it? What made you look for her there?'

'Janet, the maid, saw Ada leave through the front door. I wanted to check that she was all right before she left the Hall.'

Although we were speaking quietly, Lily, once more in her role of comforter of Helene, was listening to our conversation.

'She was unsteady on her feet after the séance. I noticed it at once,' I confided.

The doctor pursed his lips. 'Too much wine at dinner, perhaps. Cold and alcohol are a poor combination.' He glanced at me. 'Did she say to you how she had come to take such a bad tumble?'

'She wasn't able to talk very much.'

'She said nothing at all?'

I hesitated. 'I thought she told me to go away. She also mentioned a child.'

'A child? She was delirious then?'

'I got the impression she thought I was in danger.'

'From a child?'

I hesitated, unsure of how to answer. 'From someone,' I said finally.

'I believe you said she'd been attacked.'

'Yes, well. I . . . I don't know.'

'You said as much to the assembled company.'

'There was so much blood. Ada was telling me to be careful. I . . . felt as if there was someone close by who had done her harm.'

'You have proof?'

I shook my head. George came to my defence. 'Louisa is no fool. What do *you* think about Ada's death, Dr Preston?'

'I think I'd like the opinion of my colleague.' He nodded at us both and returned to his vigil at the window.

I spotted Sir Thomas whispering to Felix in one corner, urgent words accompanying restrained gestures. George followed my gaze.

'Sir Thomas isn't very happy. He put pressure on the doctor to issue a death certificate.'

'Sir Thomas? What's it to do with him?'

'When doctors start quibbling about cause of death it doesn't bode well for a family's reputation. The gentry stick together when their status is at stake.'

'What time is it now?' I had lost all sense of the hour in the commotion.

George looked at his watch and swore. 'This infernal thing's stopped again. It's late, that's all I can tell you.' Through the front window, a light appeared which steadily increased until a pair of car headlights, far brighter than those on the car Quinlivan drove, dazzled us through the window. Janet came out of the shadows and pulled open the door, letting in a man in his fifties carrying a doctor's leather bag. Dr Gosden was known to the family and when Felix went up to him, the medical man laid a reassuring hand on his arm.

'Why don't you lead the way, Felix.'

The trio began to climb the stairs as I moved forward. 'I want to come too.'

'Perhaps afterw—' began Felix, but was silenced by the younger doctor.

'Let her come.'

I shook off George, who would have loved to accompany me, and followed the men up the stairs. For the first time, Ada's room showed signs of chaos. She'd been placed decently on top of the counterpane with her hands folded across the stomach; an artificial rose had been laid next to her, its gaudiness a mockery of Ada's lifeless form. Around the bed, though, a rug was turned up at the corners and all three drawers of the large chest had been opened and not fully shut.

Dr Gosden bent over Ada, feeling for a pulse and then listening to her chest with his stethoscope. I watched as he applied a hammer first to her elbows and then, lifting up her soaking skirts, to her knees. It brought back memories of my grandmother dying, a drawn-out process, and my mother, to check she'd finally gone, had held a mirror in front of her mouth. Dr Gosden reached into his bag and produced a small magnifying glass. He parted Ada's bloodied locks and began to examine a wound extending from her hairline deep into her scalp.

'Lacerations to the skin and evidence of severe trauma to the skull,' he said to no one in particular. 'Can you get me some water?'

Felix filled a bowl from the ewer and carried it to the doctor. 'We can use Ada's hand towel for linen.'

I saw him dip the cloth in the water and gently wipe Ada's hair, following the blood trail down her scalp and, as they washed her skin, onto her forehead. When the water had turned oxblood red, Dr Gosden leant forward and peered again at the wound with his glass.

'The crack to her skull is probably from her fall.' He looked up at me. 'Was the ground hard where she was found?'

'It was iced solid under the trees once I'd waded through the drifts,' I replied.

'Can you see this?' All three of us leant forward to see where the doctor was pointing. Three clawlike marks scarred Ada's forehead, a trident on her skin.

'Neptune's victim,' I heard Felix murmur.

'Almost certainly gouges from whatever felled her,' said the doctor. 'A branch, perhaps, falling from a tree.'

'Yes, but there was no wind this evening.' I looked over to Felix. 'You surely remember. The evening was freezing but calm.'

Felix was having none of it. 'The trees in that copse are half-dead. It wouldn't take much weight of snow for a branch to snap and fall. Shall I send Quinlivan out to look?'

'I would feel better, certainly, if I found what caused that wound,' said the young doctor, frowning as he examined the gouge.

Felix disappeared for a moment and I was left with the two medical gentlemen. Dr Preston turned to me. 'She was a medium, I believe. My mother used to go to meetings when I was much younger. Did you attend the séance this evening?'

'I wasn't invited.'

'Probably wise. I've never seen the attraction myself. More than one of my patients has been fleeced by a rogue spiritualist.'

I looked down on the shell of Ada surrounded by these men of science and made a face. Dr Preston mistook my gesture and gently touched my elbow.

'How are you feeling in yourself? It must have been a frightening thing to discover.'

'I'm shaken, that's all.'

The older doctor looked up from Ada. 'If you feel any contractions you need to get to Brighton as soon as possible. There's a decent hospital there. Don't leave it too long in this weather.'

Felix re-entered the room. 'Quinlivan is searching now. There are a lot of branches littering the ground but we're looking for something of some size, I suspect, to account for Ada's injuries.' He looked over to me. 'Would you like to go downstairs?'

I sensed the force of will behind his words. He wanted me out of the room. I shook my head. 'I'd rather wait with Ada.'

I crossed to the window and watched as the beam from Quinlivan's torch arced around the trees. Occasionally it would stop and then resume its relentless search. Eventually it was shone in the direction of the house and its path became steady. Either he had found something or he had admitted defeat. I suspected the former as Quinlivan didn't strike me as a man to give up easily.

There was a knock on the door, and Quinlivan came in holding a branch, not as heavy as I'd imagined, but with one branchlet sticking out at a forty-five degree angle in that distinctive clawlike pattern. As he brought it nearer to the light, I saw the splashes of dark carmine.

'It looks newly fallen. Can you see the pale wood where it's torn away from the trunk? It's come down recently.' Quinlivan held out the exhibit to the men who gathered to inspect the splintered wood.

'Was there really a sufficient weight of snow to make that branch snap off?' My voice sounded shrill amongst the distinguished gentlemen. All three raised their heads to regard me.

'You have an alternative explanation?' asked Dr Gosden.

'I followed footprints to find Ada once I was in the garden. There were two sets, one dainty, the other much larger.'

'Is this true?' Felix asked Quinlivan.

Quinlivan shrugged. 'Another layer of snow has fallen since we brought Ada in. Any tracks have been obliterated.'

'But they were there, I promise you.'

I saw Dr Gosden take in my rumpled appearance, his eyes lingering on the swell of my stomach.

'You believe Mrs Watkins has died as a result of foul play? Do you have any proof?'

How could I explain the sense of danger I had experienced in that earthy copse? 'I heard footsteps while I was comforting Ada. Close by. Someone was there who didn't want to identify themselves.'

'That's all?' asked Dr Gosden.

I lost my temper then, sick of them treating me as if I were a fool. 'I heard the commotion after the séance. She'd been told she had to leave here immediately. Everyone was angry, and who's to say the anger didn't spill over to actual violence?'

Felix turned to me. 'Are you actually accusing one of us of doing this to Ada?'

I caught my breath. 'I – I . . .' My words trailed off as I saw the futility of trying to prove my suspicions until I'd had time to digest the evening's events.

Felix's voice was firm. 'Louisa has had a shock. Ada was not in danger from anyone here. In fact, we tolerated her nonsense for a long time.'

'But I'm not imagining the menace I felt.' The room began to swim as my voice rose. 'Ada was beaten, I'm sure of it.'

'I think a tonic might be in order,' murmured Dr Gosden, exchanging a glance with Felix.

'And that's it? Will none of you listen to me? What about you?' I appealed to the younger of the two doctors. 'You had concerns, didn't you?'

I felt all three close ranks on me, as Dr Preston held onto my arm. 'Perhaps I should take you back downstairs.'

'So you'll issue the death certificate?' I heard Felix ask as I was ushered from the room. 'Then, perhaps, I can offer you both a nightcap in my study.'

Dr Gosden closed his bag with a snap. 'That is certainly the branch which struck her and I agree that it has recently fallen. I'm happy to certify death as a result of accidental head injury.'

Furious, I wrenched my arm away from the young doctor, careering out through the door and into George, who had been pacing outside Ada's bedroom.

'I can make my way back to my room. I certainly don't need a tonic.' I marched down the passage, conscious of George's footsteps behind me. I didn't trust myself to speak. I had been ignored by three gentlemen and I felt the weight of my inferior status as a woman. Well, they would see. Ada's death did not deserve to be swept under the carpet as if she were of no importance. I wasn't convinced that, had it been me lying on that counterpane, my death would have been investigated with any greater rigour. Well, Ada now had a champion. For the rest of my stay, I would work to ensure she got the justice she deserved.

Chapter Thirty-Five

George followed me into my room. He didn't even consider any impropriety, pulling the door shut behind us with an air of repressed excitement. Perhaps it was common to all journalists, but he was more enthused by Ada's death than the séance he had come to Clewer Hall to attend.

'You need to leave me alone, George, I'm exhausted. They've ruled the death accidental.'

'I heard. You still think there was something suspicious?'

I sat on the bed, pulling off my shoes. 'There were footprints which led me to the body, Ada's and those of another. There's no proof, however. Quinlivan says the fresh snow has covered up any evidence.'

'Were they walking together, do you think, or was one following the other?'

I tried to clear my mind and conjure up the images of those footprints. Frustrated, I shook my head.

'I don't remember.'

'If Ada was attacked then it must have been someone in the house. It's too much of a coincidence that, after the consternation caused by her séance, an outsider who wished her harm happened to be lurking in the garden. We need to think back to earlier. Everyone was in the drawing room immediately after the séance when we arrived from the Adelaide Room. Don't you remember? We watched the Conan Doyles climb the main stairs to their chamber. Felix had told Ada to leave and the house was in uproar.'

'Then the Conan Doyles have an alibi. What about the others? I left Sir Thomas and Felix in the drawing room when I went upstairs to look for Ada.'

'They both left the room not long after you.'

'You didn't see where they went?'

'I'm not sure. Sir Thomas took the dogs down to the kitchen and I later heard them outside. I thought Felix went out onto the balcony to have a cigar. Only it now strikes me as a cold night to smoke out of doors.'

'And they were both furious with Ada. What about the women? Helene and Lily weren't in the hall when we arrived, although I heard one of them sobbing in the living room.'

'Which one?'

'I don't know.'

George gave a snort of frustration. 'Everything happened in a rush, so I'm not sure we can account for any of the family. What about the servants?'

'Alice was in the kitchen when I went out to look for Ada, but Quinlivan and Janet I can't account for.'

'Janet passed me, presumably to clear the Adelaide Room after the séance. Quinlivan was helping.'

We looked at each other. 'There's no one else. Horwick is laid up,' I said.

'The servants are in the clear, then. The Clewers and Sir Thomas are not.' George, I saw, had begun to write in his notebook again.

'It was a man's print that I saw next to Ada's footprints.'

'Anyone can slip their feet into a boot. What we need is a strong motive.'

I passed a hand over my face, suddenly exhausted. 'You heard what was said during the séance. Ada claimed that four sons of the house have died as part of the curse, but there were only three Clewer sons.'

'You're sure?'

'I got the history of each from Alice on the night of my arrival. There were three children apart from Lily – Archie, Richard and Cecil. So why did Ada mention four?'

'You think that statement enough to warrant Ada's murder?'

'I don't know. But I heard someone cry out, I'm sure of it.'

'You don't know who?'

I could have cried at his persistence. 'You were in the room with everyone. Didn't *you* notice?'

'I think everyone was distressed by Ada's fakery.'

Exhausted, I lay back on my pillow. 'I can't think straight. I need to rest.'

'Ada's death has been ruled an accident. The matter, as far as the family is concerned, is concluded.'

'Not for me it isn't. I have a day or so of photographs left. I shan't let Ada's death be signed away as accidental if she was killed deliberately.'

George regarded me, his expression betraying little. 'You're going to have your work cut out trying to prove anything other than the official version, especially now the doctors have had their say.'

'I'm still going to try.'

'You're tired,' he said. 'Let's talk in the morning. I'd like to see you before I return to London. Louisa, I'm sorry but I have business to attend to and can't stay any longer.'

'Of course. Goodnight, George.' I hesitated. 'I appreciate your company this evening. It's made all the difference.'

I closed my eyes as I heard him say, 'Goodnight, Louisa.'

I heard his footsteps retreat down the passageway and I was still lying on the counterpane, pulling my cardigan around me, trying to summon the energy to undress myself when I heard a knock on the door.

'Who is it?'

'Helene.'

I sat up, arranging myself the best I could. Five minutes earlier I had been discussing with George the possibility that this woman might have attacked Ada. Now I was to be alone with her in my bedroom.

'Come in.'

Helene entered, wearing a blue silk dressing gown, her hair plaited down her back.

'I wanted to check how you were feeling after tonight.'

Her unexpected solicitude put me on edge. 'I'm quite well.'

'I was worried about the baby.'

I sighed, some of the tension dissipating. 'I know. The baby's fine, too.'

'Would you like me to check?'

I shrank from her. 'There's nothing wrong. I can feel it moving.'

'I can check. I'd rest easier if I knew the baby was well.'

'Please don't worry.' I didn't want this woman touching me. I was on my own in this wing of the house and Helene's usual fragility was accented by an air of desperation.

'Please.'

Good God, it appeared she wasn't going to move until I complied. If it was the only means of getting rid of her, then I would do it. Sighing, I removed my cardigan but kept on my dress. I would not stand in my underwear in front of Helene. She placed her hands, fingers facing downwards, on my stomach.

'I can feel him too.'

'Him? I might be having a girl.'

'Your stomach is stuck out like a Christmas pudding. It'll be a boy.'

An old wives' tale I'd heard before, but I was too tense to argue. 'Its feet are at the bottom of my ribs. I can feel it kicking. The baby is the right way, at least.'

'I can feel his outline, here is his back on this side of your stomach.' Her fingers skirted across my abdomen, reminding me of Ada's touch on our first acquaintance. We pregnant women lose ownership of our bodies the minute we begin to show. 'He's quite low, though.' Helene raised her head up at me. 'How long did you say you had left?'

'About six weeks. A little less than that, now. Perhaps five.' I drew away, glad to get out of her clutches. I had a chance, however, to use my time alone with her to my advantage.

'Helene? What did Ada mean by four children? During the séance she said that four sons of the Hall had died. What did she mean?'

Helene stood. 'Ada was fallible. I see it now. Perhaps I always knew, but grief makes fools of us all. Forget about the séance. How do you know what was said?'

'George mentioned Ada's words.'

'Mr Storey? Yes, I see.' She turned away from me. 'The baby's making its way down. Some move quickly into the birth position. It would be better if you hurried to finish your work.'

So that was what it was all about. Helene wanted me gone from the house.

'I'll do my best.'

She left me and I returned to my position on the bed, listening to the house gradually grow silent, my resolve increasing. When I was sure everyone had retired, I crept across the cold, sticky carpet in my bare feet, determined to search Ada's belongings. The room had been tidied, all the drawers shut again. Janet had mentioned finding items that Ada was going to use for the séance but I saw nothing untoward amongst her things. She had been made respectable in death and even the bottle of laudanum had gone, to hide Ada's dependency, I suspected. I did find an item I remembered, however: Ada's tarot, which I slipped into my pocket.

I'm not sure why I took the pack of fortune cards. I think I wanted something of Ada's, but I'd also been fascinated by her reading of the tarot and I didn't want them thrown out. If I'd asked Lily, I'm sure she would have given them to me. As it was, I knew I was laying myself open to accusations of thievery, so if necessary, I would blame a state of confusion if I was caught.

I finished my search of Ada's things but the grubby underwear and mended dresses revealed nothing. Back in my room, I put the pack in my case and jammed my Holland jacket on top of the cards to hide my theft. I was dog-tired but I couldn't escape the prickle of fear every time the house creaked. I decided to push the little chair I'd taken from the nursery up against the door, its rusted frame squealing as I jammed it under the handle. For added protection, I placed my suitcase on the seat. If anyone decided to come into the room, everything should fall with a clatter. For the rest of the night I would be on my own in this wing, with only Ada, lying in eternal rest, to keep me company.

Chapter Thirty-Six

The Conan Doyles left the next morning. They'd breakfasted in their room, more work for Janet given that their mother had wisely told Lizzie she wasn't to return to the Hall. From my place at the breakfast table, I watched her carry two trays up the stairs in succession and return, giving me only a quick glance as she came to collect the crockery I'd used for my meagre breakfast of dry toast and weak tea. I realised I'd unfairly blamed Lizzie for the bitterness of my drink the previous morning: it tasted no better today.

'Are none of the family or guests joining me?'

'Mr George has been down already. He's back in his room working. The family have decided to breakfast in bed.'

'Even Felix?'

She didn't meet my eye. 'I think everyone is tired.'

Or doesn't want to talk to me, I thought, after my outburst the previous evening. It made me more determined that my voice wouldn't be silenced.

Sir Arthur and Jean, both looking subdued, came down the stairs as I passed through the drawing room. Although the news of the séance and Ada's death was too late for the morning's newspapers, it might make later editions, and I'm sure they were keen to leave as soon as possible to distance themselves from the Hall. To my surprise, Jean took my arm.

'Why don't you leave with us? We're expecting our driver

shortly. He could take you on to London if that would help.'

Despite myself, I was touched. I'd grown used to my loneliness here at the Hall and the sense of dislocation from my old routine. However, London represented everything that was wrong with my life and I was in no hurry to return. In any case, there were too many unanswered questions about Ada's death and I had resolved to stay, at least until I'd finished my commission.

I resisted the temptation to give Jean a hug and shook my head. 'I need to finish off here. I'll be fine but I do appreciate the offer.'

'If you don't mind me asking, my dear, don't you think your place is with your husband? Surely he'll be worried when he hears what has happened here.'

Edwin, worried? He'd be furious. That would be a difficult conversation for me to have. 'I must telephone him. You think the death will make the newspapers today?'

'With Mr Storey in attendance? I think you can be certain of it.'

'I'll call Edwin today to reassure him.'

'As you wish.'

Conan Doyle joined his wife. 'Ada was a fraud, of course, though it pains me to speak ill of the dead. But still, there's something in this house neither of us like.'

'What do you mean?'

'I've felt it before. It was in the home of another – Colonel Elmore was his name. I was woken to a deafening sound, similar to someone banging on a table with a cudgel. Years later, when the house burned down, the skeleton of a child was found buried in the garden. The incident has never rested easy with me.'

'A child?' I stared between the two.

'We'd feel much happier if you came with us, my dear. There's an odd atmosphere in this house and I don't think either of us believes the matter is finished.'

I shook my head. 'I'll stay, but thank you for the offer.'

Quinlivan, who had brought his own car around the front to await George's departure, came through the front door to tell the Conan Doyles that their own driver had arrived. I gave each of them a kiss goodbye and watched Quinlivan take them out. He came back in shortly afterwards, rubbing his hands.

'Good riddance.'

I looked at him, confused at his vehemence. 'They weren't that bad. What have you got against them?'

He shook his head.

I followed him down the stairs into the kitchen. 'Come on, you didn't like Ada either. You don't strike me as the religious sort, so what was it? What have you got against those who believe in talking to spirits?'

Quinlivan poured himself a cup of coffee from the pot brewing on the stove. 'People like Ada and Conan Doyle want everything on their own terms. They believe in something if it suits them, but if not, it's all rubbish. Take Sir Arthur. Remember those photos of the fairies?'

'I remember.' Two little girls who lived in a village called Cottingley, cousins I think, had taken photos of little figures with wings they'd played with at the bottom of the garden. A wonderful story, except the fairies were dressed in 1920s clothes, copied probably from a magazine. They were a clever fake, which I'd been able to spot at once although others had proved more gullible. 'Conan Doyle believed they were genuine.'

'Oh, he believed them all right. Two respectable girls seeing fairies at the bottom of the garden and, of course, they're real. But when it comes to the honest visions of ordinary men, it's completely different.'

'What visions?' I asked, but, as I spoke the words, something stirred in my memory. 'There were stories of angels appearing during a battle, weren't there?' I put my hand to my head, trying to remember the name of the place.

'Mons,' said Quinlivan through gritted teeth.

The tale came back to me, a fantastical story of longbowmen, St George and even a crucified soldier seen in the sky. Who knows what had entered the fevered heads of those battle-frightened men?

'And Conan Doyle has said he didn't believe them?'

'I asked him about it when I picked him up from the station. Do you know what he said to me? "The stress and tension of battle aren't the best conditions with which to assess reliable evidence."'

I was surprised. Conan Doyle had struck me as a principled believer and I wondered why he was so dubious about trusting the experiences of the men in the trenches.

'I'm sorry. I don't think he meant it as a personal insult. If it's any consolation, I rather like the idea of a sky full of angels watching over you while you fought.'

Quinlivan wasn't mollified, I could see. He sat down heavily on the chair, his polished boots gleaming against the fire on the range. 'If he'd had an ounce of the common touch, I'd have told him my own story.'

I sat next to him, refusing a cup of the proffered coffee. 'You saw something in the trenches yourself?'

He took a long slug of his own brew and placed the cup on the table, keeping his eyes on me. He knew of my scepticism and was perhaps judging my likely response. Finally, he sighed.

'We were on a march. When they moved the lines, we'd be herded into our unit and marched to the next trench. One morning – it can only have been just gone five – I saw a man walking behind me who was exhausted. You get to know the look.'

I was transfixed by Quinlivan's story. I saw, not Quinlivan's tired fellow soldier, but my own Bertie, marching with his unit, thinking of me and the boys.

'It was Private Rubin, a man I knew a little. I gave him one of my malted milk tablets, noticing his hand was icy cold, and hurried back into line. As I carried on marching, I remembered he'd died three days earlier.'

'And you looked back?'

Quinlivan shrugged and looked at me over the rim of his mug. 'Gone.'

A hallucination, perhaps. I'm sure a rational person might be able to find an explanation for it, but Quinlivan's face was firm.

'Us working people have as much right to our own experiences as anyone else.'

At his words, George came into my mind, and I was sure he'd have wholeheartedly agreed.

Chapter Thirty-Seven

I left Quinlivan, determined to get on with my work although the previous night's events hung heavy over me and I replayed my journey into the garden over and over again. The night had been still and Ada had been lying on the floor, felled by a branch supposedly fallen from a tree. She had told me of a child, I had felt a presence in the garden and Lily had appeared. As I turned over the sequence of events, the sense of being observed grew stronger, a prickle on the back of my neck, nothing more. Nerves are the last thing you need when taking photographs, so I ploughed on, conscious that the family still hadn't come to see how I was faring. If I was to get to the bottom of what had happened to Ada, I wondered if I might use this isolation to my advantage.

Clewer Hall, I was surprised to see, was observing the Victorian mode of mourning. All the statues and mirrors in the house were covered with a square of black cloth or netting and the few vases of flowers had been removed. It added to the air of morbidity as I began my work in the drawing room. When I'd finished, I took my camera upstairs to photograph two tired-looking tapestries dominating the wall of the south bedroom.

As I set up my camera, it was hard to keep my eyes averted from the garden. I told myself that I would be naturally drawn to the place where Ada had died, although I think, deep down, I was also waiting for Quinlivan to depart with George, his curiosity satisfied about his father's experience at the séance in 1896.

When, eventually, I saw the car make its slow progress down the drive, I had to resist the urge to pull the curtains shut, my mood sinking at the knowledge that George hadn't sought me out to say goodbye. Our acquaintance had only been brief, but even the insignificant fact that he knew of my work had given me the thrill of remembrance that I had a life beyond Edwin and Kentish Town. He had promised he would come to see me this morning but, clearly, London had exerted its pull and I was to be left without a further thought. Swallowing my disappointment, I took a final image and carried my equipment out of the room determined to seek solace in developing the plates.

The snow had begun to thaw and I could hear the drip-drip-drip of slush falling from the trees. I took the long route to the icehouse, keeping to the path, still unable to shake the creep of knowledge that I was being watched. The hairs on my arms were standing on end and I was seized by the desire to turn around and confront my spy. Only once did I look back at the house, but saw nothing, not even the shadow which often hung over the east wing.

The icehouse door swung open easily and I laid out the chemicals ready to begin first developing and then fixing the images. The first two plates I processed had that infernal light embedded in the glass, although, thankfully, the bedroom shots were unblemished. As I peered closer, I saw that the unexplained blemish in each of the photos hovered over the shared wall with the Adelaide Room. I wished now I'd asked Conan Doyle about spirit photography. The few examples I'd seen were clear fakes, pictures of babies or women dressed in white, clearly superimposed onto another image. As long as there has been photography, there has been the opportunity for fakery. But this light appeared at a certain point near the Adelaide Room and I had no explanation for it. In frustration, I began to pack up my stuff; then a shadow appeared at the door.

'So this is where you disappear to every afternoon.'

I stared at George's tall figure, crouching under the arched lintel as he entered.

'I thought,' my throat swelled and I had difficulty getting out the words, 'I thought you'd returned to London. I saw you leave with Quinlivan.'

'Not me. That was the sick butler. A fair sight he looked too.'

'Horwick.'

'Horwick, that's it. He's being driven to a relative in Bournemouth to recuperate.'

'His sister,' I said, steadying myself. 'Then he's delayed your return to London.'

'It isn't a problem. I've just telephoned the story in from the post office. My editor likes it because there's a human tragedy our readers will identify with. He's suggested I stay a little longer.'

'That's good.' I took a breath. 'I was sorry to see you go.'

He looked across at me, his expression hidden in the poor light. The silence lingered a little too long and was only broken by George.

'What have you been doing this morning?'

'Taking some photographs and placating Quinlivan.'

'What's the matter with him?'

'Conan Doyle was rude about the Angel of Mons – and although I don't think he believes it himself, Quinlivan won't have soldiers criticised.'

'The Angel of Mons? The whole phenomenon began as a short story by Arthur Machen which people took for fact. Conan Doyle may be a believer, but he can recognise a work of fiction.'

'Well, don't tell Quinlivan that.'

'It's funny, though.' He leant against the wall and took out a cigarette, absent-mindedly lighting it. 'When I joined up, I was determined to see action but when I realised that doing my bit involved getting blown up in the trenches or shot going over the top, I managed to wangle a job as a correspondent. My father's name helped.'

Was that a note of shame or pride in his voice? I still couldn't see his face clearly, so it was difficult to tell.

'There was this story I heard about Drake's Drum. Francis Drake took this drum with him when he circumnavigated the world and when he died he said if England were ever in danger, to beat the drum and he would return to defend the country.'

'And it was heard on the battlefield?'

'Heard at the start of the war and when the German fleet surrendered in 1918, they say.'

'And do you believe it?'

'After that war, I'm not denying anything but no, Louisa, I don't believe it. But I'll defend any fighting man's sanity who does.'

I shut my chemical bag and left everything there, carrying only my satchel with the developed plates. We emerged blinking into the weak sunlight, the air cold on our faces. I put my hand over my forehead and stared at the house with George beside me.

'You're still sure Ada's death wasn't an accident?' he asked.

'I am, but I hardly know where to begin.'

'We need to start looking for a strong motive. Something more than a person simply upset at Ada's prophecies.' He paused, frowning at the house. 'We're being watched.'

'You feel it too? I thought it my imagination.'

'I know it. Look at the window to the sitting room on the left. Someone is watching us.'

The sun was too low in the sky for me to see properly. 'Who is it?'

'I can't tell.' He glanced at me. 'Shall we see who's so keen to see what we're up to?' He paused. 'I'd have been sorry to go too, Louisa.'

Together we began to walk towards the house and, at the same time, I saw a figure move away from the window. A member of the household was watching what we were doing. The question was, who?

Chapter Thirty-Eight

When we arrived in the sitting room, Felix, Helene and Lily were all seated there, discussing the arrangements for Ada's funeral or, as I sourly thought, how to remove her body from the house as quickly as possible. They greeted our arrival with polite discomfort, Lily shifting to make room for us on the sofa while Helene's eyes kept sliding to my stomach. The fire was banked up and the screen removed. I had managed to initiate some change, at least, into that freezing house.

'I hear you will be staying with us a little longer.' I thought Helene was referring to me, but she had her eyes on George, her brown, almost black, irises little frozen coals.

George, clearly not unused to hostility in his work, nodded. 'You don't mind, do you? I've heard the roads are still treacherous and I can work as well here. I do need to type up my notes from yesterday's séance.'

'You will also have informed your paper of Ada's death?' asked Felix.

'Of course. I've also told them the death has been ruled an accident.'

I saw Felix relax, sitting back in his chair, although the two women did not. I decided I would get nothing from repeating my suspicions here and had begun to form other plans to get to the bottom of Ada's death. I could feel George squirming on the sofa next to me. He soon made his apologies and I heard, in the distance, the clatter of his typewriter soon overlaid by the faint tinkling of the piano and that familiar reedy voice. The house was officially in mourning and there would be no music playing during this time.

'I've written to the boarding house where Ada was staying and until they reply we can't do anything.' Lily put her cup down, looking at her mother for a reaction. Helene, Ada's benefactress, crumbled her thin biscuit with restless fingers, looking uninterested. How soon are we workers forgotten by those who pay us. A sour bile rose in my throat.

'May I have some tea?'

Helene reached across and handed me a cup.

'She never talked about her family?' I asked.

'Not at all. I got the impression she was from the north. Her accent certainly held traces of it, but she never mentioned any relations.'

'She mentioned Morecambe to me.'

'Anything else? A family member, perhaps?' asked Lily.

I shook my head.

Felix stirred, lost in thought. 'Then she must be buried here in the church next to the house. We can stretch to the cost of a funeral for her.'

'I don't want her buried near here,' said Helene, her face set. 'This wasn't her home.'

Lily put her hand on her mother's arm to calm her. 'It's out of the question. She needs to be back with her own kind.'

Poor Ada. If I'd had more money myself, I'd have taken her to St Pancras and buried her near my own children, but Lord knows what Edwin would have said and, in any case, who was to say if Ada wanted to be buried in London? As we sat in silence, contemplating the fate of Ada's remains, piano music once more drifted into the room. I looked at the family, none of whom made any sign they could hear anything. Ada had told me I had the gift and, in my upset after Jean's automatic handwriting, I hadn't given the piano music any further thought.

'Are any of you musical?'

Lily lifted her head, her brows knitted in surprise.

'You're thinking of Ada's funeral.'

I shook my head. 'I saw a piano in one of the rooms that were flooded. I wondered who played.'

'Only me,' said Helene flatly. 'I didn't have musical children, although not through want of trying. They all had lessons at one point.'

Lily tensed, her eyes on her father. 'Mother sang to us all through our childhood. She had a willing audience, at least.'

Helene stood. 'I don't think this is the time to be discussing music. None of you ever think of my feelings.' She rushed out of the room, Lily hurrying after her. Felix picked up his paper and, feeling the snub, I left him alone.

In the central drawing room, I heard the singing, louder this time, coming from the east passage. Not the boy, a young woman, her voice infused with grief. It's an odd thing I've noticed about songs before, but the melody can elude you forever until the lyric shifts and suddenly the whole song reveals itself. The words I could hear now were different to those on the previous occasions and I leant back against the wall to listen.

But there was one of the children who could not join the play.

And a poor little beggar maiden watched for him day by day.

It was a tune that my mother had sung and the memory of it brought back a rush of delight. At family celebrations, we were all expected to do a turn. My brother would recite the *The Rime of the Ancient Mariner* and I'd read out loud the first chapter of *Peter Pan* accompanied by actions which I thought at the time fitting to the story. My own musical mother, lamenting the fact that both of her children had tin ears, would stand next to a piano while my aunt carefully picked at the keys, trying not to make any mistakes. The song – I'm not sure I ever knew its name – was a melancholic air about a rich boy too ill to play with his friends who was watched by a beggar girl at the garden gate. If there was a significance to the story in the song, I couldn't grasp it.

I went to look for Alice in the kitchen. She was someone I might be able to quiz about the tune, but the room, although showing signs of recent occupation, was empty. Unusually, there was nothing cooking on the range, only the warming kettle occasionally hissing. Horwick's room had been stripped of his meagre possessions and, in the cold store, a lone scraggy pheasant hung from a hook. The sight of the bird induced a wave of nausea and I staggered out into the laundry room, my head swimming.

For a moment, I thought I saw Ada rising above me like a banshee. As I took a step back, I heard the splash of water on the floor and saw that Alice or Janet had washed Ada's dress, not the ostrich affair she'd been found in, but the much-mended black gown. Tears sprang to my eyes as I saw the care with which it had been washed and newly patched. As I stared at the gown, the airer from which it was suspended began to swing back and forth very slowly.

Chapter Thirty-Nine

I was sick that afternoon. Climbing the servants' stairs I felt a rush of nausea which forced me to run to the privy. I only just made it, my body expelling bile and foam until I was left heaving on the floor.

'Are you all right, Louisa?'

George's muffled voice drifted through the door.

'Can you give me a minute?'

God knows what I must look like. I splashed cold water on my face, cursing the fact that I had worn my decent day dress which must now smell revolting. I slid the bolt back and shielded my eyes, even the dim light causing spears of pain in my head.

'I came to ask you if the Clewers had mentioned anything of significance in the sitting room and I heard you retching. Can I do anything?'

'If you could help me to my bed.' I reached out to hold his arm but he put it around me, as a brother might do.

'I heard raw ginger is good for nausea during pregnancy. Or is that seasickness? I can't remember.'

He made me laugh, my stomach protesting as I giggled. 'I shouldn't be sick at nearly eight months. In any case, although I usually feel nauseous, I don't actually retch.'

'Something you ate? The food has been rather rich.'

'I've only had toast.'

'Drink, then. Perhaps the milk was off in the tea they served you. I wouldn't be surprised in this house.'

We had reached the bedroom and he pushed open the door with his foot. I pulled away from him. 'I had a cup in the sitting room. Whenever I have tea, either with the family or at breakfast, it disagrees with me.'

I sat on the bed. Lily had poured me tea on the first day of my arrival and I had fallen asleep, missing dinner and wakening with a raging thirst. Twice, during breakfast I had noticed a peculiar taste with the infusion. Today, Helene had handed me the tea and I had vomited soon after. Could there be a connection?

'What's the matter?'

I couldn't tell him. I needed him to trust me in the matter of Ada's death. If he thought my mind was made fuzzy by either my pregnancy or a reaction to food, he might think I was imagining any threat towards Ada. In any case, in the sitting room the tea had been poured in front of me and drunk by other members of the family. George had been with me the first morning Lizzie had brought me the foul brew and had drunk it too, with no effect.

'Nothing. Perhaps you could leave me to rest. I'll try to get up later.'

'There's something I need to tell you.' He pulled up the rusty nursery chair next to me and sat on it. 'I went to look for you downstairs first, and I overheard Lily suggesting to Felix that perhaps you should leave. The fact that you were so willing to believe Ada was murdered has clearly been festering in her mind.'

That galvanised me. I staggered onto my feet, hands on hips, nausea replaced by a surge of anger.

'They're going to dismiss me?'

'You're lucky. The sale of the house and contents is important. Felix said no immediately. You're to finish your work, although

I expect you'll get plenty of scrutiny as to how fast you're progressing.'

'Felix defended me? I'm surprised.'

'Why's that?'

I sat down again, wincing as the bed groaned with my weight. 'I repeated my suspicions the night of Ada's death in front of him and the two doctors. Felix wasn't very happy.'

'Well, he didn't take your concerns seriously as he insisted you're to stay.'

'Was Lily happy with his reply?'

'Not really.' I saw George laugh. 'You're looking better already. It's brought colour to your cheeks. But seriously, you need to be careful. You want to find out about Ada's death, and that's fine, but you need to keep out of Lily's way. Look, I'll tell them you've been taken ill. I'll bring up some magazines I saw in the living room. I should be able to find you a book too.'

He hurried away and I sat down on the bed again, closing my eyes as sleep threatened to pull me in. I heard him come in and place the papers on the bedside table but I was so weary, I couldn't open my eyes.

'Thank you,' I murmured as the door clicked shut.

Chapter Forty

I woke at twelve minutes to ten with a start, surprised at Bertie's alarm clock ticking next to me. George must have wound it up, knowing I'd wake in the night. My first thought was that I'd neglected to ring Edwin. How soon the poor man was forgotten . . . A stab of remorse pierced me, too late in the day. Perhaps it was this which made me restless, guilt combined with the way you get when you've lain in bed for too long.

I examined George's choice of book, which didn't appeal and, desperate for something to distract me, picked up Ada's tarot. The pack still smelt faintly of her: that familiar spicy perfume coated with mildew. As I spread the cards face down on the bed, I struggled to remember if Ada had laid them out in a particular way. I tried various configurations and settled on four rows of five with two at the bottom. Feeling foolish, I selected a card at random. The image I turned over was of a man on a cart being drawn by two Egyptian-style lions. The Chariot, the words underneath the image informed me. I stared at the picture but it was meaningless without a reader to interpret it. With a sigh, I gathered up the pack.

George had brought me dog-eared copies of the *Lady's Realm*, most over ten years old and I flicked through the top issue to see if I could find an image I had taken. One of a group of women meeting soldiers from a train was certainly mine, but the picture was unaccredited. Of course; why hadn't I picked up Ada on this at the time? She had been adamant that she had discovered my existence in the journal, but my name was not attached to any of the pictures. I picked up another issue. There was a photo I had taken at Ascot races. Again, no credit. People such as George would have known my name anyhow, as I was working and plying my trade in the business. I couldn't understand, however, where Ada had seen my name.

The answer came near the bottom of the pile where, unusually, I had appeared in a photograph alongside Christina Broom, who had blazed a trail for us women photographers with her work. We were side by side, bent over our cameras and my name was there for everyone to see. Ada had scored three thick lines with her pen underneath my image. Ada, who had brought me here for a purpose because she thought I had a role to play in this house's destiny.

'You're not forgotten,' I told the empty room.

I put my dressing gown on over my dress, double-knotting the belt so I wouldn't trip over it as I descended the narrow backstairs towards the kitchen to make myself a hot drink. As I passed through the ground floor, I opened the green baize door to look at the passageway. The familiar rot and damp smell rushed at me and the temperature dropped from cold to glacial. I took a step forward, the walls pulsating with an energy which I could only barely stand. There was a silvery light hanging suspended near the Adelaide Room. Not a reflection of the moon, but the same shape as the smudge appearing on my photographic plates. I could hear the paper breathing – in, out, in, out – as the drumming in my ears began and then the whispers. The walls talking to themselves. No, not a conversation but a monologue. A single voice.

'What are you doing out of bed?'

There was a flash of brilliance as the hallway lights came on one by one. George stood at the entrance to the passage, still dressed for dinner.

'I awoke and meant to get something from the kitchen.'

'You shouldn't come into this wing at night. Remember what happened to Horwick.' He came forward and took my arm. 'You're freezing. What are you doing here?'

'There was a light in the passageway, a phosphorescent circle near the Adelaide Room.'

'I can't see anything. Let me take you to the kitchen. It's the only warm place in this damn house.' He took my arm, guiding me down the narrow backstairs to the kitchen.

As we left the passage, the whispers became fainter and fainter and the baby, which had become restless, settled as we reached the warmth of the dying kitchen fire.

'Are you feeling better?'

'A little.'

He leant against the range and lit a cigarette. 'What are you doing here, Louisa?'

'You mean in the kitchen?'

'No, I don't mean that. Why are you in this house and not with your husband?'

I looked down at my hands. 'I need to work.'

'Is money really that short? Your place is with your husband. No, don't look at me like that. I'm simply stating the fact that this house isn't safe for a woman about to give birth. It's too remote, for a start. I've heard that the baby's not your first. What happened to your others?'

By the dying embers of the fire, I told George the story of three children. My first two, Hugh and Philip, and of the love with which they'd been brought into the world. I also told him the story of the baby inside me, which in a few weeks would be emerging into this new modern world, a different era from the one my first children had inhabited. I made no mention of love in relation to its conception. George was an astute man and he must have noticed the omission.

He was silent for a moment, smoking while he kept his eyes on me. 'Where did your first husband die?'

'The second battle of Ypres, in the spring of 1915. I still dream of that time. My last real moment of happiness with my mother and I playing with my children in front of the fire before the knock on the door to tell me Bertie had died.'

'You must have been bereft.'

'Taking photos helped. I'd already started earning a little from the images I took of London street life. Suffragettes, workers' marches, street sellers.'

'That's a long way from *Lady's Realm*.'

'Once Bertie had gone it was a case of beggars can't be choosers. The journal gave me a steady income.'

'And a fine reputation.'

I looked down at my hands, pleased. So the name Louisa Drew still carried some weight. A surge of warmth began in my chest as George continued his questions. You could never mistake him for anything other than a journalist.

'How did you start? It's an unusual choice of profession.'

'Charles, a friend of the family, had bought a camera, dabbled a little with it and got bored. I think he liked taking the pictures but the fiddling around afterwards dampened his enthusiasm. Our fathers were colleagues in the shipping company where they were both managers. Rather than let the camera gather dust around the house, Charles's father suggested passing it onto me. He knew I liked painting, although I wasn't much good at it.'

'And you found you had a talent for photography instead?'

'Yes, and when my husband died it seemed a respectable way to try to make a living. I didn't just have us three to support – I lost my father and brother at the Somme in the following year, so I had my mother to think of.'

'Christ.'

'There's this myth it was a young man's war, but my father was in his forties. He died a few days after my brother – and both telegrams arrived together.'

'I'm sorry, Louisa. I've heard similar stories. Brothers going down together, fathers and sons. It must have been terrible to have had to deal with the loss of your children afterwards.'

I looked down, fighting the impulse to delve into those dark memories. 'There are no words to describe it. I reached the bottom of the pit. It was a blessing I had my mother.'

'Is she still alive?'

'She died a few years ago. I think she drew some comfort that I was engaged to be married again, even if she didn't like Edwin.'

'Did he serve too?'

'He survived the Western Front, although he lost a brother.'

'And what does he do now?'

'He works in a men's outfitters. Dunn and Co. in Kentish Town.'

'I've heard of it. It's an honest job.'

For the first time in my pregnancy, I desperately craved one of the cigarettes George was smoking but I was cross at him for giving Edwin a seal of approval. However, I'd been too focused on his words and not the manner in which he asked his questions. When I looked up, I caught sight of George's expression. It was a look I recognised from Bertie and, if I was honest with myself, once or twice from Edwin. The gaze of desire. Flustered, I drew my gown around me, trying to regain my composure.

'There's something I want to tell you. Since I've been at Clewer Hall,' I said slowly, 'I've experienced odd happenings. A drop in pressure alongside distortions of my senses.'

'It's not unusual for women—'

'In my condition, you mean? This is true, but I experienced nothing of the kind before my arrival here.'

'One of my sisters, she used to crave chalk. She didn't actually eat it although she wanted to.'

I shook my head. 'I also hear music which has no explanation.'

'All right. Here's something different. After my father died, Edith, my eldest sister, was pregnant with her second child and said she used to be able to smell his tobacco smoke when she was dozing on the sofa. And her husband doesn't smoke – he has a weak chest – so there's no explanation from a member of the household.'

I reached towards the range, putting my palms against the cast iron.

'I know you're being kind but I'm not reassured. I can't rid myself of the feeling that the house doesn't want me here. It's mystifying, because I have nothing to do with Clewer Hall. When I arrived, Ada asked me if I'd been here before and I haven't. So why did she feel drawn to ask for me?'

'Didn't she explain?'

'She said it was forecast in the tarot, that I would be a catalyst for change.'

I smiled as I saw George raise his eyes to heaven. 'Even if music was playing I'd probably not notice it, but for what it's worth, I've not heard a piano since I've been here.'

'I can even remember the tune.' I sang a few notes, the only line I could recall, and he shook his head.

'It means nothing to me.'

A shadow crossed the doorway and I looked up. Lily, also wearing her dressing gown, was standing in the doorway.

'Do you need a chaperone?'

George stood, stretching. 'I need to get myself to bed – I've stayed up far too long. Perhaps you could make something for Louisa to help her sleep?'

I panicked and stood. 'I don't need anything now. I feel much better.'

'Nonsense, Louisa. A drink will do you the world of good.' Lily went into the cold store and returned with a jug of milk which she poured into a pan, placing it on the range. 'It's what my nanny used to make for me before bed when I was a child. Hot milk. I'm not sure it helps you sleep, but it does soothe a disturbed mind.'

I noticed that her long hair, which cascaded down her back, was turning grey at the roots. The range was cooling and the milk took a while to catch. Alice must have been cooking apples for the family supper because the air was infused with the smell.

'Did you recognise the tune I was humming?' I tried again, the melancholy air rising up and mingling with the steam from the milk.

She flinched slightly. 'The tune,' I asked again. 'Do you recognise it?'

'It's a song from the last century, that's all. I haven't heard it for years.'

As she walked towards me, holding out the cup, the smell of apples grew stronger. 'Drink your milk. It will help you sleep.'

I took the cup up to my bedroom and left it cooling as I slid between the cold sheets. I would not drink anything I hadn't prepared myself until I was sure I was not being given anything to harm me. It was only while I was drifting off that I remembered when the air had last smelt of spiced apples. In Ada's room, when I had caught the scent of the laudanum bottle. The bottle was now missing but the scent, I realised, had been carried on Lily's nightclothes.

Chapter Forty-One

Edwin arrived the next day to take me home. I'm not sure if I was more surprised by the fact that he had made the trip out of London or that he came alone. I'd been fooling myself that he'd receive my note and wait for my return, seething, but with no choice but to leave me to my work. I misjudged him. Edwin has a strong sense of duty, if little else, I found.

I'd woken late and I was still pulling on my clothes when Janet came in, her face red with exertion.

'I met your husband loitering on the driveway. He looked like he was plucking up courage to come to the house. He was ever so ill at ease.'

My stomach lurched as I paused, one arm stuffed into my cardigan. 'Where is he now?'

'I suggested he go to the tea room in the village.' She paused. 'You don't mind? I told him you could join him there.'

Edwin would be a fish out of water in this rural setting. Janet had seen the problem at once and had dealt with it efficiently. I felt a rush of gratitude towards this young woman. 'I don't have a coat. Mine was used to cover Ada. What shall I wear?'

Janet shrugged off her own navy gabardine. 'Use mine. It won't cover your stomach but it's better than nothing.'

I noticed a few curious faces turn to me as I walked along the main street, people stepping out of my way when I drew near. Ada's death had made me an object of interest, I saw. The tea room was housed in a single-storey building at the far end of the main street. Edwin was sitting at a table in the window, examining the menu. Through the steamed glass I could see him squinting at it, too vain to put on his spectacles. He'd clearly left home in a hurry. His hair, usually parted on the side and fixed with cream, was sticking up on one side. As I opened the door, he turned to see that it was me and returned to his reading. Swallowing my annoyance, I took the seat opposite him.

'This is a surprise. I assume you got my letter.'

'It arrived yesterday. I would have come straight away but I needed to get a day's holiday from my employer. They weren't best pleased.'

'I'm sorry,' I said, accepting a menu from a girl with a starched white cap. 'I never thought you'd make the trip down here.'

'You hardly left me any choice.'

I sighed, refusing to rise to the bait. The girl was idling next to the table, waiting for me to choose.

'I'll just have tea,' I told her, watching Edwin's lip curl as he ordered the same.

'Have something to eat. You've come a long way.'

'I know it's a long way. I've paid for the train ticket. It doesn't leave me much for food.'

'Which is exactly why I took this commission. We need the money.'

He waited for the girl to disappear into a room at the back before replying. 'Not at any price. I've seen what happened to that woman. Mother showed me the article yesterday. You didn't mention any death in your note to me.'

'For goodness' sake! Ada died after I sent the letter. I was going to telephone you after the accident, but . . .'

'I slipped your mind.'

I felt sorry for him then. We were speaking to each other like strangers and yet this decent man in front of me was my husband. I reached for his hand.

'I'm sorry, Edwin. It's been absolutely awful. When I accepted the assignment, I thought it would be a case of taking some photographs and sending my plates onto the auctioneer.'

'Isn't that what you're doing?' His voice rose and I looked at him in alarm.

'Of course it is, but Clewer Hall has been full of guests. The séance took me by surprise, I promise you.'

'You should have left as soon as you heard it was due to take place.'

'Edwin,' I hissed, 'we really need the money.'

'That's right, rub it in! I'm not able to support my own family. Mother has offered to help, you know, if it will stop you gallivanting around the country.'

I bet she has, I thought.

'I think it would be a good idea if she moves in with us when the baby's born.'

'What?' My shout carried across the tea room. 'I'm not having Dorothy in our house permanently.'

'We can discuss it when we get home as I can see you're in no state to see sense now. How long will it take you to pack?'

'What do you mean?'

'Don't be obtuse. I asked how long it would take you to pack your case. I'm taking you back with me today.'

'And I'm not going. I'm three quarters through my commission and I won't get paid unless I complete it.'

'I don't care!' Edwin's voice rose. 'You're my wife, carrying my baby, and you're staying in a house where all sorts of goings-on are happening. That woman deserved everything that happened to her.'

'Don't you dare say that!' I saw him shrink at the anger in my voice. 'I *liked* her. She was kind and dignified and I'm not going home until I've finished my assignment.'

The waitress was staring at us, open-mouthed. She had her back to the wall and was listening shamelessly until a voice from the kitchen shouted, 'Violet Jessop! What are you doing dawdling there?'

I turned my attention back to Edwin, whose fury mirrored mine.

'Don't tell me you believe all that communing with the spirits nonsense?' he hissed. He saw me hesitate and pounced. 'You attended it, didn't you?'

'Of course not. It was a recreation of the original. Why would they invite me along?'

Edwin's face flushed purple. 'Listen to you, "a recreation of the original". You sound ridiculous.'

I steeled myself to reply. 'I'm staying for a few more days until the commission is completed. I'm sure you can fend for yourself until then.'

'And after?'

'What do you mean, after? I'll be coming back home.'

He looked gratified, his mouth settling into a line that so reminded me of Dorothy.

'There'll be no need for you to be working once the baby's born. You said there would be money to put aside.'

Until the baby was weaned. That's what I'd told Dorothy but she'd shaped my justification to suit the pair of them. This, if they both had their way, would be my last commission. I had nowhere else to go. My parents and my brother were dead. I had friends, of course. Emily, for example, who had first introduced me to

Bertie. But I couldn't impose myself, if I were a separated woman with a young baby, on any of them. I had no choice. After this week was out, I would be returning home.

Chapter Forty-Two

I waited with Edwin for the bus back to Brighton to arrive. A charabanc passed us, stuffed full of people in high spirits on their way to the coast, braving the biting wind. Their good humour made Edwin more morose.

'I'll see you in a few days,' I said. 'It won't be long now.'

Edwin turned his head. I'd thwarted his plans to bring me back to London and I wasn't to be easily forgiven. 'There's a man staring at us over there.'

I followed his gaze. George was on the opposite side of the street, sheltering under a giant fir tree, the branches twisted from the weight of the recent snow. I wasn't sure how long he had been watching us, but he showed no embarrassment when he saw he'd been spotted. He crossed the village street, picking his way between shallow puddles and debris of dubious origin.

'I've been to Mrs Ellis to telephone through a story for today's later edition. Do we have another guest at Clewer Hall?' He looked to Edwin, who shuffled his feet. 'I'm George Storey.'

Edwin had no choice but to accept the proffered hand, although I could see he would have liked to have refused.

'Are you family?' he asked.

'Goodness, no. I'm a journalist. My editor has suggested I stay here a few days longer than I'd intended. Do you live in the village?'

'Edwin is my husband.' Both men turned to look at me as I said it, their eyes assessing. 'He's getting the bus back to Brighton.'

'It's natural you were worried about your wife after Ada's death.' George's voice was contemplative. He took a step back, as if to give us more space as a couple.

Edwin shot me a look, his gaze difficult to fathom, and we were spared any further embarrassment because the bus appeared around the bend. George watched as Edwin gave me a dry peck on the cheek before climbing up, taking the seat on the opposite window so he couldn't see me wave goodbye.

As the bus pulled away, George moved towards me, his manner detached.

'Why didn't you go with him? Your photos are surely nearly complete. Given the circumstances of Ada's death, I'm sure your employer would forgive you cutting short your assignment.'

'Cutting sho—' I stopped, remembering the confidences we'd shared in the kitchen the previous evening. 'Why would I want to cut short my stay? You know I'm determined to discover what happened to Ada.'

'For what purpose? Ada's death has been ruled an accident. Why don't you leave any investigating to me and go back to your husband?'

'Because I can't let it go! Don't you see? Ada's death? The story of the fourth child. Remember? Ada mentioned a fourth child in the séance.'

I looked at the George who, for all his metropolitan gloss, understood nothing at all.

'I shall leave when I please. The arrangements I've made with my husband are nothing to do with you.'

He looked away from me. 'I only want what's best for you. You can change your mind at any time. I'm sure Quinlivan would be more than happy to drop you at the station.'

He walked in the direction of the house without a backwards glance, the thin thread of mutual understanding stretching until I felt it snap as he turned into the drive.

Sick at heart, I picked up a newspaper from the village shop. It was a day old, which would allow me to read the article about Ada's death. Before returning to Clewer Hall, I retraced my steps to the tea shop which was still empty, the girl once more in her position behind the counter. She looked up, puzzled.

'Did you forget something?'

'Your name is Violet Jessop, isn't it? Are you related to the Jessops who lived in the garden of Clewer Hall?'

Her expression didn't change. 'I think so.' She raised her voice. 'Mam, there's a lady here asking about Clewer Hall.'

From behind bead curtains, a woman emerged, her apron bearing traces of flour. 'Clewer Hall?' Her voice radiated suspicion as she looked me up and down.

'I had tea with my husband just now and I heard you call your daughter. The name Jessop is the same as that of the old gardener's cottage and I wondered if you were related.'

Her expression didn't soften. 'On my husband's side, we are. Tom Jessop was head gardener for the Clewers for over forty years. He was a relation of my father-in-law. Uncle, I think, or maybe great-uncle. There are plenty of Jessops around here.'

'Do you remember him?'

'A little.' She paused. 'Why do you want to know?'

A good question, and not one I could answer easily. I decided on a version of the truth.

'I'm taking photos of the house and I saw the old cottage. I wondered about its history.'

'Not much to say about Old Tom. He kept himself to himself, and his wife was worse. An outsider, I think she came from Norfolk way. Arrived at the Hall as laundry maid, met Tom Jessop and never left. She did the laundry right up until Tom died.'

'They're both dead now?'

'Long gone. Old Tom died first, his wife not long after. She didn't stay in the cottage after Tom went – a woman in the village took her in. Well, she was probably glad to leave. She lost a child there, you see.'

'A child?'

'That's what I heard. They had just the one and it died.'

'Boy or girl?'

'A boy, I believe. They had the poor little thing late in life. It quite took everyone by surprise, even the Jessops. It happens to some couples like that. Their first at an improbable age. But the child died and they never had any more.'

A child who had died. Could this, I wondered, be the fourth child? 'How did he die?'

'I don't know. All I remember is that the child died young.' She paused. 'I'm not surprised, in that old house.'

'What do you mean?'

'I've heard the stories. Hauntings, curses, warnings. No place for a child.'

'But the haunting was *by* a child. Surely not a danger to them.'

'Are you sure? What about the curse? There's something not right about that house when it comes to children.'

'And you know of no other stories in relation to the Jessops' child?'

She paused. I've never had much trouble working out if a person is hiding something. My own children could never pull the wool over my eyes. Violet Jessop's mother knew something more, and I needed her to tell me what it was.

'I've lost children of my own,' I said. 'I can spend hours berating myself for not protecting them even though I know their illness wasn't my fault.'

I was on the wrong track, I saw. Although she looked sympathetic, Mrs Jessop showed no signs of revealing more. I tried another tack.

'Children aren't easy, are they?'

This, at least, produced a response. 'They never stop being a worry. Vi over there's only fourteen but the boys are already after her. I've tried to tell her the essentials, you know.'

I did. Now I looked properly at Violet Jessop, I could see the attraction for men of the village.

'You've brought up a decent, honest girl, I can tell.'

Mrs Jessop flushed with pride. Violet was the key to her mother's secrets. Praise the daughter and Mrs Jessop's hostility began to disappear.

'It must have been quite a job for Jessop and his wife with both of them working. Plenty of opportunities for mischief.'

'Oh, I don't know. Most children are able to look after themselves. I heard he was a little magpie but I doubt there was any harm in it.'

Magpies, those piebald crows with their reputation for thievery.

'The child stole?'

I'd been too direct, I saw at once. Mrs Jessop lifted the hatch and began to straighten the cruet set on one of the window tables.

I called over to her. 'I'm sorry, I wasn't being disrespectful. I remember my sons collecting their own little treasures and keepsakes. Fragments of glass, brass buttons. There's no harm in it.'

'That's what I said to my Joe. He was just being a child. Anyway, it's all long ago in the past, isn't it?'

I nodded and made to leave. 'Of course it is.' But I wasn't so sure. Lily hadn't liked me being so near Old Jessop's cottage and I knew, from past experience, that employers didn't like thievery amongst domestic staff, even if the culprit was only a child. A small crack had opened into the past, one I might be able to prise open further.

Chapter Forty-Three

I took the newspaper to the Adelaide Room and read the article, holding the print up to the light. There wasn't much. The small column didn't even have George's name next to it but there, tucked in between an advert for an indigestion remedy and cigarette paper, was an article headed SÉANCE MISHAP detailing the events of Ada's death. To George's credit, he had stuck to the facts and there was nothing to suggest her death was anything other than an accident.

I folded the newspaper and tucked it under my arm, looking around the room. I shouldn't really have been there. My work on the curios was completed but it was hard to drag myself away. Although it was the jewel in Clewer Hall's tarnished crown, I always thought of it as Ada's space, from the round table which she had manipulated for dramatic effect, to the wallpaper which had added to the sense of mystery during the séance.

Over by the window, the case of marble limbs glinted in the weak sunlight. I crossed and looked through the glass. All seven arms were back in place, untouched, I thought, since I'd last studied them with Horwick and Janet. The words of Felix returned to me when he'd described them. Four were of his children, the others made from casts of the arms of servant children. Perhaps the Jessops' son had been one of them.

A tread in the corridor alerted me to the fact that someone was loitering outside. I crossed quickly to the door, surprising

George, who was examining the wall between the passageway and the Adelaide Room.

'What are you doing?' I kept my voice neutral, determined he wouldn't see how hurt I'd been by his suggestion that I accompany Edwin back to London.

'Trying to find the source of the light you saw yesterday evening. Mediums use phosphorus, camphor and quicksilver to create their effects. Some of Ada's powders may have been taken after she died.'

'I saw nothing in her effects.'

He stopped what he was doing. 'You went through Ada's things? When?'

'The night of her death. I wanted to see if there was anything interesting, but I discovered nothing.' I didn't mention the tarot cards.

'For God's sake be careful. Can't you leave the actual investigating to me?'

'I don't remember you being particularly concerned about Ada the night she died.'

'Me? I had no sense of danger that evening, I was going on what you said. Why should I have been concerned about Ada? You heard how she went on during the séance.'

He wouldn't look me in the eye. Oh, bother George Storey! I turned to go. 'Never mind.'

'What's in here?' He pointed to the door next to the Adelaide Room.

'A little sitting room. All the rooms in this wing have been closed off since a flood. It's strange they never attempted to repair the damage. The family had money, surely, if Felix was collecting all these beautiful objects.'

George opened the door, taking in the peeling wallpaper and floor pitted with plaster and paint flakes. 'The flood must have happened some time after 1908. Felix invested heavily in an Indian company which was found to be trading fraudulently. He lost heavily and family finances have been much stretched since then. I did my research before I came.'

'And they've been struggling ever since?'

'I suppose. There's no evidence of any money here, is there? The house has been left to rot and the sale of the contents must be to pay for the passages over to India.'

'If Lily had made a good marriage, she might have been able to help the family fortunes. She wouldn't have been the first woman to have exchanged her freedom for a pot of money to help her family. I wonder why she never married.'

'She's no beauty like her mother but by no means unattractive. Perhaps she was unlucky in love.' George wrinkled his nose. 'The smell is terrible. Let's get out of here.' He pulled the door to with a crack and I heard a piece of wall dislodge.

Chapter Forty-Four

25 June 1896
5.03 p.m.

Lily marvelled at her mother's fury, so different from her languid mood earlier that day. She should have remembered how impossible it was to keep anything secret in the house. Recently, she'd read a book where the heroine had prised open a floorboard in the corner of her room and placed her love letters from the groom's son in the space. They'd remained undiscovered until long after the girl had died from a riding accident.

Lily hadn't been so fortunate in her choice of hiding places. The space where her deep mattress met the metal springs had seemed a good idea at the time. Her bed sheets had recently been changed and it would be at least a week before one of the chambermaids would be rooting around there again. She'd forgotten, however, about Helene's ability to wheedle out any secret she might try to keep, however minor.

The bundle of letters, tied with an emerald-green ribbon, now sat between them on the table. Her father had gone out that morning, off to another sale, Lily suspected, and the closed door meant the servants wouldn't come anywhere near them while Helene's fury raged.

'How long have you been seeing Samuel?'

'I've seen him since I was a child.'

Helene crossed to Lily and slapped her. The act of violence shocked her, but Helene's half-smile contained a sense of satisfaction.

'I've read your letters. You're meeting him again. How long has it been going on?'

'A few months.'

'How many? Two? Eight?'

'Since Christmas.'

'Six months? And why didn't you tell me about it?'

'Because I knew you'd behave like this. If it's not about you, then it can't be about me.'

Lily thought that her mother would strike her again but instead she picked up the letters.

'Remember what happened the last time you two got close? Or have you forgotten so easily?'

Now, Lily thought, it was she who might strike her mother, but she swallowed. 'I remember. Can I have my letters back?'

Her mother pretended she hadn't heard her. 'It's too hot for a fire in here; I'll get Jessop to add them to the bonfire in the garden.'

'Jessop? Then he'll know my secret.'

'He'll be discreet. He always is. You're not to see Samuel again. Do you hear me? Leave Sir Thomas's son alone.'

Her face still stinging from Helene's slap, Lily wove through the cypress trees, making her way towards the walled garden. Bending her head she went through the arched gate and entered the little churchyard, making her way around the cool wall until she stood on the threshold of Sir Thomas's estate. Samuel was waiting for her, his fair hair wet; perhaps he'd been for a swim in the sea before meeting her. She felt a disagreeable pang as she wondered who he had been with. He turned and smiled at her with the ease of someone who cares little about the response.

'My Lily.'

'Mama has found your letters.'

'Again?'

At the thought of the former time, Lily felt a deep shame at Helene reading her most intimate thoughts.

'I've been told not to meet you again.'

He flushed, more with embarrassment at her upset than from any deep feeling. She sensed his agitation, his desire to be anywhere else than with her. She was well aware that the teasing phrases in his letter might as easily have been directed towards any other girl he was idling with. Blast him, she thought. He could at least try to look sorry.

'Papa is looking at us going to the Lakes for August. Mama doesn't like the heat, as you know, and it will be cooler there.' Samuel kicked a stone, the flint spinning into the air.

'Can't you persuade him to change his mind?'

Samuel looked away. 'It really is for the best.'

'He's coming to the séance tonight. Perhaps I'll try to persuade him then.'

Samuel's tension was etched in his face as he turned to her. 'I really don't think that's a good idea.'

'You cared last time.' She watched him as she spoke. 'You cared when we were forced to stop meeting.'

He took a step forward and she shrank from the dislike in his expression. 'Do you want to know what I discovered today?'

'What do you mean?'

He grabbed her wrist. 'Let me tell you what somebody finally thought worth mentioning.'

Chapter Forty-Five

We buried Ada the following day. Felix got his way, of course. I'd begun to think of him as a man who, despite his relaxed manner, usually achieved what he wanted. The parish church was a fine flint building with a square tower topped by a squat, pyramid-style roof. Inside it was surprisingly plain, none of the ornate Victorian furniture that had invaded many of the churches of my childhood. I spotted three faded wall paintings around the chancel and one I recognised as the martyrdom of St Thomas à Becket, with a knight about to strike the archbishop at the altar. The second was harder to distinguish, although I thought I could make out a huge set of weighing scales. George saw me looking at it.

'St Michael weighing the souls of the departed,' he whispered.

We made a strange crowd, sitting in that bare church in clothes cobbled together for the occasion. Helene was in full mourning, wearing a dress in the modern style, her head covered by a veil. Lily had contented herself with a black suit, a little old-fashioned, worn with a cloche hat. Alice, who sat a little away from us, looked as if she had just removed her apron for the service. George was in a suit not quite right for the occasion, which made me feel better in my shabby work skirt and a coat borrowed from Lily. Neither Quinlivan nor Janet made an appearance, although I wasn't sure if they had made a joint decision to forego the ceremony or each, for their own reason, had decided not to come.

There was a mourner at the back of the church. A woman in her late forties, plump and bound up in a coat too tight for her. I turned and gave her a smile before the service started led by a young and disapproving priest. He'd no doubt been told the occupation of the person he was burying that afternoon, but gamely intoned the burial rites of the Book of Common Prayer. Afterwards, we trooped out to see Ada buried in sight of Clewer Hall. When the verger opened the door, a gust of wind brought in a few flakes of snow but it was too mild to settle onto the existing layer. I looked at the hard ground and then away again. It wasn't a place I'd have chosen, and I thought Ada might have had something to say about it too.

Instead of joining the family back at the house, I returned to the church to gather my thoughts and snatch a few precious moments of silence. I hadn't liked to look around during the service but sitting in a pew near the back of the church, I could see the names of the three Clewer sons at the top of the marble memorial and their respective death dates: 1914, 1916 and 1918.

After my back began to ache, I wandered around the church, taking in the faint smell of incense which intermingled with the smell of rot, reminding me of Clewer Hall. I inspected the nave, looking at the carved choir stalls, each with a head jutting out from the wood. One of them depicted a Red Indian, a man dressed with a plume of feathers lying flat upon his head. What had Ada called her spirit guide? Black Hawk, that was it, someone she was familiar with and trusted. It must be mere coincidence that here he was, represented in a place of worship. Well, Black Hawk had told her there would be a disaster that evening and he had been right.

I turned at a noise and saw the stranger at the funeral had come back into the church, driven in by the snow I supposed. I went to pass her to leave her in peace but she stopped me.

'You're family?'

I shook my head. 'Just a guest of the Clewers.'

'But you knew Ada?'

'Only a short while. Were you friends?'

'Not friends, no. I read about her death in the paper and I thought I'd come along today. I expected more people.'

'It was a while since you'd seen her?'

'Over twenty years, I'd say. Nearer thirty.'

She had a curious accent, part Sussex overlaid with a faint London drawl.

'Can I join you?' I took the pew opposite and twisted around to speak to her, not easy in my condition. 'You've travelled down from London?'

'Yes, but it's not a hard journey.'

I thought of Edwin's complaints that morning. No, it wasn't a difficult trip to make if you cared about the person at the other end. A thought occurred to me.

'Are you family? We still have some of Ada's things.'

'Oh, no.' The woman laughed. 'I'm one of the villagers. Or I was. I met Ada when she visited the Hall that first time. I was one of the parlourmaids.'

'Then you'll remember Alice. Did she recognise you?'

'I wrote to Alice after I read of the death. She told me the date of the funeral. She's offered me tea in the kitchen, but I'll not be going. I've heard the house isn't what it once was and, anyway, it's hard to go back to something you've left behind, isn't it?'

'Yes, yes it is. Do you have family left in the village?'

She shook her head.

'Then you're returning to London tonight?'

'I'm taking the four o'clock bus. I'm a little early, so I thought I'd wait in here.'

I'd have liked to leave this frigid church with its centuries of tears, but I sensed this woman had come to Ada's funeral for more than old times' sake.

'Do you work now?'

She nodded. 'My husband's a butcher in Camden.'

'Camden. That's not far from me at all.'

She smiled, looking at her hands. 'What was she like, Ada? At the end?'

I paused, wanting to do Ada justice. 'A little impoverished, dignified. Still working as a medium.'

'Oh, yes, the séance. The family were terribly upset after that first time, you know. I had to stay up, you see, to clear the Adelaide Room. People think parlourmaids had it easy. No laundry, no slops like the chambermaids had to deal with. But they were late hours. We had to wait up until all the downstairs rooms were clear, then tidy up for the morning.'

'When were you at the Hall? I'm sorry, I don't know your name.'

'I'm Gladys, although everyone calls me Glad. I arrived in early 1896 when I was fourteen.'

I thought of Lizzie, Janet's sister. 'It must have been a daunting place if you were so young.'

'The family liked to take village girls and we knew, growing up, there was always a place for us in Clewer Hall if you were respectable. It wasn't so bad going there.'

'You liked it?'

Gladys shrugged. 'It was hard days. I was glad to leave at nineteen and marry my Fred. He was down here on a day trip to Brighton and we met near the pier.'

'You like Camden?'

She brightened. 'Oh yes.'

'But you came for Ada's funeral?'

She looked away and I could see the tip of her nose was red from the cold. I waited for her to speak. She needed no prompting, just a little time to get her story out.

'The newspaper article got me thinking about the Hall and the days after the séance. It was a funny time, and I thought I'd forgotten all about it. But seeing her picture – it must have been an old one they used, because she looked exactly the same as I remembered her – got me thinking of the past.'

My back had begun to seize up in the cold. Although Gladys didn't notice, the vicar stuck his head through the door but withdrew when he saw us talking, leaving behind a blast of icy air. I pulled my coat tighter and turned my attention back to Gladys.

'We put her in the little sitting room in the east wing when she arrived. It was where the seamstress used to go, so a room not used by family but not a servants' place.'

'I understand. The room's now closed off.'

Gladys nodded. 'I'd only recently started at the Hall so they didn't give me one of the main rooms to look after, just some of the smaller ones in the east wing. I waited on Ada that day, bringing her tea and biscuits and then a spot of dinner before the séance.'

'She didn't eat with the family?'

'Oh no.' Gladys looked shocked. 'She wasn't of their class.'

Ada had inveigled herself into the family circle by the time she died, but times had changed in the last thirty years.

'I made a mistake.' Gladys shivered, finally feeling the cold. 'I told her my mother had second sight. She wasn't much interested but I thought it might show that I was on her side. You know, not all the servants were happy about her being there. Alice was fair steaming and gave Ada the cheap water biscuits she normally reserved for the coalman.'

'So you told Ada that your mother had second sight. And how did she react?'

'A bit bristly. She wasn't very happy. But she kept asking me about the family and how I was a good girl and I must know some things about the Clewers.'

I kept my expression fixed. No doubt Gladys would have told her all manner of things about the family . . .

'They're an interesting family. I'm sure what you passed on was innocent enough.'

I paused. A flush of colour had crept up her face and was staining her jaw and the tops of her cheeks.

'Did you tell her about the ghost child?'

She looked at me. 'You've seen him?'

'I've heard the story.'

Gladys's eyes dropped to my stomach and she looked suddenly tired. 'I thought he'd been forgotten about.'

'Did you tell Ada?'

'Oh no. She'd already mocked my talk of second sight, so I was hardly going to tell her about a ghost that only ever appeared to the servants and visitors.'

'But you told her something.'

'She was persistent.' Shame radiated off Gladys, causing me to hold my breath. I waited, to the sound of the cheep of a bird settling in the bell tower.

'Ada was good at wheedling out secrets. It was a long time ago, Gladys.'

She pulled up the collar of her coat. 'I told her about something that was talked about late at night by the older servants. They always shut up when I came in, but I heard it in dribs and drabs and found out soon enough what they were talking about.'

'And what was that?' I leant forward and Gladys's voice dropped to a whisper.

'It was a story about Noah, a boy that once belonged to Jessop the gardener.'

Chapter Forty-Six

The church was still, the bird had flown off and there was only the rattle of loose slates above us to interrupt Gladys's story. There was already more colour in her cheeks, as if the anticipation of telling the tale was a cathartic act, shedding years of guilt and worry. My back was in agony from twisting to speak to her, so I went to join her on the pew; in any case, I thought the story might be better told with someone next to her, rather than her being observed across a chilly aisle.

Gladys took her time to begin. 'When I started at the Hall, it began as a joke with one of the grooms. When I'd go outside, he'd say, "Watch out for the spooky child", but back then the Hall wasn't like it is now. It was well-cared-for and there wasn't anything to be scared of. I went about my business and never saw a thing.'

'Did the other housemaids mention anything?'

Gladys thought and shook her head. 'I don't think so, but it was common knowledge: a ghost child that some had seen but no one knew who he was. The thing was, behind the story of this supernatural boy, there was another tale that was told.'

'About Noah?'

'Exactly. Us servants knew our place. Amongst us girls, at the bottom was the scullery maid who had her hands in sudsy water from morning to night. Then it was kitchen maid, parlourmaid, chambermaid and then Daisy, Mrs Clewer's lady's maid. At the top was the housekeeper and cook, although they were both a bit apart. They were older, too.'

'So many staff. And I suppose there was a similar hierarchy for the men?'

'Exactly, and every evening, as we were winding down, the seniors as I called them would sit down and have a cup of tea and a chat together. Mrs Perry the housekeeper, Alice and Horwick. It was common knowledge you weren't to disturb them unless it was urgent, and you weren't to listen in.'

'But as you passed, you'd be able to overhear the conversation?'

'Of course we could. But funnily enough we never discussed it amongst ourselves. It was as if that part of the day was allowed to them and if, for example, the mistress wanted something which really Mrs Perry should sort out, one of us girls did it.'

'And you heard a story about the Jessops?' I prompted.

'There was one tale that they spoke of, only in fragments, and it involved Mr and Mrs Jessop's child. They'd had a baby, only the one, and he'd been a sickly child and had died recently. Perhaps that accounted for their personalities. Old Tom was plain miserable and his wife no better. She was in charge of the laundry, sharp-tongued and forever complaining about her work.'

'They weren't popular?'

'People kept out of their way, but I always felt sorry for Mrs Jessop after I heard that and tried to be kind to her, even when she was sharp with me for mess on the tablecloths that I hadn't made. She'd lost a child, and that was enough for me to be sorry for her.'

'And they used to talk about this around the table?'

'They did. Enid Jessop wouldn't have heard, as she lived in the cottage with Tom. The laundry was done in the morning and hung out to dry in the afternoon, so she'd be gone by evening. Us parlourmaids knew to soak any tablecloth stains in salt or borax. The thing was, whenever they talked of the Jessops, there were a lot of knowing looks. You know the type I mean. Then one day, I was in the laundry room. I'd upset a cup of coffee down my apron so I had to change into my spare one, and I wanted to soak the cotton in the sink so the mark didn't stain. I don't think they realised I was in the room, but they talked about a place in Torquay and a baby being born.'

'Torquay?'

'That was the place, I'm sure. A baby was born and brought back to Clewer Hall for the Jessops. That's what they said. *For* the Jessops. I was interested, now, so I held my breath and listened. They were talking about the Jessops and how it was ridiculous as the child looked nothing like them and, anyhow, they'd tried to have children in the past and nothing had come of it.'

A cold shiver began at the bottom of my spine, spreading up my chest.

'When was this?'

'They were mulling it over as if it had recently happened. The boy had died at four years of age and it must have been just before I arrived, because cook was still upset as she liked the boy.'

I frowned, trying to make sense of the story. 'A child was born in Torquay and brought back to Clewer Hall to be given to the Jessops?'

'Yes, and the thing is, Miss Lily and her mother went to Torquay each year.' Gladys leant back in her seat, her eyes on the wall painting. 'I used to mull it over in bed. Miss Lily and her mother going to Torquay each year for the summer season, and the Jessops unexpectedly having a child which had since died.'

'And you told this to Ada?'

'I wanted to impress her, you see, with something I knew about the family, although I didn't know all the facts.'

'And did you tell the servants afterwards that you'd told Ada this?'

'Not Alice or Mrs Perry – perhaps just one of the other parlourmaids.' She looked at me with an appeal in her eyes. 'Do you
think it made any difference?'

Chapter Forty-Seven

I was pretty sure Gladys's revelation had made a difference. In 1896, she had revealed the existence of the child to Ada – who had milked the knowledge in the subsequent séance and spiced things up by revealing a curse. I didn't blame Ada for that. Like me, she had probably experienced the malevolence of the Hall and the condescension of the family. She was a show-woman and had put on a spectacle for the family. On Wednesday evening she had gone one step further and announced to the company that four sons had died. The three Clewer boys and Noah. She had kept that one card up her sleeve and announced her knowledge to the assembled company that night; a final revelation to seal her reputation as a communicator of the spirits.

What I couldn't fathom was how that might have contributed to her death, but I was sure the secret of Noah's death was key to why Ada lay bleeding on the icy ground after her revelations. It had stirred up old wounds, and whoever had felled her had been determined she would never leave Clewer Hall.

I walked with Gladys so she could catch her bus, trying to make sense of what she'd told me. She prattled on next to me, glad, I think, to be returning to London. I used the servants' entrance when I returned to Clewer Hall. In the kitchen, Alice was standing by the range. When she saw me, she slipped a small box behind a jar on the mantelpiece. I saw that she'd been crying, as on the night of Ada's death.

'Can I do anything to help?'

She dabbed at her eyes with the corner of her apron. 'I'll be started on dinner shortly. How are you feeling after the funeral?'

'Better. Much better, in fact. I ate something which disagreed with me yesterday evening.'

My words didn't have the calming effect I'd anticipated, causing Alice to well up once more.

'What's the matter?'

Alice shook her head and took a copper stockpot from a shelf. I watched her throw bones into the pot and fill the pan with cold water. In the distance came the faint sound of horses hooves labouring up the drive. Alice wiped her hands on a cloth.

'Keep an eye on the pot while it boils, will you, Louisa? I can hear the delivery boy outside.'

As soon as she'd left, I retrieved the box from behind the jar. It was no bigger than a soap dish, with a label which read, TOWLE'S PENNYROYAL AND STEEL PILLS FOR FEMALES. I opened the box which had one pill left in it and looked at the accompanying circle of paper.

Woman's unfailing friend Towle's Pills for females are the Oldest, Safest and only Reliable Remedy for all Ladies' Ailments. Quickly correct all Irregularities, remove all Obstructions, and relieve the Distressing Symptoms so prevalent with the sex.

I had come across these pills before. They were to ease the symptoms of irregular menses in women, I remembered, and in the days when diet was poor, even amongst the gentry, women bled much less – a problem if a woman wanted to conceive. I studied the text more closely. *Remove all obstructions.* My hand began to shake as I realised the significance of those words. Towle's pills were shrouded in the language of the last century but the meaning was clear: the tablets were of a type to induce miscarriage. A woman in the past must have used this medicine for either a menstrual problem or had attempted to rid themselves of a child. In either case, they would be seriously dangerous if I ingested them.

I remembered the foul tea and the sensation of dislocation I'd felt since I'd arrived. Were these pills the culprit, and had Alice guessed? I placed the box back on the shelf just as Alice brought the delivery boy into the kitchen and began a negotiation for the following week's supplies. I dithered, wondering whether to confront the cook once the boy was gone, but remembered her loyalty to the Clewer family. If one of them was responsible, she was hardly likely to reveal the culprit. Even worse – there was the possibility that she too had a hand in the appearance of the pills.

I hid my face so she wouldn't see my panic and slipped out of the kitchen, making a rapid calculation of the chances of completing my assignment tomorrow, for I could no longer stay here. It wasn't me that was at risk; it was my baby.

Chapter Forty-Eight

Felix, Helene and Lily left for church the following day. I was surprised at Felix accompanying the women but perhaps, given Ada's death, he thought it would look better to be seen supporting the family, which must now surely be the focus of gossip in the village. After they had gone, I made some tea straight from the kettle on the range – which I'd filled myself – and sawed a hunk of bread from a loaf I found in the pantry, the first food I'd taken since my discovery of the pills. Retrieving my photographic equipment from my room, I counted the number of plates I had left and resolved to get everything finished that day. Tomorrow I would leave Clewer Hall.

The house was subdued but not asleep. The baby shifted, its little limbs occasionally pushing against my belly as if in response to my voice, proving to me, at least, that he or she was unharmed. I began by taking a photograph of an ebonised cabinet-on-stand, painted with scenes of the Old Testament. It was placed in a bedroom which I suspected had once belonged to one of the Clewer sons. Over on a mahogany tripod table was a collection of photos. The first was of a boy dressed in boating clothes, which consisted of a woollen jumper and pale striped linen trousers. There was a hand reaching out to him in the punt, but the photo had been cut so just the boy remained, laughing up at the unseen person. In the second photo, the same boy – I could tell by a small birthmark on the side of his face by his eyebrow – was in his twenties and dressed in uniform, his expression sombre.

Feeling like a thief, I opened the drawer of the cabinet and began rifling through the contents. There was precious little to reveal the personality of the dead boy. Some postcards, a small flute and a magnifying glass.

'Find anything?'

I slammed the drawer shut, causing the photo to tip and fall face down with a clang.

George was standing in the doorway, watching me as I righted the photo.

'You gave me a shock. Why did you creep up on me like that?'

'I'm sorry. I like the element of surprise. You never know what you're going to catch someone doing. Rifling through Richard Clewer's drawers, for example.'

I laughed, half-ashamed. 'I couldn't resist having a look, although I'm unlikely to find anything of interest.'

George came into the room, taking the photo frame from my hands, checking it for damage. 'You don't think the sons are important?'

'I didn't say that. It's just, they're gone, aren't they?'

'But their lives are more than how they died, surely? Each boy had an individual personality, different hopes and dreams, all now vanished. Take Richard — what do you notice about the photo?' He turned the frame towards me.

'That it's been cut to remove the other person in the image.'

'Not cut, folded.'

I watched as he took the back off the frame. He opened out the photo and I saw the other arm belonged to a boy in his twenties, similar in age to Richard in the second photo. He'd adopted a mirror position, gazing down at his friend, laughing back at him.

'They must have been close,' I said, handing back the photo. 'I wonder why they bent the photo over?'

George took the photo back, smiling slightly. 'Close, yes. As I said, every person in this family has a story. Richard's, although interesting, is almost certainly lost to time. What we know of him will be what the family choose to remember. Hence the folded photo.'

I gathered up my camera, refusing his offer of help, and made to move onto the next room.

'Going to search that one too?'

'It's now or never.' I was still cross at him but found I couldn't remain angry for long in his presence.

George frowned. 'What do you mean?'

'I'm leaving tomorrow as well. This is no place for me.' I took a deep breath. 'I would like, before I go, to find out what happened to Ada – but it will not be at the expense of my child.'

'What's the matter?' George pushed the door shut. 'Tell me.'

I felt the blood rush to my face at the memory of the previous evening. 'I found some pills. They're for a variety of women's ailments and would certainly not be safe for me to take. The box, although old, upset Alice, and I've been sick, as you know. If someone is trying to poison me, I can't stay.'

'But it's an old box, you say? The pills weren't purchased recently, which means they were acquired for someone else.'

'You think I'm ridiculous, leaving?'

'Of course not. If it wasn't Sunday, I'd say you should leave today.'

'This way, I can finish my assignment before I go.' I paused. 'And I am going to search the upstairs rooms while the family are at church.'

'And what exactly are you hoping to discover?'

'I'm looking for evidence of the fourth son.'

He frowned. 'Ada's words from the séance. You think she was telling the truth?'

'There's something I need to tell you.'

I sat on the bed and told him the story Gladys had revealed in the freezing church. About a child of the Jessops arriving when they were older and perhaps past bearing their own children. A child which arrived while Helene and Lily were holidaying in Torquay. He sat in total absorption as I laid out the mystery to him, every sense on alert. When I'd finished speaking, he sat on the bed beside me, a gesture devoid of any sexual overtones.

'You're right, we must search the bedrooms. The discovery of those pills might be significant. There was not only an unwanted child but efforts were made by the mother to rid herself of him before he was born.'

'Lily?'

'Possibly.'

'And you think it important in relation to Ada's death?'

'It certainly looks that way. The only solution is, as you suggest, to start searching for clues.' I saw him smile. 'The intrepid detectives. Would you like a Watson to your Sherlock?' He put his arm around my shoulder.

I pretended to consider, glad that I would have company after the discovery of those pills. I pointed at the door. 'Lead on.'

Chapter Forty-Nine

George had already discovered which room each of the Clewer boys had slept in. Richard in the north-east chamber where I'd just taken my plate, Cecil in the one adjacent to it and the eldest, Archie, in the south-east bedroom opposite Ada's. I let George carry my camera and plates between each room. We needed the equipment so we'd have a legitimate excuse if we were caught. While I set up the shots, George searched through the room, rifling through drawers, looking inside and behind wardrobes and under beds.

To my surprise, the bedrooms weren't shrines to the dead young men. Each had been cleared of the boys' clothing, despatched perhaps to some charitable cause. As in Richard's chamber, there were photos of Archie and Cecil displayed in a prominent place in their rooms to mark their territory. Archie's showed him as a very young boy and in uniform. Of Cecil, there were only photos of him as a child. Perhaps the idea of him in a sailor's uniform was too distressing, as slow death by drowning is surely terrible to contemplate.

I lingered too long over each of the images, George growing impatient. 'There's nothing to be found here. Let's move to the women's rooms, starting with Lily's. She's the most likely to have birthed an illegitimate child. Any son of Helene's could simply be passed off as legitimate offspring.'

'Unless, for example, she and Felix weren't sleeping together?'

I could feel a blush rising on my face as we discussed the intimate details of my hosts. 'In that case, a pregnancy would be impossible to explain away.'

George frowned. 'Would the dates fit? Gladys's assertion is that Helene and Lily went to Torquay every year. Did she say what year the child was born?'

'She arrived not long before Ada first came to the house and she thought the child's death was a recent event.'

'Do we know how old Lily is?'

'Late forties, I would say. Which would have made her nineteen or twenty when the séance took place and around fourteen or fifteen when the child was born. Gladys said the boy was aged about four when he died.'

'Do you think it possible?'

I almost laughed. 'Girls can certainly have children at fourteen. If the child given to the Jessops was born when Lily was fourteen or fifteen, then Helene would have been in her late thirties or early forties. Helene could also be the child's mother.'

I could see him weighing up the possibility. 'I wonder who the father was. A guest here, perhaps. When my father came down, the Clewers had a reputation as one of *the* places to go for the long weekend – tennis parties, dances, that sort of thing. There would have been plenty of guests coming in and out of the house.'

'We're unlikely to guess the child's paternity. It's the mother we need to discover.' A sobering thought came to me. 'Perhaps she had no say in the conception.'

George groaned. 'The plot thickens. Horwick was around at that time but he's now left, so I've lost an opportunity to question him. What about Alice?'

'She was here, too, I think, but she's very protective of the Clewers. Look at her attempt to hide the box of pills.'

George began pacing around the room. 'We need to be careful who we speak to. How much time do we have?' George looked at his watch. 'I don't believe it. This thing has stopped again.'

'Let me look at it.'

Irritated, he shrugged me off. I pulled up the sleeve of my jacket to check the time according to my watch. I had wound it before going to bed and had heard it ticking when I'd fastened it on my wrist that morning. When I looked at the dial, however, the hands were still. The time said twenty past five, although it was not yet gone midday.

'What time does your watch say?' I asked George.

'What does it matter?'

'What time?' I repeated, my voice rising.

With a sigh, he looked at his wrist. 'It says twenty minutes past five.'

'But mine says the same!'

'Show me.'

He pulled my arm towards him and I could feel his breath against my skin as he lifted my arm.

'Someone's playing tricks on us. Let's not lose sight of what we need to do while the family are at church. I know which is Helene's room, I saw her come out of it this morning. We'll start there.'

With a final glance at my wrist, I followed him through a door at the end of the passage which gave onto a feminine room where the dark panelling present in the rest of the house had been painted white. A canopied bed with floral curtains sat in the centre of the room and next to it I spotted a redundant bell rope and suppressed the urge to give it a sharp tug. Despite the luxury of the furnishings, the room was bitterly cold, the freezing air squeezing inside through a cracked window. I could smell

Helene's perfume, a heavy floral scent which hung in the air as I opened a chest of drawers.

'It feels more fitting if I go through her underclothes. Why don't you look in the wardrobe?'

My hands grazed cotton and linen underwear, all beautifully made. 'There's nothing here.'

'Nor here.' He looked around. 'She doesn't even have any mementoes of her sons. I wonder why not.'

'Perhaps she spends time in their rooms. She can see their images there. What's this?'

I opened a door next to the bed and saw the edge of the bath. 'Surely this isn't the sole bathroom, accessible only through Helene's room?'

George glanced at me. 'There's a door which leads onto the passageway, too. You just have to ensure both doors are locked when you wash. We should try the door at the end of the passage. It's the only room on this side we've not been in, with the exception of mine. It must be Lily's.'

Lily's bedroom was like her mother's, though less elegantly furnished and without the trace of expensive perfume. On a burr walnut chest of drawers, there was a photo of her three brothers larking around for the camera. I showed it to George. He took the photo out of my hands, studied it for a moment, and pulled the back off the frame.

'George!'

'It's an old trick. Did you see how the photo didn't sit properly in the frame? It's one of the places where people hide their secrets.'

'I've never had anything to hide.'

He looked up at me and back down quickly. As the back of the photo came away in his hands, a much smaller image, tucked in behind the larger one, was visible. I watched him peel away the photo and look at it.

'I think we've found your child.'

I took it off him and stared at the boy before turning the print over and reading the name printed on the back. NOAH.

Chapter Fifty

The boy in the photo was dead. I would have been able to tell, even if the pose hadn't been that of a carefully staged memento mori image. I'd never had to take such a picture. Such things held no appeal for me and fortunately, by the time I'd begun to take my own photographs, the Victorian tradition of capturing dead relatives to produce a keepsake had died out. What I had of my boys was locks of their hair, kept in an envelope, some photos of them as babies, and a treasure trove of memories.

Noah had been placed on a quilted blanket which lay on a piece of furniture I recognised – the chaise longue in the sitting room, a highly decorative seat which I'd never seen any member of the family use. The little boy was dressed in a long nightgown, embroidered at the neck and sleeves, and probably used as a shroud. His eyes were shut. Whoever had taken the photograph hadn't submitted the child to the indignity of painting artificial pupils onto the boy's eyelids, but his arms were crossed, as Ada's had been, in the familiar pose of the dead.

'I've heard about these but never seen one,' said George, taking back the photo of the child. He turned it over, ever curious and read the name on the back.

'Noah. What was the Jessops' child called?'

'The same.'

'And Lily has hidden it here beside the photo of her dead brothers. Her child?'

'It looks that way. I wonder who took it? It's not an amateur image.' I inspected the back of the print but there was no photographer's mark. Brighton was near enough. Perhaps a professional had been paid to come to the Hall from the town. This, however, suggested complicity from both family and servants as this wasn't a rushed or secretive image and would have taken time to set up and photograph.

'We need to put the photograph back,' I said, 'so Lily doesn't know we have discovered it. I am going to take a duplicate of it first.'

'What on earth for?'

'We can't come back here, can we? I want proof of the Clewers' connection to Noah, and this is it. Give me a moment.'

George crossed to the window, looking at the tower of the church. As I put a plate in the camera, steadying my hands for the shot, he remarked, 'The image is Victorian, but that's all we know. It's impossible to date it more precisely. We need to discover when Noah was born and also when he died. Do you know where he's buried?'

'Gladys didn't say.'

'If he's a village boy, he must be in the churchyard. There's a Methodist chapel in the village but it's without a cemetery. I checked with Janet earlier when I asked about Ada's funeral arrangements. He'll be in a grave at St Peter's if someone cared enough to take a photo of him.'

As I replaced my camera and plates in my room, before following George out of the house, I felt malevolence pour from the walls. The room darkened and the smell of rot intensified, making me want to retch. I was tired of making excuses for these episodes. I had never been mistaken. The house was unhappy about the discovery of the identity of Noah.

*

In the cemetery we passed Ada's grave, which lay alongside the back wall. The Clewer family's sparse flowers were still there, wilting alongside the bunch of snowdrops I'd picked from the hedgerow. George, at last noticing that I was out of breath, pointed at a wooden bench.

'You sit there. The ground is uneven amongst the headstones and you're likely to fall if you try to help me. The churchyard isn't large, so if the grave's here, I should find it easily.'

I watched his tall figure roam between the graves, checking each headstone before moving on.

'Jessop is a village name. What were the parents called?'

'Old Jessop and Mrs Jessop.'

I could hear him laughing. 'That's very helpful, thank you.'

I thought for a moment. 'I think he was Tom and her name was Enid, or perhaps Edith.'

George paused at a small gravestone to trace a name which had become indistinct from exposure to the elements, stretching down to clear away moss and lichen.

'Have you found it?'

'It might be what we're looking for. The inscriptions are just initials. No other information, not even a date.'

'Initials?'

'N. J.'

'Let me see.'

'Be careful.' He came towards me and stretched out his hand then led me to a small, square stone, carved with the two initials, sandwiched in between two full-sized headstones bearing unfamiliar names.

'You think it's him?'

'It's not a pauper's grave but neither is it the one of a wealthy family. It's the sort of thing I'd expect servants or the poorer classes to pay for.'

'If he was a Clewer son, surely the Jessops would have expected a handout? Remember, the boy was dressed in finery for his memento mori photo.'

George shook his head. 'That's easy to disguise once he's in the coffin. If he was placed in a wealthy grave, it would have given rise to speculation.'

'But this is so sparse. Even the child of respected servants might have expected more.'

'There didn't need to be any more details. Whoever the child's real mother is, she knows where he is.'

We looked down at the small bunch of early crocuses left on the grave.

'He's hardly been forgotten, has he?' said George.

'So what's the connection to Ada's death? One of the women, probably Lily, had an unwanted child and Ada discovered the secret from Gladys. If Lily had the child in Torquay while Helene was with her, both women would have been aware that Ada knew something during the séance of 1896. Can you remember exactly what was said?'

'According to my father's transcription, it was something along the lines of "a child here today, gone tomorrow".'

'Which fits exactly with the story of Noah.' I shook my head. 'So why was Ada allowed to return to the house, time and time again?'

'Helene wanting to commune with her grandchild and her dead sons?'

'At the risk of exposing the child's existence to society? That can't just be it.' I leant back against the yew, inhaling the ancient, pungent scent of the foliage.

'At Wednesday's séance Ada made clear to everyone that there was a fourth child. She was no longer hinting at another child, she was *telling* us there was a fourth Clewer son. It's almost as if she was forcing the issue out into the open. Was Ada trying to save the family and the house by telling us what she knew?'

'But it brought about her death.'

'I know.' I couldn't keep the despair from my voice. 'She over-played her hand. Poor Ada. My time here is nearing its end and I'm afraid I'm not going to find the answers I want.'

Chapter Fifty-One

George left me to see if Quinlivan had a railway timetable he could consult for the times of the train departures the following morning. The temperature had dropped, so I put a jumper on over my cardigan and crammed myself into my Holland jacket, looking, when I spotted myself in a mirror, a little like an over-stuffed child's toy. To keep myself warm, I made a cup of tea with water straight from the chipped kettle on the range. I took two gulps in the kitchen, the tea scalding the roof of my mouth, and carried a top-up with me to the icehouse, the cup rattling on the saucer as I picked my way over the icy ground.

As I developed the plates, the air inside the icehouse stretched thin in the late-afternoon. I'd recently read an account of George Mallory's fatal attempt on Everest, and his team's use of oxygen tanks to counteract the effects of the altitude. I felt the same breathy sensation, even though I could smell the sea that evening a mile or so distant. The only other time I'd felt the same way was when my brother had pushed my head under water in a river near our house. As the unexpected current pulled me away, I'd felt the same heady elasticity of time.

As the moon was nearly full, I left the door slightly ajar as I lit the oil lamp. The cold must have got to the fuel as the flame immediately began to smoke, hitting the back of my throat and causing me to cough. I wasn't confident as I mixed my chemicals, my hand shaking a little, and I had difficulty reading the labels with my stinging eyes. I took my time, aware I was struggling to breathe while my raw throat remained unsoothed by the tea.

Eventually, the developing mixture began to work its magic and each image, although a little fiddly to get right, eventually appeared clearly in negative, even the memento mori of Noah. I was studying this plate when the door of the icehouse opened. I turned with a smile, expecting to see George back from the village, but my heart nearly failed when I saw the ghost of Ada, all black taffeta and rustling petticoats. Or was it her? The smoke had gathered at the entrance to the icehouse, the night air drawing the fug away from me. All I could see through the choking fumes was a woman clothed in black.

'Who's there?'

I moved to extinguish the lamp. Even the moon would give me more illumination than the foul light emitting from the brass lantern. When I looked again, the woman had moved closer, although I still couldn't tell if it was Lily or Helene.

'Do you want something?'

The fear was evident by the tremor in my voice and I saw a gloved hand reaching out for me. I hit away the woman's arm but was seized with a lassitude so great that it was all I could do to open my mouth, although no sound emerged. I groped for the table, missed it and dropped to the ground, my fall broken by the horse blanket on the earthen floor. Then, with a roaring in my ears, everything dimmed.

They all came to me at that moment: Bertie, my boys, Mother and Father and my brother. I would have gladly joined them if they hadn't taken a step backwards as I moved towards them. *Not yet time*, although I could feel joy spreading over me at the knowledge that they were together. Abruptly, another voice broke into my thoughts: the sound of George shouting at me.

'For God's sake, Louisa! Wake up!'

The white smoke had become a foul yellow-brown and I could hear him coughing as he pulled me outside.

'Are you all right?' He had pressed a handkerchief to his mouth and his voice was treacle thick. 'I thought I'd lost you.'

'I'm not sure.' I tried to sit, although I would rather have stayed under the trees as Ada had, fading into the night air.

'There's a foul odour inside that hut. The chemicals have reacted with the heat of the lamp. Stay here while I get as much air in as I can.'

George opened the door and entered the icehouse. I could hear the clink of glass being gathered.

'Is there damage to the plates?' I shouted across to him.

'Don't come inside. One of them has smashed and I need to collect the others to see if any more damage has been done.'

'Where are they?'

'On the floor.'

I'd placed each plate on the drying rack with the exception of the one that I'd been examining when I'd been disturbed. 'Let me see.'

'Don't come inside!' I could hear the ferocity in his voice. 'I'll bring them out to you.' His outline emerged from the icehouse and I saw he, too, was struggling to breathe as he dropped down to the ground next to me. 'Only one is cracked, but the other four are fine.'

'Four? I took six images. There should be six in total.'

'I could see only five. Let me look again.' He disappeared once more into the foul smoke.

'There will be a leather oblong case. The plate might be in there.'

'I have the case, but it's empty.'

'Bring them to me.' I knew, before I even checked, which image would be missing. Still, I checked each plate. The broken one was of a box ottoman in one of the bedrooms. Unimportant, and I wouldn't need to retake it.

'The missing plate is the one of the memento mori. We must have left traces of our presence.'

'Do you mean this wasn't an accident?'

It was like trying to recall a dream as I chased fragments of my memory.

'A woman came into the icehouse. Helene or Lily, I believe, but I don't know which. I'm not sure I could tell at the time.'

'Helene and Lily are very different in manner, although similar in looks.' His wrath was back. 'This damned house. Let me take you inside.'

In my room, he lit the kindling placed in the grate by Janet and added plenty of coal to it. The flames licked up high into the chimney and the bite gradually disappeared from the room.

'We're leaving tomorrow. Helene or Lily has what they want, so they're likely to leave you alone now. It might be as well if you have your dinner in your room, though.'

'I won't take the chance. I'm not eating anything I haven't prepared myself.'

'I'll ask Alice for a tray this evening, too, so I can eat with you. I'll say we have some work to discuss. We can swap trays when they arrive and I'll eat whatever is meant for you. Does your door have a lock?'

I shook my head. 'I wedge a chair under the handle in the evening to give me at least a warning if someone tries to get in.'

'I'm going to speak to Alice now. Put the chair next to the door and only open up when I return.'

He was longer than I expected and I listened in silence for his footsteps to return, examining my bag of developed plates. They were tidy enough, but the top of the case had not been latched properly and this was something I always checked. At last I heard

George's heavy tread at the bottom of the servants' stairs and a loud rap on the door.

'Louisa, it's me.'

I pulled away the chair.

'Alice is bringing us food up here. We'll use that small writing table to eat. What's the matter?'

I pointed to the bag. 'I think some of these plates have gone too.'

'Are you sure?'

'Pretty sure, but I need to check against the inventory.'

We did it together, George reading off the items which had a tick against them and me searching for the plate. Finally, I identified which were missing: two from inside the Adelaide Room, both with the bright light in the corner. Professionally, it was no tragedy. I'd already written off the plates as I was running desperately short of time and wouldn't be able to retake the photos. But the light, I'd thought, might represent the boy and he meant a lot to one of the Clewer women.

'I'll have to accept that the images are lost. You were gone a long time. Is Alice fine with you eating in this room with me?'

'I was distracted by Sir Thomas's dogs in the kitchen. They're handsome beasts and better tempered than their master. He's in the Hall, visiting one of the family.'

'Sir Thomas?' I remembered Lily's aversion to him on the night of the séance. 'He had a son, didn't he?'

'Samuel Jensen. Sir Thomas was most put out you thought he might be a Liberal.' George stretched his legs out in front of him.

'Never mind that. Samuel would be Lily's age, wouldn't he?'

'Samuel?' George drummed his fingers on the bedside table. 'Now that's a thought.'

Chapter Fifty-Two

25 June 1896
2.20 p.m.

Sir Thomas Jensen wasn't to everyone's taste, Helene knew. On her frequent trips to London, Torquay and Buxton, he was the topic of conversation and source of much speculation. Polite society looked to her to add fuel to rumour as they were known to be near neighbours. Sir Thomas had harboured hopes of becoming the parliamentary candidate for Brighton the previous year but had been unexpectedly passed over, putting him in a perpetual foul temper which had only enhanced his ruddy good looks. Marion, his sickly wife, knew the attention her husband drew but appeared unconcerned by it. She lived for games of bridge, her nerve and brain tonic, and the frequent massages and other treatments which she toured the spa towns of the north to enjoy.

The general consensus was that you pitied Lady Marion married to her florid husband, but Helene had long ago decided it was Sir Thomas she felt sorry for, wedded to a perpetual invalid. She knew, of course, she had struck lucky with Felix and should count her blessings, but, since his first trip abroad quite early in their marriage, nothing had been the same, and the first few years of matrimonial harmony were a distant memory.

Sir Thomas's note had come that morning, brought over to the house by his valet and passed onto her through Daisy. His missives, although infrequent, followed the same, terse style. *Meet me at the usual place. Make sure you're not seen.*

It had been harder than anticipated to get away. Preparations for the séance were in full swing and all the guests had arrived. Theoretically, the entire staff should be busy, but each time Helene had stepped out into the garden, either Jessop or one of the other servants had been loitering. Eventually, at half past one, as the staff gathered to eat their communal lunch, she'd managed to slip through the garden unseen.

The usual place alluded to by Sir Thomas was inside the church. No one ever went there on a summer's afternoon, not even the vicar. If, by chance, the door opened, Helene would stay – it would look less unusual her being there – and Sir Thomas would leave by the vestry door. As usual, such plans were unnecessary. They were undisturbed as Helene took the Clewer pew while Sir Thomas hovered by the door. She saw his face and knew at once what the problem was.

'They've been meeting again?' Even as she asked the question, she was aware of the absurdity of condemning her daughter for a secret assignation along the lines of the one she was currently conducting.

'John spotted them in the churchyard and beyond the village near the potter's field.'

At first Helene struggled to recall who John was, then remembered him as the valet who would have brought Daisy Sir Thomas's message to pass onto her mistress. Her second emotion was a grudging admiration for Lily, who had moved beyond the confines of the Clewer estate into an area beyond the village where, theoretically, she should have had more privacy. It was both brave and risky because, if they were spotted, as indeed they had been, there could be few excuses that would explain what they were doing together, unchaperoned, so far from home.

'I'll have to speak to her once more.'

'It didn't do much good last time.'

Helene gritted her teeth, now regretting the effort she'd made in changing her dress for this meeting. 'Samuel bears some responsibility for this, too. Why don't you talk to him?'

'And tell him what? He knows Lily is a respectable girl from a decent family. He doesn't understand why he shouldn't be allowed to see her.'

Helene sighed. Lily was the daughter of a big estate, as was Samuel Jensen. There should be no reason, in the normal course of things, why they should need to keep their romance secret. She looked up at Sir Thomas, still so handsome and, if gossip was to be believed, soon to be a widower.

'Isn't he just dallying with her?'

Sir Thomas's shrug infuriated her but she kept her tone calm.

'Dallying or not, the affair needs to come to an end. You talk to Samuel. There's not much point me trying to persuade Lily if he wears her down with his persistence. It's something you both have in common.'

'I'll speak to Samuel. I'll think of something. But you need to talk to Lily, too. This needs to be stopped. Remember what happened last time?'

'I remember.' Helene drew her shawl around her and tried to stop the cold chill settling on her. 'I'm hardly likely to forget, am I?'

Chapter Fifty-Three

Dinner with George was a wonderfully cheery affair. We didn't talk about the Clewer family. Perhaps he thought I needed a break from our suspicions. Instead, he told me of his family and life in London, including stories from his work, entertaining me with the antics of politicians and public figures. It reminded me that there was more to London than Kentish Town. I had once known this, of course; I had been out amidst the throng, photographing city life, and his tales brought a pang of longing. I was kidding myself, of course. It was much more than that. I didn't want to return to London and never see him again, knowing he was living and working in another part of the city. I was angry that he'd wanted me to go back with Edwin, but I'd have hated it if he'd taken my affection for him for granted. I suspected my feelings for him were reciprocated but there was nothing we could say to each other.

At first, when he'd gone back to his room, I found sleep impossible, but I must have drifted off because I woke at five. I knew the time as I heard the chimes of the church at the bottom of the garden striking the hour. Through the window, the pale light of the near-full moon seeped through a gap in the curtains. As I moved my head to block out the light – turning was pointless, for I could only sleep on my back – I heard the steady tread of feet climbing the stairs. Not the purposeful steps of Alice, making her way to her room at the top of the attic, nor the thumps of

Gideon the tom wandering around the house at night. No, this was the step of someone light on their feet, slowly making their way upstairs.

I'm ashamed to say that fear turned my insides to liquid. I lay in the darkness, praying the footsteps would continue up onto the attic floor, but as they reached the passageway outside my room, I heard the half-familiar sound of the nursery door squeaking on its hinges. Footsteps crossed the room, followed by the sound of an object being dragged across the wooden floor and then the door closing again. I held my breath as the feet took a few steps and stopped just outside my room.

I listened, with my heart fit to burst, as I heard the sound of the door handle turning. My hand groped for the little brass bell that Janet had given to me early on in my stay here, but I knocked it from the table and I heard it clang as it rolled under the bed. It had the effect of bringing me to my senses and I sprang from the bed, knocking over the chair, feeling the splintered wood gouge into my leg, and flinging open the door. The pain in my thigh was unbearable, as if someone was biting me through my nightgown; when I put my hand to the spot, it was slick with my blood.

I pushed the door shut, my mind racing. I had hit my leg on the chair and the wood had splintered, but surely it shouldn't have caused so much blood? The pain reminded me of the bite I'd received that first time in the icehouse, as if I was being attacked by a presence I could not grasp hold of.

I felt as if I were going mad. Where had the rational Louisa disappeared to after ten days in this house? I was about to climb back into bed, nursing my sore leg, when I heard a scream, a cry of pain and a bump and thud as someone fell down the stairs. The abrupt silence was worse than the noises which had come before it and, despite my terror, I flung open the door, limping out into the passageway.

The stairwell was empty. I switched on the light and looked up towards the attic and then down to the ground floor, and beyond it to the basement. There was no one to be seen, injured or not. I pushed open the nursery door, groping for the light switch, until I realised that this was a room where electricity hadn't been connected. The passageway light illuminated the dust on the floorboards and I could see tracks where an object on wheels had been dragged across the room.

Leaving the door wide open to light my way, I crossed to the window. The moon was in full light and there, in the middle of the lawn, was a shadow moving towards the gardener's cottage.

Chapter Fifty-Four

Monday, my final day at Clewer Hall, dawned bright with the sun rising through clouds split with orange tiger stripes. The brightness couldn't dispel the fear I'd experienced the previous night. Alice and Quinlivan brought me up the copper bath from the laundry room and together filled it with hot water, carried up in huge preserving pans. I shielded my leg from them. There was nothing they could do for me now but as I lay in the water, the heat stinging the wound, I remembered my mother telling me to avoid hot baths in my final months in case it brought the baby on early. Another old wives' tale, I thought, but I was aware that the baby had just had a growing spurt and my skin was taut over my stomach. I still had the stretch marks from my other pregnancy – Edwin had made a face when he first saw them – but the red marks were now filled to silver by the baby inside me.

Eventually I heaved myself out and got dressed, then I carried my camera down the main stairs into the central drawing room. Out on the lawn, I took a photo of Clewer Hall. It looked grim, forbidding and utterly cold, but there was no shadow over the east wing to mar the photo this time.

I developed the plate straight away. This was the image which would appear on the front of the brochure and I was anxious to get it right. I steeled myself for what carnage I would have to clear up before I could begin, but the icehouse had been tidied, swept clean of the shards of glass, and my chemicals placed on the table in a neat row. I pulled out the zinc bath and began.

The negative took my breath away. In the clear light, I'd managed to sweep away the death and decay and the house appeared as fresh as when it had been first built. Before I could doubt myself, I poured fixing fluid over the glass and placed it carefully on the rack to dry out.

The icehouse was beginning to close in on me; feeling claustrophobic, I stepped out into the frozen morning and spotted Janet making her way up the drive. She walked with her eyes straight ahead, her expression fixed.

'Hello!'

Perhaps Janet's composure wasn't as deep-rooted as it seemed because she jumped when she heard my shout, relaxing when she saw me with my camera. She crossed the lawn, her neat movements at odds with her haste to speak to me.

'Has anything happened?'

'I wanted you to know that I'm leaving later. Alice and Quinlivan know, but not the family yet. I'm going to try for the evening train.'

'Will you be all right travelling at night?' she asked.

'George might make the journey with me.' I made a face. 'I don't want to spend another evening here.'

'What's happened? I notice you're not eating with the family any longer.'

I hesitated, wondering how much to reveal. It couldn't matter now, on the day of my departure. 'I found a box, Janet. It was nearly empty but Alice was trying to hide it. The tablets inside were for inducing women's menstruation.'

Janet frowned. 'Quack's cure, I'm sure.'

'They were popular herbal remedies in the day – pennyroyal was a common ingredient. When they say induce menstruation, they're actually for ridding yourself of unwanted pregnancies.

And that drug is dangerous for me.'

Janet shrank away from me. 'And you think . . .? Louisa, I'm sure it isn't so. Everyone here is set in their ways, but they don't wish you harm. Talk to Alice. There must be a harmless explanation. Please. Alice will see you right.'

Chapter Fifty-Five

There are various ways to wheedle a secret out of its keeper. One method, popular with my mother, is to use charm, employing clever tricks so that the informer barely knows they've been indiscreet. This would never work with Alice. She had years of loyal service, and an overwhelming desire to protect the Clewer family after the tragedies of the past.

As I walked across the damp lawn, my shoes sinking into the thawing grass, I decided on another strategy. I would confront Alice with what I knew, tell her of my discovery of the memento mori in Lily's room – and hope that she confirmed my suspicions about the role of Samuel Jensen in Noah's conception. If I was lucky, I might then find out why either Helene or Lily had tried to poison me and had followed Ada into the snowy night.

I found Alice in the kitchen writing a letter, a laborious task judging by her pained expression. I took the chair opposite her, watching her hand form the unfamiliar letters.

'I'd like to talk to you about Old Jessop and his wife.'

'Oh, Louisa, don't be bothering about that now. I have this letter to write before lunch.'

'There was a child.'

I saw Alice's hand stall and falter, leaving a blob of thick ink on the paper.

'I've heard about the child from two people. First, Mrs Jessop, who owns the village tea room. She said there was a child. A magpie, she called him.'

'What of it?'

'Then I spoke to Gladys after Ada's funeral. She told me about the Jessops' attempts to have a child. It can't have been easy. Servants often have to forego having children. But you managed it, and so did Tom and Enid Jessop.'

'It was easier for them. They had their own house. My husband and children lived in the village.'

'Easier for them to bring up, perhaps. But not straightforward for them to conceive.' I touched my own stomach. 'Enid had miscarriages. Then Noah arrived.' I paused. 'From Torquay.'

I saw Alice freeze and slowly screw the cap onto her fountain pen.

'And what else did Gladys tell you?'

'About talk in the servants' quarters on the origin of the child.'

'And you've come to some conclusions, have you?'

I saw I would have my work cut out extracting information from Alice.

'I want to talk about Noah.'

'There's nothing to say.'

'I heard he was sickly.'

'All children are at that age. The cottage wouldn't have helped. It's the clay soil – it holds onto water and there's nowhere else for it to go.'

'They didn't think about moving away? There must have been plenty of house jobs going in those days. They didn't think of finding somewhere more suitable for the child?'

Alice opened her mouth then shut it.

'They couldn't, could they? For the past and, come to that, the future of the child was married to this family.'

Alice stood. 'You'll get no gossip from me.' I saw she was resolute and would tell me no more. I tried another tactic.

'Then tell me about Towle's Pennyroyal pills. Who did they belong to?'

Alice's eyes slid to the spot where the packet was still resting.

'Don't you know they're dangerous to pregnant women?'

'Dangerous? But that's what they're for.'

'Only if you want rid of the baby! Who's been putting them in my tea?'

Alice clutched her chest, staggering towards the fire. I ran to help her. 'Hold on, sit here.'

Alice was wheezing. 'My goodness, you've given me a fright. Those pills aren't for you.'

'How can you be sure they haven't been given to me? Every time I've drunk tea, I've been ill.'

'Louisa Drew! You and your active imagination. Those pills are from long ago. The family is beginning to think about their India trip and we are sorting through things. I discovered the medicine and meant to throw it out.'

'But you were crying.' I pulled up a chair next to her and gripped her arms.

'Oh, how you put two and two together to make five. They're a reminder of times I'd rather forget. Can't you leave it be? Let little Noah rest in peace.'

'It's Noah who holds the key to everything. Gladys told me all she could but I know there's more.'

'Gladys? What would be the use of asking her about Noah. He was ten or fifteen years in the past when she arrived.'

'But I thought . . .' I gaped at Alice, trying to make sense of her words.

'Thought what?'

'Gladys gave me the impression that the boy's death happened just before she arrived at the hall.'

'Gladys?' Alice's voice oozed scorn. 'She never knew what day of the week it was. Noah died a long time before she arrived at Clewer Hall.'

Chapter Fifty-Six

As the pieces of the puzzle fell into place, I felt the house breathe out a sigh of putrid satisfaction. Noah wasn't Lily's son, but Helene's. Noah had lived and died long before Gladys arrived at Clewer Hall. I had been nearly there, but my perception was distorted by the discovery of the memento mori in Lily's room. My dismay revived Alice.

'You've got half a story from Gladys, which is no surprise. If it puts your mind at rest, I'll tell you the details, but don't be repeating it to anyone else.'

'Please.' I looked over my shoulder, praying we wouldn't be interrupted.

'Tom Jessop was called Old Jessop long before he was actually old. I guess it was from all the time he spent in the sun, but he was whippet-thin with one of these brown, wrinkled faces. When he met Enid, she was young, only in her twenties, but she had the sour expression of someone much older. They married not long after Colonel and Mrs Clewer and became something of a fixture at the Hall.'

Alice kept her eyes on the flames licking up the chimney.

'In the heyday, there was a lot of linen to wash and Enid was invaluable. Neither the master nor mistress were particularly interested in gardening but you were supposed to have proper flowerbeds. Tea roses and delphiniums, that sort of thing, so Old Jessop had quite a responsibility.'

'I can see there was once a beautiful garden here.'

'The mistress soon got pregnant. Her lady's maid told us that the mistress wasn't easy when she first started to work for her but, funnily enough, whenever she was pregnant she became more tranquil. She relaxed, if that's the right word for it. When Miss Lily was born, there was a nanny employed for her. Then the Colonel got called away to war.'

'What year was this?' I asked.

'I think around 1878.'

'Felix said he'd fought in the Anglo-Afghan war when I first met him,' I said.

'Before he went, he asked Sir Thomas Jensen to keep an eye on his family while he was away. Mrs Clewer's mother was supposed to come down from Derbyshire to stay with them but her husband, a reverend I believe, took ill and she never came. So Mrs Clewer was all alone in the house with baby Lily. And she and Sir Thomas, you know, became . . . close.'

'They had an affair?' I asked, causing Alice to look down.

'Well, yes. And the maid soon noticed that she wasn't tying the stays so tight. The problem was, by the time the mistress was expecting, the Colonel had been gone over eight months, so even if the child had been born early – and there's no guarantee of that, of course – it still couldn't have been the Colonel's.'

'So she went to Torquay?' I asked. 'Gladys mentioned the town.'

'She managed to get that right at least. Yes, she went to Torquay, accompanied by her servant, leaving Lily behind with the nanny. About the same time a new laundry maid arrived to take over from Enid, who had taken ill and gone back to live with her parents in Norfolk to recuperate.'

'Norfolk?'

'Exactly. Then Tom told us that Enid wasn't ill at all but was expecting and she'd return to the Hall when she'd had the baby. Enid had already lost about five babes by then. She could get pregnant, all right, but she couldn't keep them. I think she went back to her family to try to hold onto this one, away from work, away from the Hall.'

'What did Tom have to say about it?'

'He didn't say much at the best of times.'

'So who came back to the Hall first?' asked Louisa.

'Enid, with her little baby, Noah. I was surprised she'd carried the child to nine months; those who keep losing them rarely manage to produce a live baby, but I thought it was God's providence, nothing more.'

'And Helene?'

'About three weeks later, so a decent interval in between, the mistress arrived.'

'And what you're saying is that the Jessops' baby had died back in Norfolk and they took in Helene's child, Noah.'

'That, it seems, is what happened.'

'How did the original child die?'

Alice looked at her apron, shrugging. 'I don't know. She had no luck with children, did Enid Jessop.'

'Was Tom Jessop with her?'

'Oh no. He stayed at Clewer Hall. It was all arranged between Enid and the mistress. I doubt he had any say in it at all.'

'So how did she get hold of Helene's child?'

Exasperated, Alice sat up. 'I don't know everything, Louisa. I assume Enid travelled to Torquay to pick up Helene's baby. The mistress must have found out, somehow, that Enid's baby had died. Perhaps she wrote to the mistress to tell her. The point is, at some time, Enid was given Helene's baby.'

'She must have been desperately sad about her loss, so the news of Helene's illegitimate child would have been a godsend.'

'You might think so, but the child never got any affection off either of the Jessops. They treated it as a cuckoo in the nest, which is what it was. It was the saddest thing I ever saw. Mrs Clewer would have been better giving up the baby to complete strangers.'

'How was Helene with Noah?'

'The servants began to notice that she showed an unusual interest in the child. Some laughed it off, believing that she was desperate for a boy, but it was a stronger affection than that. Then the Colonel came back from the war and everything resumed as normal.'

'Helene would surely have changed?' I said.

'Helene – and the master too, but in different ways. But it was still a happy house, with perhaps a shadow hanging over it.'

'Shadow?' I asked. 'What do you mean by a shadow?'

Her eyebrows rose at my sharpness. 'Just a turn of phrase. On the surface, everything looked the way it had been before, but underneath there was a sense that the world was a bit skewed.'

'And how did Noah die?' I asked.

Alice looked down, ashamed. 'An accident. No one to blame, really. You can't keep your eyes on children all day long.'

'An accident in this house?'

'Of course not! In Old Jessop's cottage.'

'And how did Helene take it?'

'It's difficult to say. Master Archie had arrived by then.'

'A mother never forgets her sons.'

Alice looked down. 'No.'

'If Noah died in the cottage, why is the story that the child haunts the gardens?'

'Stuff and nonsense! I've told you not to take any notice of the rumours. The groom thought he saw Noah a few years after his death, although I never held much truck with the story. Still, it frightened the life out of him – and his wife was about to have a baby, too. Poor little mite didn't survive, sickly thing she was.'

'The child was born in the house?'

'Good gracious, no. In the groom's quarters above the stables, where Quinlivan lives now.'

Still on the Clewer estate, though. No child born in this house since Noah's death had lived into adulthood. Ada had been right about a curse. She had been right about the Clewer family. For a moment, the room stilled, the only sound the tap of the forsythia bush against the window.

'The night of Ada's death, you saw me leave through this door. Do you remember? You gave me a flashlight to help me find my way. After I'd left, did one of the family come in through that door? Or Sir Thomas, perhaps?'

'I saw no one.'

I slumped. 'Then I'm never going to get to the bottom of what happened to Ada.'

Alice sniffed, rising to her feet. 'Ada's best left in peace, Louisa. She brought nothing but trouble on this family, full of tricks and suchlike.'

She was, I knew, a complicated person; but I began to think that it was Ada who was the catalyst for everything. She thought I'd be the catalyst for change but it was, in fact, her.

Chapter Fifty-Seven

25 June 1896
1.31 p.m.

Ada shifted in the trap, her legs stiff from the lengthy journey. The June afternoon air had been graveyard-still when the morose man had tapped the horse into a trot with the tip of his whip after picking her up from her room in Croydon, and the wooden bench, two painted slats spanning the trap, were hard on her rump. She was forced to bite her lip in agony as they covered the endless miles of the new macadam road.

As town gave way to open countryside, she tried to make conversation with the driver. Fletcher, the letter had called him, but he kept his eyes on the horse's mane, answering her questions with non-committal grunts. Ada gave up. The wealthy classes were becoming wise to the tricks used by mediums to spice up their evening, and the man had probably been given instructions not to speak in case he revealed any information about the family. He remained in the same position until they entered the South Downs where, in familiar territory, he raised his whip in greeting to people he recognised in a succession of small villages.

As they turned into a driveway, the smell of the sea arrived on a blast of wind, Ada wrinkling her nose at the briny tang. It had been a painful scrabble to leave her origins in Morecambe and she didn't welcome the reminder of what she'd left behind.

Ada suspected, however, that this genteel stretch of coastline wouldn't be dominated by cocklers returning to do business with keen-eyed fishmongers. She shook away thoughts of her unmissed home town and fixed her gaze on the lush vegetation which swayed above their heads. Purple wisteria, intermingling with overhanging elm branches, clashed with feelers of yellow climbing roses. Ada leant back for a moment, savouring this last time alone before she'd adopt her refined veneer for yet another influential family.

'Clewer Hall,' said Fletcher, pursing his lips in satisfaction as the house came into view. Ada saw first the west wing revealed and then the full house, grand and forbidding with a blank, outward stare.

She frowned. Her booking for that evening had been made by a letter signed by Mrs Helene Clewer, the tone of the message the type she was used to: condescension masked by a courteous plea. *Do come.* And so she had, desperate for both the money and the possibility of shining in front of a man doing much to make mediumship, if not respectable, then at least accepted in society. Ada had been unsurprised by the impression of wealth and conventionality the letter conveyed. This, however, wasn't what she was sensing here today.

'You can drop me off here.'

Fletcher raised an eyebrow so overgrown that it fanned up onto his forehead. 'My orders is to take you to the house.'

Infuriating man, she thought as the old nag finally sped up. 'I'd rather walk the rest of the way.'

Still he carried on, taking her around the house towards the side entrance where he pulled on the reins. Ada stood with difficulty as he remained sitting, hunched in his seat.

'I'll be back at nine thirty,' he muttered into his chest.

She nodded, distracted by a movement at the corner of her

vision. 'I won't announce my arrival straight away. I want to stretch my legs in the garden for a moment.'

He didn't reply but set off at a gallop, leaving a cloud of dust in his wake. The garden had a summer's afternoon stillness, although in the distance she could hear two male voices, servants probably, talking and laughing. She tried to spot the speakers but it was difficult to judge the direction of the sounds. The jollity of their tone was at odds with the uneasy creep on her soul. She moved away and listened instead to her inner voice, the one that told her older, much darker secrets, the voice that drew her towards a copse of Italian cypresses, their pillar forms standing sentry for her arrival.

'Is anyone there?'

There came the snap of branches and, peeping out from a tree, a little boy stood watching her, his coat torn near the hem. She saw at once that he was from the other side, his eyes ringed with fatigue and his breathing heavy. They regarded each other for a moment. It was sometimes better to let them speak first, because you could do so much damage if you mistook their intentions. This boy, however, looked young, of an age when it was hard to articulate your deepest fears.

'Don't be shy. Why don't you come out from behind the tree?'

He continued to stare at her.

'Do you need me? I can help you pass over if that is what you need. Can I come nearer?'

As she took a step forward, his expression turned to rage. Ada stopped. She'd learnt the hard way that not all spirits are benign, and she'd become careful. Old habits, however, are hard to change.

'I can help you,' she said again. The boy looked unsure and she thought he might move towards her. She was wrong. He bared his teeth at her and Ada felt a shadow behind her. She spun round but could see only the great house with its manicured gardens stretching into the distance. She turned back to the boy, who had lost none of his fury, trying one last time.

'If you want me to, I can help you pass over. Don't ally yourself with the house, child. Once you're inside a building it makes it harder to move on. Do you see what I mean? I can help you more than the house can. There will be people waiting for you on the other side. Your mother, perhaps?'

Her words trailed off as Ada shrank from the expression in his eyes. Accepting defeat, she made her way back to Clewer Hall.

Chapter Fifty-Eight

It was time to go. I was no longer simply weary but overwhelmed by an all-embracing exhaustion. The house, the family and, ultimately, the truth, had left me battered and bruised and now the time had come to return to London, to my stale life, and settle down with the baby. No one had poisoned me. The pennyroyal tablets were left over from that time when an unwanted baby had come into the world despite the attempts of Helene to rid herself of it beforehand.

In my room, I packed what little I had in my leather case and took care to ensure all the finished plates were carefully secured. I would ask Quinlivan to take me to the station. George had said he might come with me, and I would worry about that farewell when we reached London.

One of the guests at the séance had killed Ada, I was sure of it. Perhaps Felix, who had been at such pains to ensure the elderly doctor would state that the death had been accidental; or one of the Clewer women, desperate to protect Helene's secret. Or possibly Sir Thomas. He too would want his reputation protecting. Whoever the killer was, it was no longer my business. I could not prove that Ada's death had been anything but an accident.

I took a final look at the room where I'd rested my head for the last ten days. I might never have been in there, so little impression had I left on the space. There would be no more governesses here, and I hoped to God the Hall would be sold to a family with no women in their childbearing years. This was a house which disliked, even hated, children. As a final act, I picked up the chair I had taken from the nursery and carried it back into that unloved space. I crossed to the window, the one I had looked out of my first night, and gave the garden a final look. I hoped, I think, for something to show me that my brushes with the supernatural hadn't been down to my fervid imagination.

I heard a click behind me and my stomach somersaulted at the thought that I'd been locked in the room. I spun round and saw that the key had been turned in the lock – but the person responsible was standing in the room with me: Helene, in a shimmering lemon silk dress, her arms blue with the cold and her pale, wispy hair hanging in damp tendrils on her shoulders. I looked around me, remembering that the nursery window was barred and instinctively took hold of the chair I'd just carried into the room. Anything to create a barrier between me and my child and that woman.

'Why did you take a photo of Noah? Don't deny it. I've found the image amongst your plates.'

I gaped at her, realising too late the light of madness in her eyes. I swallowed. 'I was in Lily's room, doing my work, and I saw the photo of Noah.'

'Inside a frame? You were prying where you had no right. Why did you photograph the image?'

I swallowed. 'It was an impulse, that's all. It was the first proof I'd had of his existence. I'm sorry, I hadn't realised how much your dead son meant to you.'

There. It was out. In my terror, I had shown that I knew about Noah, told the secret which had only recently been revealed to me. My words, however, had little effect on Helene. Her eyes held mine as she took a step towards me.

'It was a foolish thing to do. You can keep the plate, I don't need it!' I was babbling in my panic. 'I'll be leaving soon, the matter is finished.'

'Finished? You're just the same as the others. Everyone thinks it'll be finished when I leave this house. Take me away to India and it will all be over.'

I looked towards the locked door, wondering how hard I might have to bang on it to make someone hear me. I needed to distract Helene somehow.

'His death must have been a terrible shock. Was it so dreadful?'

She trembled as she moved closer to me. 'A needless accident. He'd been rude to Enid Jessop and she'd locked him in his attic room in the cottage. It meant he couldn't see me in the east wing.'

'He visited you there?'

'He liked to listen to me sing. They couldn't stop him, of course, but Enid locked him in as a punishment, knowing how desperate he was to see me.'

'What happened?'

'He managed to get out, rushed down the stairs.'

'The stairs of the cottage?'

'His little head bumped down the two flights. I shall never forget the time. Twenty past five. I was waiting for him in the room. I had Lily, and Archie had just been born, but my times with Noah were special.'

'Twenty past five?' I asked.

Helene's eyes narrowed. 'What of it? Does the time mean anything to you?'

I couldn't tell her while she was in this state of how mine and George's watches had stopped at that hour. I began to edge around the wall, away from the window. 'Would you let me out of this room, Helene?'

She took a step backwards, her hands shielding the door frame. 'You've heard the music, haven't you?'

I tried to decide which answer would most placate Helene. If I said no, perhaps she would take it at face value and let me out. But I had told the assembled family in the sitting room that I heard a piano playing, so she would know it was a lie. 'I heard something.'

'And the light appearing in the plates of the Adelaide Room? I have them, so don't pretend you don't know what I'm talking about.'

'You can keep the plates. You're welcome to them.'

'But why did they appear in your images? Why *you*?'

'I don't know.' I could feel the hysteria rising in me. 'I don't even know what Noah's connection to the Adelaide Room is.'

'One day I showed him the wallpaper. He was being fractious and even my piano playing wouldn't soothe him. So I showed him the animals in the wallpaper. He loved them, and from then on he'd always ask to see the room.'

'And he was called a magpie?'

'He was a child and liked bright things. He was caught with some oddments in a handkerchief – a teaspoon, a shiny button – some things of value, others not. But there was nothing important. I only found out about Enid Jessop beating him afterwards.'

'Why have you locked me in here, Helene? Will you let me go? I am leaving today. You'll never have to worry about me again.'

'I don't understand,' Helene drew a circle in the dusty floor with the tip of her toe, 'how my son appeared to you and to Ada, but never to me. The music you hear, the lights you have photographed . . . It's him.'

This was it. Helene might be missing her son's death photograph but I recognised a more fundamental need in her, one I understood with my very being: the wish to see her son again. I clasped my hands together.

'I don't know why I hear the music. You have to believe me,

Helene. This house, it has a strange effect on everyone. I'm nothing special.'

'I so desperately want to see him, Louisa. You understand, don't you? I gave him to the Jessops so that he would still be with me. I heard their baby died and it seemed the perfect solution.'

'I do understand. Helene, perhaps if we went downstairs—'

'Ada saw him, you know. That very first evening, she saw my son. It's why I invited her back time and time again. I wanted to see what she saw, what *you* see.' Helene looked across the room at me. 'I am Noah's mother and he never once appears to me.'

'He's at peace. Along with your other sons. Like my children. They're allowed to rest in peace.'

'*He's not at peace!*' Helene bellowed, her voice hysterical. 'He haunts this house! He has destroyed my family with his appearances. And I want to see him before I leave.'

'Didn't you ask Ada how?'

Helene moved over to the window, finally opening up a gap between me and the door.

'Every time I saw her, but she refused. Told me you either have the gift or you haven't. The night of the séance, I put on a pair of Felix's boots and followed her into the garden. I knew it was my last chance. She wouldn't be allowed back into Clewer Hall and I wanted to know the secret to seeing my child.'

'And . . . what did she say to you?'

'She refused to say anything. She was sick of her life, of us, of the house. She wouldn't talk to me about my son. I remember her scornful look and her words. *You'll never have the gift.* So I picked up the stick from the ground and struck her over the head.'

At that moment, I hated Helene. Seizing my chance, I rushed to the door, banging hard on the wood.

'Help me! For God's sake, help me!'

My fists pummelled the door, the sound of my desperate hammering echoing around the room.

'Tell me how I can see my child, Louisa!'

'I don't know,' I shouted. 'It's not a good thing.'

I'd said the wrong thing. I saw her face fall.

'I'm in danger,' I shouted. 'For my child's sake, help me!'

I was trapped, and Helene responded to my desperation with fury, crossing the room in an instant. She slapped me across the face, the sting of the blow causing my legs to buckle and, seizing her advantage, she grabbed my arms and dragged me to the floor, my head hitting the wooden boards with a crack. I tried to rise but she was upon me, her fingernails in my hair, tearing at my skin. I fought her, for my sake but most of all for my baby's, but I could feel myself growing weaker. When I could resist no longer, my throat hoarse from my screams, I finally wrapped my arms around my body, in a last attempt to shield my child.

Chapter Fifty-Nine

My shouts of agony brought Felix out from the study and Lily hurrying up from the sitting room. My cries even carried down the servants' stairs as Alice struggled up two floors to come to my aid. George got to the nursery first – I heard his muffled voice urging me to open the door – but it was Quinlivan who had the working man's strength to break into the room. The door bowed and splintered and he rushed to pull Helene from me.

I stared at the sea of shocked faces as they took in my appearance, blanching at my numbed skin stained with rivulets of blood.

'Mother! What have you done?' Lily knelt next to me, removing her shawl to place it against the wounds on my face.

Helene, always beautiful, was majestic in her wrath. 'I want to know why Noah appears to this woman and not to me. Ada refused to tell me and I made her sorry.'

'For God's sake, Helene! Be careful what you're saying. Lily, take your mother to her room.' Sickened, I listened to Felix's determination to protect his family.

I pulled the bloodied shawl away from my face. 'It's too late. She's already told me that she killed Ada.'

The group turned to Helene, struggling in Quinlivan's firm grip.

'All I wanted was to see my son. Is that too much to ask?'

I appealed to George. 'She hit Ada with a stick the evening of the séance. Ada claimed to have seen the child who haunts the garden and Helene demanded that Ada reveal how she too could see Noah, her son.'

'Is this true, Mother?' asked Lily. 'Did you kill Ada?'

'Why does he never appear to me?' Helene's wraithlike figure was proving difficult for Quinlivan to hold onto as she twisted to get away from him. 'Why can I not see my son?'

'Quinlivan, please take my wife to her room. I'll help you.' Felix showed no emotion as he clasped Helene's arm. 'Alice, would you come too?'

I heard them pulling Helene down the corridor, her melancholic voice still pleading she be allowed to see Noah. Lily helped me to my feet but I shrugged her off. 'Let me go. I need some time alone.'

I stumbled out of the room and ran down the stairs, out of the servants' entrance and into the garden.

'Louisa!' George was close behind me but I couldn't face company nor comfort from a man who would disappear from my life in a day or so.

'Leave me alone, please!' I shouted back at him, plunging further into the garden.

He let me go.

At the ornamental pond, I stopped. Any further and I would be out of the grounds and at the mercy of the village's curiosity. I stood at the pool's edge, contemplating my turgid expression in the dank rainwater. I saw three deep gashes where Helene's fingers had gouged my skin. Petals of blood were dropping onto my Holland jacket and, as my tears finally came, they stung the open wounds on my face. I tore myself away from my reflection and took in the marble fawn sitting in the pool, its face, eaten away by the salt air, representing everything gone bad about the house.

I had discovered the killer of Ada and I should have felt satisfaction, but I was overwhelmed by a wave of sorrow. Ada, who had latched onto the family and been felled by the repercussions of one of her prophecies. Poor, pitiable Ada. George would write his story and there would be another scandal, possibly with my name attached, which would add to my sense of dislocation back in my London life. I could already imagine Dorothy's shocked but satisfied face.

The minutes ticked by. No one came to me and I was glad of the time alone as I began to say goodbye to this enigmatic, unwelcoming house. The wind was strengthening and the winter sun, which had shone bright throughout the day, began to set over the row of elm trees. I heard a tread behind me and, without turning, felt Lily join me at my side. The first member of the Clewer family I'd met on my arrival and the one I thought had held all the secrets. We stared at the brackish water together for a moment until she spoke.

'Dr Gosden is here already. We're lucky – he was visiting a patient in the village.'

I turned to her, observing the tremor in her voice and her expression of despair.

'He has stated that Mama is of unsound mind. She has had a breakdown, and Alice is with her in her room until we decide what to do.'

'What do you mean?'

'We have two options. She has attacked you and admitted to the killing of Ada. The natural thing to do now is to call the police. Father knows the Chief Constable a little, Sir Thomas does too. The doctor has said Mama is not fit to be questioned and Ada is buried, of course. Any investigation would involve an exhumation . . .'

I recognised the plea and fought to keep my emotions steady. That she should use Ada to bargain with me made me feel sick to the pit of my stomach.

'And the other option?'

'Dr Gosden knows a good hospital further along the coast. It takes both public and private patients and a room could be found for Mother.'

'Permanently?'

'That would be down to the doctors. There would be no interference from us. We will sign the necessary forms and Helene will be incarcerated until the doctors consider her fit to be released.'

Which was likely to be never, I thought, for how many women who'd entered lunatic asylums, voluntarily or not, were later released? I wondered if it was a ploy, an attempt to hoodwink me so that they could whisk Helene off to India as soon as I was back in London. Lily guessed at my thoughts.

'Mama is quite mad, Louisa,' she said wearily. 'She won't be coming to India with us now. We had hoped to take her with us, but I see that's not possible.'

'Did you not even slightly suspect the depths of her insanity?'

'We have tried to protect her from herself. We indulged her by allowing Ada into the house, thinking it might help. She's had a lot to cope with, and I can see now that it only made things worse. I also realise our decision to go to India was a catalyst for much of what has happened. It made her all the more desperate.'

'And Ada's death? Don't you think even Ada deserves more than a hurried burial and the swift escape of her killer, even to an asylum?'

Lily didn't answer. I hoped it was from shame but thought it more likely a decision not to incriminate herself.

'What about George? It should be his decision too. He's a journalist who will have to suppress a story.'

'He says he will do whatever you decide.'

I looked down at my expression and saw the despair on my face mirrored by Lily's. I tried to think what Ada might have wanted.

She was the victim, after all; my own scars would heal soon enough. Ada had been a woman of contradictions. She might have enjoyed the notoriety that the press coverage of her murder might generate, but surely would have hated any investigations into her mediumship practices.

I felt weary with the responsibility of it. Perhaps I was giving too much weight to the dead when it was the living who really mattered. Me and my unborn child. Felix and Lily, who would have to add another tragedy to the Clewer history.

'I don't think there is any justice to be served in calling the police,' I said finally.

Lily let out a long sigh and I realised she, too, had been uncertain of my reply. That she hadn't taken my agreement for granted was a relief.

'I suspected you, you know.'

'Me?' I'd shocked her. 'Why?'

'The night Ada died, you had blood down your dress. A lot of blood. I had covered Ada with my coat, which should have given you protection while you sat with her.'

Lily looked across the pond. 'I too examined Ada. There was blood everywhere. You were right, her injuries were too great to have been caused by a mere branch fall.'

'I also saw you replace one of the marble arms in the glass case.'

'I'd retrieved it from Mama. She occasionally removed Noah's marble cast along with the memento mori in my room. A link to Noah, I suppose. It's how she spotted so quickly that you'd seen Noah's photo.'

'I see. And Ada's laudanum?'

'What do you mean?'

'I could smell spiced apples on you when you made me the cup of hot milk in the kitchen. The same smell as in Ada's room.'

Lily looked down. 'It helps me sleep too.' Now she'd secured my agreement to her plan, Lily was in a hurry to go. 'I'll tell Dr Gosden to arrange for an ambulance for my mother.'

My mind was still on the dead and the uncared-for little boy, Lily's half-brother.

'When I found the photo of Noah with those of your brothers, I thought he was your child, but you'd put him there because he was a son of the Clewer House.'

'No, I put him with the others because I miss them all.'

'You remember him?'

'Of course I remember Noah. He loved the garden, and I'd see him from the nursery window, dragging his little wooden duck along the grass.'

'He came into the Hall, you know.'

Lily nodded, her eyes still on the pond. 'I caught him in the nursery once. It was when Archie was a baby and, as Clewer heir, he was getting all the attention. My governess, Miss Lewis, was unwell and Noah had sneaked into the nursery with his little duck.'

'Did you speak to him?'

She shook her head. 'He was trying to show me something but we were interrupted by a maid. He had a handkerchief full of shiny objects. I suppose he was trying make friends. I used to try to see him in the garden but it was difficult. My governess didn't want me playing with the servants' children.'

'And when did you realise he was Helene's child?'

'Well, I knew he didn't belong to the Jessops early on. Servants talk, and I overheard something about a changeling in the gardener's house. Then Noah died and no one really talked about him.' She took a deep breath. 'When I was sixteen, I had a secret affair with Samuel, Sir Thomas's son. It could have been a dalliance but Samuel was persuasive. It went a little further than was proper.'

'You mean—'

'There was no child, but there could have been. We were lucky I wasn't left in the same position as Mother fifteen years earlier. Somehow, though, Helene found out about our affair. There were letters I wrote which revealed too much.'

'Helene was upset?'

Lily pushed back her hair. 'She was livid. I thought Mama's fury was because of what happened but it didn't quite make sense. My virginity had been taken, but there was nothing to stop me marrying Samuel once I was of age, with both our parents' permission. There had to be another reason I wasn't allowed near Samuel, and it used to eat away at me during the endless hours I spent alone.'

'You worked it out, though?'

'Not exactly. About six months before the séance, Samuel returned at Christmas from London where he was articled. He was studying to be a lawyer and we met again, more out of curiosity than anything. Mother found out that we'd been meeting again the day of the séance. We'd been spotted by one of Sir Thomas's men. I slipped out to see Samuel, as he'd been upset on the previous occasion we'd been made to part, but this time he couldn't wait to get away from me.'

'He knew about Noah?'

'He knew it all. Sir Thomas had told him so that he would keep away from me.'

'Were you in love with him? There's no blood relation between you two, so while any marriage would have been difficult for Helene and Sir Thomas to stomach, it would hardly be abnormal.'

'I think, once we both knew what had gone on, our appetite for each other soured. Then I had to endure that séance with Ada and her insinuations about Noah. I still don't know how she could have found out about him.'

I kept Gladys's secret safe. It would do no good to reveal it to Lily and, in any case, I was still reeling from Helene's response to my revelation.

'Ada knew so much. Probably some servant talking. I was so incensed I scribbled a note while I was consoling Mother that evening. I wrote CHARLATAN in capital letters and left it for Ada to find.'

'And Samuel? Did you meet again?'

'Of course, but our affair was finished. He has since married and has children. You know that.'

'Then I'm sorry.'

Lily shrugged. 'It doesn't matter. After the séance, everything fell apart anyway. Helene's nerves went, Father lost much of his money, then the flood came and we couldn't afford to fix the damage. My suitors, such as they were, fell away – and then came the war.'

'And the ghost child the servants talk of? There is an odd atmosphere in this house. Unwelcoming. I have never felt comfortable here.'

Lily looked so weary, I thought her head would drop onto her chest. 'I like to think Noah is at peace in the graveyard, not lost for eternity in the garden.'

'Except this house is overwhelmed by lost children. You never saw the child yourself?'

'As I have told you time and time again, it is nothing but a rumour.'

'Then why were you so unsettled when you realised I was pregnant?'

She didn't speak and I thought I wasn't going to get an answer. Eventually, her eyes on the cottage, she said, 'There is no ghost child, I'm sure of it. But Clewer Hall is no place for children.'

Chapter Sixty

The ambulance which came to collect Helene was the type you might find on a London street. A small motorised vehicle with seats at the front for the driver and accompanying nurse, with windows of darkened glass stretching out at the back. The nurse bustled about in her starched linen, her hair covered like a nun's. I peered as the driver opened the doors at the back of the ambulance, taking in the long bed covered in a thin blanket. The chair next to the bed was probably for the nurse rather than Felix, who hadn't mentioned accompanying his wife to the asylum. There were no signs of manacles of any kind and I wondered if Helene would go willingly.

Dr Gosden came out and spoke briefly to the ambulance driver. He gesticulated to the bed and I saw that it did have restraints; not the chains of my Gothic imagination, but fabric straps by which the patient's body could be bound to the bed. Helene had been confined to her room and it was Alice who had offered to sit with her, not her husband or Lily. Alice had come down to inspect the ambulance the way a neurotic mother might look over a new cot. I saw she had the old housekeeper keys around her waist, had probably locked Helene's bedroom before she came downstairs. George was next to me with his hands in his pockets, his casual stance belying his curiosity, missing nothing. I wondered if he would keep his side of the bargain, stopping the story becoming public knowledge.

We watched the group enter the Hall.

'I'm not sure I can stand watching Helene put in the ambulance.'

'She tried to kill you.' I could hear the repressed anger in his voice. 'You and your baby. I'll never forget your screams in that nursery. Don't feel sorry for her. She's getting off lightly.'

My belly, stuck out like a Christmas pudding as Helene had said, was lower this morning, the baby making its way down before birth. The wind whipped across the grounds as we heard sounds of consternation from the Hall; raised voices and a shout of alarm.

'Something's up,' said George, moving towards the doorway.

I was already ahead of him, taking the steps upstairs as fast as I could manage and pushing open the door of Helene's room. I remembered the time I had searched the chamber with George, the cracked panes of glass letting in slivers of ice. The room was empty but the door to the adjoining bathroom was open. I moved to it and saw that the second door there, leading onto the corridor, was open.

The family would have known to keep all of the doors locked, but Alice, who rarely came upstairs, must have forgotten about that door's existence and had let her mistress use the bathroom in peace, allowing Helene to make her escape.

'Where do you think she's gone?'

I was talking to an empty space. George disappeared into the bathroom, out through the door Helene had used and hurried back down the stairs. The family and medics had already dispersed to look for Helene. I could hear Alice calling for her mistress, pushing open doors as she checked each bedroom in the family wing. I rushed to the window and watched as a group fanned out over the garden. It was Lily who drew my gaze. Unlike the others, whose movements were random and unfocused, Lily was heading towards Old Jessop's cottage, her long strides unfaltering.

I shouted to George, who emerged from the east wing as I hastened downstairs. 'We must follow Lily.'

He ran in front of me as we hurried into the garden. The others, noticing our urgency, followed us to the cottage as Lily disappeared through the front door.

'Be careful!' I shouted, remembering the rotten board splintering under me when I'd stepped through the entrance.

'Stay back, I'll go!' Quinlivan ran into the cottage as a crack of thunder split the afternoon air. I glanced up at the cloudless sky.

'No. Not thunder,' said George as an explosion of rubble and grime burst around us.

From inside the cottage I heard a scream. George took off his jacket. 'Something has collapsed. I'm going in to help.'

Lily emerged from a cloud of dust, coughing as Felix rushed forward to put his arm around her. He caught my eye and held it. 'Stay out of there, Louisa. This might be for the best.'

Felix, I saw, wouldn't be making an attempt to rescue his wife, and I was sure it wasn't from cowardice.

'I couldn't get up the stairs,' said Lily. 'The steps disintegrated as Mama made her way to the top. I think the floor has given way.'

'Be careful!' I shouted into the cottage, as I sucked in centuries of brick dust and ash. 'George! Please be careful.'

I retched from fear, sinking to my knees as I heaved over and over again. Finally, the air began to clear and Quinlivan emerged with Helene in his arms, her eyes open, sightless as he laid her on the ground.

'Where's George?' I shouted, getting to my feet.

'I'm here.' He leant against the cottage, holding a handkerchief to his mouth. 'We were too late. I think she fell two floors as both levels have collapsed.'

I watched as Dr Gosden knelt next her, feeling for a pulse.

'You knew she had a means of escape through the bathroom!'

I shouted at them all. 'Why didn't you check?'

Felix and Lily stood together, their eyes fixed on Helene, the epitome of the upper classes, who I would never understand. It struck me how convenient an ending this was for everyone. Helene would not be incarcerated. She could be buried in the family plot and Felix and Lily would go to India as planned.

'Why?' I asked them. 'Why did she go to the cottage again?'

Lily looked down at her mother. 'I saw her across the lawn when I looked from her bedroom. She appeared—'

'Yes?' asked the doctor.

'She appeared to be following someone . . .'

'Who?' I shouted. 'Who was she following?'

Lily shook her head.

Sick at heart, I left them, walking through the little picket fence and across the scrubby garden unobserved by the others. The staircase had collapsed beneath Helene, bringing down the first floor and its ceiling, leaving a gaping hole up to the rafters. Amidst the rubble I saw the remains of a little truckle bed, not much more than a cot, and little else.

I turned back to look at where Helene had been laid on the ground. Her face was turned towards me and her expression of contentment was unmistakable. I hoped, against all reason, that Helene had finally seen her son.

Chapter Sixty-One

I was desperate to get away from everyone. I had the answer to Leo's manner those ten long days ago. He had known – or suspected – that Clewer Hall was rotten and I wanted to be away from it all, although London held no welcome. I would have to slide into my old life somehow and forget everything that had happened here. But anywhere would be better than this house. I joined George, who was staring down at Helene, his face pale. At a loss, I touched my cheeks. I could hardly feel Helene's scratches on my frozen face.

'I need to leave now if I am to catch the train.'

George began to reply but stopped, averting his eyes as Helene's corpse was placed on a stretcher and carried away to the ambulance. Together we watched Felix and Lily accompany Helene to the house, their arms linked.

'You don't want to delay your departure even by a day?'

'I want to go now. Nothing's changed.' I turned away. 'I'm sick to death of the place.'

'There is a seven o'clock train. It gives us plenty of time to gather our things. I'll see you as far as Victoria station.'

His voice was preoccupied, distant; his mind, I assumed, already on the work which awaited him in London. I looked around the garden. The air was still with not even a sliver of wind to disturb the evening.

'I can't believe it's all over. Did you notice the look of

contentment on Helene's face? It was as if . . . Oh, I don't know, as if she'd finally seen Noah.'

He didn't scoff but I saw he was unconvinced. 'There's nothing supernatural about what's gone on in this house.'

'What about your watch?'

He pulled back his sleeve. 'What of it? It's working perfectly well now.'

I sighed. George belonged in this world. He didn't have one foot in both the living and the dead like me. 'This will be my last commission for a while. Possibly ever.'

He turned. 'You're surely not giving up photography completely?'

I shrugged. 'Times are changing, but not fast enough for me. I need to look after the baby, and besides, as you said, my camera belongs in a museum. I do have one request, though.'

'Go on.'

'I have a few unused plates left. I was going to take some photos of the family as a remembrance of my time here, but that's out of the question now. How about if I take one of us?'

He looked at me in astonishment. 'Of us?'

'I know I don't look my best – my face must be a mess – but I'd still like a photo.'

'Who'll take it?'

'It is possible for an amateur to take a photograph. My mother tried it once years ago with me and the twins. It was slightly blurry because we were laughing too much but it's my most precious photo. I'll ask Alice or Janet to drop the lens cover while the image exposes.'

'You don't carry the photograph with you?'

I thought of it sitting by my bedside table back home in Kentish Town and was glad I hadn't brought it to Clewer Hall. Let those two rest in their little graves. 'It's too precious.'

'Let's have a go then, shall we? Where were you thinking of taking the photo?'

'In Alice's kitchen. The fire and lights should be enough for me to take an image.'

This pleased him, I could see. 'I couldn't have chosen anywhere better.'

Alice, Quinlivan and Janet were sitting at the scrubbed pine table when we entered. They were silent, a plate of untouched bread and butter sitting on the table. Janet made to rise but I told her to sit back down.

'I want to take a photo of you as you are now. The three of you in the kitchen.'

They were too stunned by the day's events to argue. I set up the camera, angling it towards their table. I had to leave the exposure a little longer than I had done with the upstairs but, when I was satisfied, I slotted in a plate, took off the lens cap and captured the scene.

I moved the camera so that it was facing the range and changed the plate.

'Quinlivan, could you help me for a moment? When I tell you, could you drop the lens cover from my camera and wait ninety seconds before replacing it?'

He stood, wiping his hands on his trousers, his scarred face impassive. Alice and Janet watched as George and I stood in front of the range. At a nod from me, Quinlivan took off the lens cap.

'We need to keep perfectly still,' I said as I felt George slip his hand into mine.

Chapter Sixty-Two

I went to Felix in his study; the room was a mess of jumbled papers and old ledgers. If Felix was making an effort to clear up before the move, it wasn't noticeable. The change in Felix was, though. His face was creased with exhaustion and he'd loosened his tie and stiff collar, as if the constriction pained him.

'My commission is complete. I think it's probably for the best if I leave immediately.'

He nodded. 'Of course, Louisa. I'm sorry it turned out not to be the task you were expecting.'

I hesitated. 'I'm sorry too.'

'You? There's really nothing for you to apologise for. Helene's secret was bound to come out one day. I should have realised that. If anyone's to blame, it's me.'

'You knew everything?'

He nodded.

'From the beginning?'

He looked at the desk. 'Not immediately. I came home from India to find Helene, I thought, much the same. It was me who had changed.'

The catch in his voice was unmistakable.

'There was someone else, out in India?'

'Yes. It's easy to forget your responsibilities when you're seduced by the gaudy flowers and dark heat. I bear Helene no ill will for what happened while I was away.'

'Does Sir Thomas know Helene has died?'

Felix sighed. 'I have sent a message. I suspect the news won't be unwelcome.'

'He won't be sorry?'

'Helene was beginning to lose her grip on reality. You saw that. I don't think any of us realised how fearful she was of the move to India. I knew she was attached to the house but her desperation was unnatural.'

I touched my gouged cheeks and nodded. I stood in silence for a moment as we listened to the house groan and creak around us.

'So,' Felix clapped his hands. 'Quinlivan will take you to the station, of course. Lily and I need him briefly as we have to make a few house calls but, when we're back, he'll take you to Brighton.'

'I appreciate that. George will be accompanying me part of the way.'

'And your husband will meet you at Victoria, I presume?'

I hadn't wired Edwin to tell him of my arrival. I'd rather return to the house first and face the consequences in person.

'I'll be met at the other end,' I promised Felix.

Lily, hearing voices, came into the study. Unlike her father, she looked as if a weight had been lifted from her shoulders. The close bond between mother and daughter had been an odd one and, I suspect, she alone knew the depths of Helene's despair. I looked around the room, so full of Felix's personality, and tried to imagine him in the relentless Indian sun. There were so many questions I still wanted to ask, but for these two at least, the story of Clewer Hall was nearing the end.

I found Alice, as ever, in the kitchen. She put a cup of dark orange tea in front of me and joined me at the table.

'Are you all right?' I asked. 'You've known Helene for years. It must be hard to digest everything that's happened.'

'It's broken my heart. The mistress a murderer. She might have killed you too.'

'I know. In the nursery, I thought my time was up.'

Alice sighed. 'I'll be glad to retire. I'm going back to family in Cornwall. I'd leave tomorrow if I wasn't worried about the master and Miss Lily. They'll need me to help with the funeral and closing up the house.'

'They'll be glad of having you close by, Alice. They might not say so but they'll appreciate your presence here. Hopefully you'll be in Cornwall in time for the summer. Will you manage?'

'I have money set, and you never know, I might be a grand-mother myself soon before long.'

'You won't miss here?'

She shook her head. 'I'm tired of change in the house. It's always been for the worst.'

'And do you think the sightings will stop now Helene and Noah have been reunited?'

Alice placed her cup in its saucer with a clank. 'Still this non-sense over the boy? Let go of it, Louisa.'

I should have been reassured. The secret of Noah's birth and the tragedy which had ended his short, miserable life was out in the open. How Helene had thought to hide him in plain sight struck me now as complete nonsense. I didn't even know where the Jessops' own child had died. Enid had gone to Norfolk for her confinement so perhaps he was buried in a small grave there. A puzzle, and one I wasn't likely to solve, but I did, at least, under-stand their motivations. We, as mothers, are driven to desperate measures, and it must have seemed logical at the time.

I looked at the plain, honest face of Alice and tried to feel re-assured, but I was beginning to feel not myself. The pounding in my ears began, at first a gentle throb until it became like a fever which would not be shaken off. Alice saw my face.

'What's the matter?'

I shook my head unable to speak as the pounding got louder. The child might have gone but the house had not. I opened my mouth to try to articulate the words but my body was racked with a pain that suffused every fibre of me.

'What's the matter?' asked Alice, standing in alarm.

I felt my skirt dampen underneath.

'My waters have broken. The baby is coming.'

Chapter Sixty-Three

There's plenty to panic about during childbirth. Is the baby coming out head first? Will the placenta follow easily afterwards? Is there anything unclean which might give me a childbed infection? My dread was none of these, but that the baby might be born inside Clewer Hall. The child was on its way. The twins had been born like this, my waters gushing out of me and the contractions beginning soon after. I tried to remember how long it had taken for them to arrive after the breaking of the water bag. Six hours, perhaps, but that had been my first pregnancy and I'd heard it was often quicker with the second.

'I can help you upstairs.'

'I'm not having my baby here. The house is damp and mouldering. I will catch an infection if I stay. I need to go to hospital.' My voice came out stronger than I'd have dared imagine. I locked eyes with Alice, trying to keep the fear from her, persuade her that my determination was based on rational thought, not fear of a curse which she didn't believe in.

She nodded. 'Stay here while I find Quinlivan to take you to the hospital in Brighton. Have you had a contraction yet?'

I shook my head. 'I don't think so.'

'Sometimes the waters break before the baby's ready. You might have plenty of time. It's good news the contractions haven't come yet.'

As I felt a wash of relief, I was gripped by a spasm so violent that I had to hold onto the range, even though I could feel the heat searing into my skin. When it had finished, Alice folded a tablecloth and handed it to me. 'Place that between your legs. It will mop up the fluids. I'm going to look for Quinlivan.'

'But he has taken Felix and Lily out in the car. A few house calls, Felix said. I saw them leave through the front door as I came down to see/you.' I'd begun to breathe quickly in my panic.

Alice considered. She'd had two children of her own, I remembered, and wasn't to be flustered.

'Old Fletcher's son still uses his father's trap now and then. If you can't be driven, you'll have to go by horse and cart. It's eight miles to the hospital. Young Fletcher will get you that far. He knows these roads like the backs of his hands. I'll change you before you go.'

Her kindness broke me and I reached out to her.

'Come with me, Alice.'

She shook her head, steering me up the servants' stairs. 'The family will need me up until their move and my place is with them. We've got a lot of history between us. They can't spare me nor Janet. I'll get Mr Storey to go with you.'

'George? Do you think that's wise?'

'Wise or not, that young man's got his head screwed on, which is what you need in a crisis. Worry afterwards about wisdom, get through this first.'

George paled when he saw how much panic I was in. I tried to manage my breathing, because my heart was racing so fast it felt as if it might burst through my chest. Although I hadn't had another contraction, my pelvis was on fire. Pacing up and down the room made the pain easier to bear and for a few minutes, while we waited for Alice, I held onto him as I crossed the floor over and over again.

'I need you to get me to the hospital. You can leave me there, but I can't stay in this house.'

'I'll get you there, I promise.' He looked out of the window, his face creased with anxiety. 'I don't think you should have the baby here, either.'

Alice came back in and handed a bale of towels to George to carry.

'I've told Young Fletcher that if you feel the baby coming – and I'm relying on you, Louisa, to tell him if you reach that stage – then he is to call at the nearest house and let them know what's happening. No one between here and Brighton will refuse you help. Is your case packed, Louisa?'

I nodded. 'I did it earlier.'

'Then you're ready to go.'

I hobbled after her without a backwards glance at the room where I'd spent the last ten days. Alice began to descend the servants' stairs and, in her haste, missed a step near the top. She shrieked, began to tumble, and I heard the thud of my case as it hit the wooden steps falling through the space. Alice might have followed my effects down the stairs but George held onto the back of her dress as it ripped and then held. She recovered and clattered down the rest of the steps.

'I can't go down these steps.'

My panic, I think, had infected George, and the next moment he half carried me down the main stairs, through the front door and out into the garden. Young Fletcher was coming up the drive as we emerged, the horse shying with nerves as it neared the house. George pushed me up into the seat while Young Fletcher, who must have been all of seventy, reached down to pat the panicky horse. Alice, full of efficiency and unflustered by her fall, handed me the case with my belongings.

'My camera. I can't leave without that.'

'I'll make sure everything is sent on,' said George. 'There's no point taking it to the hospital. After the baby is born, I'll come back and send all your things onto your home.'

I nodded. It made perfect sense, although I was distraught at the thought of leaving all my developed plates at the mercy of the Clewers. Janet, who I saw hovering near the entrance, came over to me.

'I'll get Ma to find some baby clothes to send to the hospital.'

'Please. I'd appreciate that.'

I was desperate to leave. I hadn't had another contraction and was determined to get going before my insides were clamped once more. George climbed up so I was jammed in the middle between him and the silent man to the right of me. Dark clouds were gathering overhead. We would have a stormy ride to the hospital and I was worrying at the thought that perhaps Young Fletcher might refuse to take me in this weather.

'Ride on,' he said to the horse.

We began to move and as the horse picked up speed, I felt co-cooned between the two men and another presence. For the first time since Ada had died, I felt her next to me. Had she ever ridden in the trap? I wasn't sure, but I sensed her spirit. Not troubled Ada with her dubious mediumship practices, nor slightly pathetic Ada in her mended gown. No, this was the essence of her, Ada's spirit strong and firm, urging me forward, away from the Hall. Perhaps the horse sensed it too as it sped up into a gallop, approaching the bend so fast I thought the carriage might upend. Young Fletcher, however, kept his hand steady.

I couldn't resist a look back at the Hall before the house passed out of sight. It was as it had been when I first arrived, unloved, decaying and with that shadow once more hanging over the east wing. For the last time at the Hall, I felt the familiar drop of pressure and the band of constriction around my head tightened.

There was movement in the undergrowth, a squirrel I thought, but no; a boy emerged from the shrubbery. The child's jacket had a tear in it, a flap of material hanging down towards his waist. He held out his toy duck, his brown eyes imploring. His expression reminded me of Pip, my youngest, who'd once had a similar way of pleading with you to join in with his games.

I shook my head and his eyes dropped to my stomach, his lip curling into a snarl before he ran off into the trees, the little green jacket merging with the undergrowth so that I could no longer tell what was vegetation and what was the child. It struck me that the child not only resembled Pip but had, unmistakably, had the look of Helene too. The child was still here and Helene's death had resolved nothing.

I gripped onto George's arm as the sky darkened and we sped away from the shadow of Clewer Hall.

Chapter Sixty-Four

My memory of the journey to the hospital was of being jolted from side to side as I kept my eyes on the road in front of me and, as we neared Brighton, a contraction which ripped through my body. Although the agony was intense, the fact that it was an hour or so after my previous one gave me the courage to believe that I might make it to Brighton after all and have my baby in the hospital. George took charge of my admittance, and from then on it was the gripping, ripping pain where nothing else counted except me, my body and the little soul trying to enter the world. Day slipped into evening and finally I was handed my daughter, her auburn hair flattened against her head. I put her onto my breast and watched as she began to suckle.

I was left alone after the midwife had finished tending to me. A nurse poked her head around the door, saw that I didn't need any help and withdrew again, her shoes squeaking against the wooden floor. I took comfort from the peace of the room I'd been given, although I was surprised I hadn't been put on a ward with other mothers. I could hear the distant cries of babies and, in another ward, the murmur of conspiratorial female voices.

My thoughts, of course, turned to the two babies I'd wrestled to birth that first time around with the help of a stern-faced nurse. Here, the staff appeared more relaxed but busier. Nineteen twenty-five was going to be a bumper year for babies, if this hospital was anything to go by. I looked at my daughter snuggling against me and was glad I had delivered a girl.

Reluctantly, I considered Edwin and I wondered if George had managed to get a message to London. The thought of seeing my husband again turned my stomach to liquid, but I needed to dig deep to find the courage to take next steps. The nurse reappeared and took the baby from me.

'It's best to not let them sit there all night. I'll bring her back in the morning. Mothers need their sleep.'

I found her tone irritating and thought about telling her the baby wasn't my first, but a lassitude was descending over me. At the door, the nurse hesitated.

'Have you decided on a name yet?'

'I thought I'd call her after my mother. She was Margaret, but Father called her Maggie.'

'An excellent name – and I'm sure your brother will approve.'

'Brother?' I stared at the nurse, my mind a fog through which the raw pain in my pelvis was trying to cut through.

'The gentleman who came with you. He said he was your brother.'

'Of course, George. Yes, I'm sure he'll approve.'

'If you're feeling up to it, I could send him in? We've put you in this room as you lost a fair bit of blood, but once you're a little brighter, we'll move you onto the main ward. Plenty of other mothers to chat to there.'

I kept my smile fixed but inwardly grimaced. I wanted to stay in the cocoon of me and my baby and not exchange niceties with others. I watched her carry Maggie out of the room and, a short while later, George came in, taking a seat at the side of my bed.

'How are you feeling?'

'Sore.'

He winced. 'I'm not surprised. I saw how you were when you were having your contractions. Why do women go through it?'

'You don't think about it until you need to.'

'I suppose that's a good thing. How are you feeling, seriously? Apart from being sore, and so on. It hasn't brought back any painful memories, has it?'

'It's brought back wonderful memories of my children.'

George smiled, looking around the room. 'I sent a telegram to your husband saying you had gone into labour. Should I send another to say the baby has been born?'

I made a face. 'He has to know, I suppose.'

Most people would have been shocked at my words but George's manner was brisk. 'I'll send another in the morning. They say you'll be lying in here for about a week, so he can make arrangements to come down.'

His face was pale, I saw, but unlike so many others, he turned and looked me in the eye. 'I told them I was your brother. Sorry about that. What was yours called?'

'George,' I said, and started to laugh, because sometimes, what else can you do?

He laughed too. 'I didn't want to cause a scandal. Not because I don't like rippling the water, but because I would never do anything without your permission.'

I looked up at him, trying to read his words.

'You mean, they might be upset, me being brought here by a man who isn't my husband?'

'There was that, yes. The thing is, when I said that I was your brother, it gave me something I hadn't expected. A sense of everything falling into place. That you were my family.'

'Like a brother?'

I wanted him to touch me, but he stayed, unmoving, at the side of the bed.

'No, Louisa. Not like a brother. Do you really want to go home to Kentish Town?'

'What are you saying?'

'I'm asking you, Louisa, what you want for your future. So, first of all, do you want to return to your home with Edwin?'

'I never want to see that place again – or Edwin, for that matter.'

'Not going home might be solvable. Not seeing Edwin will be more difficult. You'll need to see him at least once to tell him what you've decided.'

'What have I decided? My options are virtually non-existent, and I can't land myself on you. Have you heard a new baby cry in the night?'

I'd hurt him, I saw. He stood and went to the window, a distant echo of something I'd done long, long ago.

'I've heard my nephews cry and nannies getting up to soothe them. I can't offer you that. I'm a working man and, although I have my own home, it's modest, with a woman who comes in daily to do the heavy chores. But I can offer you the chance to live a different life than the one ahead of you. A life where you work.'

I must have cried, for he came over to me.

'Well, why not? Nothing will change unless it becomes common for women to earn a living, too. My money will stretch to someone to look after the child when needs be, and there's nothing more I'd want in the world, Louisa, than for you to come back with me. You have the choice of respectability and boredom – or that of minor scandal and a life of earning your own keep, accountable not even to me. How does that sound?'

Chapter Sixty-Five

THIRTEEN MONTHS LATER

The baby's gulping cries filled the bedroom as I rolled into the empty space next to me, the sheet still warm from George's imprint. From the kitchen, the smell of coffee, pungent and inviting, drifted up into the bedroom. There was a heavy tread on the stairs and George appeared in the doorway, mug in hand, which he placed on the bedside table. He lifted Maggie from her cot and hung her over his shoulder, patting her back until her sobs subsided. She soon settled at his familiar touch, her red face hanging over his shoulder as she caught my eye.

I'd started to wean her; my milk was beginning to dry up and she readily accepted a bottle of cow's milk with a little lime water which George had also prepared. I watched her for a moment as she sucked at the teat, her eyes focused into the distance.

'What time do you need to be at the auction room?' George was dressed, his mind on the office.

'Sometime this morning, the earlier the better. It's a case of taking the prints to J. C. Stephens and picking up my payment. You're sure Edith won't mind having her for an hour or so?'

'I telephoned last night and she said bring Maggie along. If she's out, the maid will take her. She'll let the servants know to expect you.'

Edith, the eldest of George's sisters, had proved to be a

godsend. While the younger Storey girls, concerned about their social standing, had steadfastly refused to invite me to any family events or attend any function at which I might be present, Edith had George's lack of regard for convention. She had visited me on the first day I took up residence in her brother's house and we had taken to each other straight away. Although not a blood relative, Maggie was growing fond of her much older cousins and I was glad of the presence of a family, which I'd missed so much. Even George's mother had paid a visit the previous month, and I hoped that eventually his other sisters might thaw, although our unmarried status might prove to be a barrier to that. There was little I could do. Until my divorce from Edwin was finalised, I remained married to him, although we were both keen to release ourselves from the unfortunate union.

There had been many surprises in the last year. Perhaps the biggest one was Dorothy's determination to stay in touch with her granddaughter. We met every Tuesday in St James's Park if it was dry and in the ABC in Regent Street, as the Aerated Bread Company tea room was known, if it was not. We'd never be friends, and God knows what she said to Edwin afterwards, but every week she came. This, I reminded myself, showed the power of children to help make amends, a much-needed reminder after the events at Clewer Hall.

I rarely thought about the house. So much had happened over those ten days, events that had changed me forever. I kept Ada's tarot in the drawer beside our bed. I had enough faith in the future not to need another reading, but I liked to have a reminder of Ada.

After Maggie had finished her bottle, I put her in the perambulator and, ensuring I had my photographic prints with me, wheeled her around to Edith's. The maidservant opened the door and took Maggie from me, the pair of them all smiles and dimples.

'I'll be back before midday,' I promised, and hurried to the auction rooms so that I might speak to Joseph Stephens Junior before the day's work began. I was a few minutes late and I could hear Joseph's distinct baritone as the bidding started, always a mesmeric sound, and I inched towards the open door to listen for a while as lot after lot was dispatched in an efficient fashion. The sale of the contents of Clewer Hall had taken place six months earlier. All of Felix's beloved collection had been dispersed around the world, and I wondered if he'd breathed a sigh of relief as those precious items had moved from his guardianship to that of others.

Clewer Hall had not sold. Leo had called me into his office before Christmas to tell me that there'd not been a single bidder for the place. I don't suppose the story of the infamous séance, nor the muted coverage of Ada's death had helped, but the extensive decay and the cost of renovation must have put off many possible buyers hard hit after the lean war years. There were simply too many old family homes being sold off and not enough people with the funds to acquire them.

The last I'd heard, there were plans to sell the Hall to the county borough for conversion into a school for female orphans. I didn't like the thought of any children inside that decrepit building, but it would at least prevent any new sons being born on the Clewer estate. The marriage bar extended to teachers and the school would be staffed by a legion of spinsters. I was lucky that Leo had proved to be generous with new commissions. Did he approve of my rebellion? If not, he had still shown himself to be adaptable.

I caught the eye of Stanley, one of Joseph's clerks and went over to him. 'I have the prints of the jewellery items Mr Stephens asked me to photograph.'

He gave them barely a glance. 'Look fine to me. I'll pass them onto the governor after the auction.'

I knew I could leave them safely with Stanley. He might have the accent of a barrow boy, but he had his eye on working his way up to the top in the auction house. Nothing would go missing in his hands.

'How's Miss Maggie?'

I smiled at the name he gave my daughter. 'Growing. She'll be walking soon. She crawls around the floor so fast it's an effort to keep up with her.'

Stanley, who had ten children, laughed. 'Wait till she starts walking. Bring her when you come in next time. If there's no auction on, we don't mind her squeals. Mr Stephens likes the sound of children, too.'

'I will.' I turned to leave. The day was mild for March, and we might still get a walk in the park.

'You're not staying for the auction?'

I looked at him in surprise. 'There's nothing to tempt me – and even if there were, I could hardly afford to buy anything.'

'The next lot is the place where you stayed to take them photos.' I realised he'd been listening to the bidding all through our conversation. He pointed at my stomach. 'When you was expecting.'

'Clewer Hall?' My voice came out as a squeak.

Stanley didn't notice. 'Mr Stephens suggested we have a second pop at it, now all that business of the séance is out of the news. There's been a rush of Americans, recently, looking for houses. It's boom time in the United States.' He affected an American drawl. '*And you can get a glass of liquor here, too*. He's hoping he can snare someone today. If you wait a mo, you can see it go under the hammer.'

With my heart thudding in my chest, I crept to the open doors and looked at the packed saleroom. It was just like Joseph Stephens to have a second go at a sale, and I cursed myself for so readily believing that he would be content with offloading the Hall to some tight-fisted public organisation.

Salerooms had changed since I'd started attending them during the war. At first, they'd been bastions of black coats and cigar smoke, but more recently women had taken an interest in collectibles and the dynamic had begun to change. In the room, I could see cloche hats, women's umbrellas clasped by hands sheathed in kid gloves and, intermingling with tobacco smoke, the faint aroma of Chanel N°5, already, only four years after its creation, one of the most famous perfumes in the world.

There was a buzz in the room as a property in Yorkshire was sold after a protracted wrangle between two men, clearly down from the country. Why a London auction house was selling it, I couldn't tell, but then probate often dictates odd arrangements for sales. Next up was Clewer Hall. Was it my imagination that the room hushed when my photo of the house was placed on a board to one side of the room?

'Lot number 73. Clewer Hall, eleven miles outside Brighton. Famed for its restoration architecture, spacious rooms including one with leather wallpaper. Extensive repair needed, particularly to the east wing of the house, but it will make someone a fine family home.'

There was a murmur of appreciation around the room and I moved in from my place in the doorway and stood to one side at the back. Joseph Stephens, with his experienced eye, spotted me at once, and after giving me a wink, began the bidding. It started slow. One bespectacled man made a low offer and I suspected he was a representative of the county borough; his bid was met by a man in the middle of the room who had the air of a property developer about him. As the house inched towards its reserve price, another hand appeared at the front of the room, pushing the house into a figure which the Clewers would accept a sale at. I watched, fascinated, as the price climbed. The house would be sold today, whatever agreement was reached. The property developer dropped out soon after and it was left to the bespectacled gentleman and the disembodied hand I could see being raised at the front until the sale was concluded.

'Clewer Hall sold to the gentleman on the front row,' said Joseph Stephens, raising an eyebrow at me.

It was recess time and the seated crowd rose for a break while the next lots were assembled. I stood on tiptoe to see the purchaser of the Hall but a group had gathered around him, shaking hands in congratulation. Stanley sidled up to me.

'See, I told you. An American buyer from Arizona. He bought a job lot of furniture from Lord Marsden's sale last week.'

'Does he intend to live in the Hall?'

'Like a lord. Made his money in copper mines, but his wife's mother is British, from the South Coast. I only hope he knows how much work he's going to have to do.'

The crowd parted and I was relieved to see a man in his fifties step forward. An older couple might be just what the place needed. Stanley stayed at my side, watching the scene with relish.

'Second marriage, of course. He wed the daughter of his partner. It's his wife who really wants the house – and what she wants, she gets.'

A young blonde woman stepped forward, her hair bobbed in the latest fashion, although it was so thin you could see her scalp under the lights. But it wasn't her face that caught my attention, but the unmistakable swell of her stomach.

Acknowledgements

Thanks to Katie Brown at Trapeze for her vision, enthusiasm and attention to detail when editing this book, and to Sam Eades and Isabelle Everington for their input. Thanks, as always, to my agent Kirsty McLachlan at David Godwin Associates.

The Adelaide Room is inspired by the Cleves Room in Preston Manor near Brighton. A séance did indeed take place there and the leather wallpaper is wonderfully Gothic in style. The rest of Clewer Hall is a figment of my imagination. Arthur Conan Doyle was a huge figure in the spiritualist movement and I'm a great admirer of him. Louisa's character is inspired by the early photographer, Christina Broom, another woman who took up photography to support her family. A list of all the books I consulted as research for *The Quickening* can be found on my website www.rhiannonward.co.uk.

Thanks to my husband Andy Lawrence for his advice on spiritualism and for introducing me to some seriously great ghost stories in books and on film. Thanks to the rest of my family for their continuing support – Dad, Adrian and Ed – but also to my other relations, especially those in Wales. I'm lucky, living in Derbyshire, to be blessed with some fantastic local festivals. Thanks, in particular, to Vicky Dawson at Buxton International Festival and Sian Hoyle and the rest of the team at Derby Book Festival. Finally, thanks to fellow writers, reviewers, supportive booksellers and, of course, readers who make it all worthwhile.

Credits

Trapeze would like to thank everyone at Orion who worked on the publication of *The Quickening*.

Editor
Katie Brown
Rachel Neely

Copy-editor
Kati Nicholl

Proofreader
Jenny Page

Editorial Management
Sarah Fortune
Isabelle Everington
Charlie Panayiotou
Jane Hughes
Alice Davis
Claire Boyle

Audio
Paul Stark
Amber Bates

Contracts
Anne Goddard
Paul Bulos
Jake Alderson

Design
Loulou Clark
Rabab Adams
Lucie Stericker
Joanna Ridley
Nick May
Clare Sivell
Helen Ewing

Finance
Jennifer Muchan
Jasdip Nandra
Rabale Mustafa
Elizabeth Beaumont
Sue Baker
Tom Costello

Marketing
Helena Fouracre

Production
Claire Keep
Fiona McIntosh

Publicity
Alex Layt

Sales
Laura Fletcher
Victoria Laws
Esther Waters
Lucy Brem
Frances Doyle
Ben Goddard
Georgina Cutler
Jack Hallam
Ellie Kyrke-Smith
Inês Figuiera
Barbara Ronan
Andrew Hally
Dominic Smith
Deborah Deyong
Lauren Buck
Maggy Park

Linda McGregor
Sinead White
Jemimah James
Rachel Jones
Jack Dennison
Nigel Andrews
Ian Williamson
Julia Benson
Declan Kyle
Robert Mackenzie
Imogen Clarke
Megan Smith
Charlotte Clay
Rebecca Cobbold

Operations
Jo Jacobs
Sharon Willis
Lisa Pryde

Rights
Susan Howe
Richard King
Krystyna Kujawinska
Jessica Purdue
Louise Henderson